THE GUMBEAUX SISTAHS

Get your gumbeaux on!

Jax

THE GUMBEAUX SISTAHS

A NOVEL

JAX FREY

The Gumbeaux Sistahs
A Novel

Printed in the United States of America
First Printing, 2019

ISBN paperback: 978-1-7331582-0-6

Cover Illustration – *Gumbeaux Sistahs Celebrate* © Jax Frey

For my morning stars—
Tony, Jessica, Erika, & Lizzy

"We changed the course of America in this restaurant over bowls of gumbo. We can talk to each other and relate to each other when we eat together."

—Leah Chase, The Queen of Creole Cuisine
Dooky Chase Restaurant, New Orleans

"My mother's gumbo is better than your mother's gumbo," said every Gumbeaux Sistah, ever.

CHAPTER 1

Judith Lafferty had never been a violent person, but it felt like it might be a good day to start. It was a little after ten o'clock on Monday morning, and she felt a steadily rising derangement as she waited, third in line, at St. John's Coffeehouse. The cafe was crowded with late morning caffeine seekers. The music from the overhead speakers was bouncy, the weather was glorious, the baristas were smiling, and Judith was seething. Normally she would be bouncing right along to the music in the popular cafe and eyeing the lemon bars in the glass case. Not today. Today, Judith would have enjoyed flinging one of the lemon bars across the room like a frisbee. Or maybe she could just punch something. Yes, she would very much like to punch something—anything at all. The life-sized, cardboard sign near the front counter of a smiling man overly enjoying his bag of coffee beans seemed a tempting target. She balled her fist and considered it. His young, smiling face reminded her of the man responsible for her current mood. If she truly believed that punching the fake smile on the cardboard figure would somehow make her feel better, she would flatten him. But she did not think anything could help right now.

She had just walked over from the Covington Art Museum which was two blocks away from the cafe. The museum sat right in the middle of downtown Covington, Louisiana, on Columbia Street. Along with the museum, the street sported two art galleries, three restaurants, a popular bar, the St. Tammany Art Association, the courthouse, a clothing store, Mo's Art Supply, an old-fashioned hardware store, the police department, an ancient cemetery, and a small park with a gazebo. Every Saturday, a popular farmers market was held around the gazebo while local musicians played. Covington was a small, southern-adorable city of around nine-thousand people and was once home to author Walker Percy, and Stephen Stills of Crosby, Stills, Nash & Young. Covington loved its old houses with white columns and welcoming porches, its live oaks covered in Spanish moss, and its calm, lovely way of life.

Judith was brought up across the lake in her beloved New Orleans, but Covington was now her adopted home and the place that she had cherished since moving over ten years ago. She was only sixty, but she already planned to spend the rest of her years living there.

St. John's Coffeehouse sat in the middle of the popular downtown area. Judith considered it to be her own personal coffeehouse, put there for her sole pleasure, that she was somehow obligated to share with neighbors and strangers. A good cafe can make a customer feel this way. The old tile floor, pressed-tin walls, tall ceilings, and dark wooden bookshelves filled with board games and a lending library added to the atmosphere she loved. It was unusual for her be in St. John's at this time of day or even on a Monday at all. She often came earlier in the morning on her way to work at the museum or on Saturdays after a visit to the farmers market. Monday mornings, however, usually found her home, as it was normally her day off. Nothing was normal today.

Her coffee order was unusual today too. Instead of her regular sugar-free, vanilla latte, she ordered a straight, black coffee—which she hated. She wanted the bitterness of the drink to match her mood.

"They let me go!" she thought incredulously, squeezing her balled fist even tighter. She still could not believe it. She felt anger mixed with disbelief, stirred in with a good dollop of horror. *"'Let go'—their words! After ten years as Manager of the Covington Art Museum, they pull this on me? Unbelievable. And let's face it, they didn't let me go— they fired me. No sense in prettifying-up the language. Hell, they might as well have set me on fire!"*

A vision of Thomas McMann's young face suddenly bloomed in her mind. She pictured him sitting at the front desk of the museum that morning. She had been forced to pass by him before joining the museum board members in the conference room. Thomas was a thirty-four-year-old snake in the grass with a vile smirk that he never bothered to hide when dealing with Judith. And now he was her replacement. Judith should have known something was up, as he had worn an extra big smirk that morning. The picture of him in her mind choked her. He had already known where he stood this morning—that much was apparent. And he knew where Judith stood too, even before the board meeting started. That meant that they had been meeting with him about her behind her back. They had planned the whole thing, and that plan included kicking Judith to the curb and replacing her with the younger Thomas, the Amazing Smirking Jerk. And for what? In her mind, Judith called him "Little-as-Possible-Thomas." His official title was Assistant Manager. Judith was Manager. She thought on numerous occasions, *"Doesn't that mean he should take direction from me?"* She had assumed that at first, but it never happened. Not once. The only person Thomas answered to was Lillian Deslattes, the board Chairwoman. And his main duties seemed to be answering the phone at the front desk and doing as little as possible.

"And they let ME go?" she thought.

They did not even give her a chance to think about it and had asked her to leave right then and there. Judith knew that it had been handled that way so she would not have a chance to retrieve museum information from her computer. They also clearly wanted to avoid a tongue-lashing over their badly handled "letting go." They fully expected her to make an ugly scene, and maybe she should have. But she had surprised herself, and them, by leaving quietly with a modicum of grace. She had simply been in shock.

The most galling of all was the reason they had cited for letting her go. In fact, it was laughable. They said that she had not met her fundraising quota for the last event—a quota that they had raised for that event alone. And now Judith knew why. They had been planning to get rid of her for months. On top of that, they had said that they were eliminating her job—that a manager was not required by the museum anymore. They said they would be reorganizing and restructuring.

"*Seriously?*" she thought. "*What could they possibly do in that place without a manager? The place is a zoo!*" Between art shows, intake, display, advertising, marketing, social media, a million hours of paperwork, not to mention the two big fundraisers they gave each year to keep the place afloat, the Covington Art Museum needed plenty of managing. And Judith had done most of it with the help of her assistant, Bitsy. It was so much work that she barely had time to paint anymore in her home studio. And she had a Masters of Fine Art from the University of New Orleans which had helped her land the job at the museum. But she had pretty much given up painting, which she loved, along with her heart, soul, and ten years of her life, to make sure that Covington had one damned-fine art museum.

To think she had walked in there bright and early that morning feeling her usual cheerful self. She had worn one of her favorite artsy outfits—a white tunic, long black skirt, colorful scarf, and at least a dozen bracelets on one arm. She had been feeling very much alive on a gorgeous, early spring morning. There were some heavy showers predicted for the afternoon, but at that moment, the sky had been a brilliant blue.

Lillian Deslattes, Chairwoman of the board, had sent her a text the night before requesting that she join the usual board meeting on Judith's day off to talk over some "important developments." Judith figured that the board wanted to discuss plans for the next few exhibits, and Judith was ready for that. She had lined up some amazing works that would fill the museum walls and was excited to share the news, hoping that the board would be as excited about it as she was. She got to work a few minutes early, carrying her briefcase and a box of muffins she had bought for the board members. Expecting to find a quiet building and to be the first one there as usual, she was surprised to find the conference room not only occupied, but buzzing with noisy voices. She was also surprised to see Thomas already at the front desk. She walked past him and said, "Good morning," but he only nodded slyly at her in return. *"He actually looks a little extra smug this morning,"* thought Judith, wondering what that was about. She walked to the conference room, stuck her head in the door, and looked around.

All of the board members were present. They were a diverse group in race, age, and degree of friendliness toward Judith. Then she noticed Lillian Deslattes sitting at her usual head-of-the-table spot. Lillian had been chairwoman of the board for several years, and secretly, Judith had given her the title of "Sour-Puss-in-Chief." Lillian and Judith often knocked heads over creative ideas and notions about what was right, progressive, and best for the museum. There was quite a bit of conflict between all the board members over that same subject, but Lillian usually managed to lead the other members around to her way of thinking. In fact, Lillian always got her way—through sheer bullying. She tended to be super-traditional, while Judith and several of the board members wanted to let loose with creativity—especially at big events. Lillian sat in her head-honcho seat this morning with her black hair in its usual painfully tight-looking but elegant chignon. Her bright red lips were pursed in disapproval at Judith's very existence. Judith called a cheery, "Good morning, everyone."

Lillian spoke first, wasting no time. "Judith, please go set your things down in your office and then join us." Her voice was frosty and clipped, but that was normal enough. Judith opened the box of muffins and left it on the conference table for the board to enjoy. Then she went down the hall to her office and set down her purse and bag. She gave a quick look around her office and felt a prickle of premonition. As she hurried back to the conference room, an actual shiver ran up her spine. Something was up.

She sat down at the conference table and helped herself to one of the muffins. The apple cinnamon confection was halfway to her mouth when Lillian hit her with, "Judith, I'm afraid your services will no longer be necessary."

The look on Lillian's face matched Thomas' earlier expression. Both had delighted, mean little smiles. Judith spluttered, "Wait, what?" She plopped the muffin back down on the table top.

"That's right. We're letting you go. The reason for your termination is that you didn't reach your fundraising quota at the last event. On top of that, we're eliminating the position of manager. Thomas will be running things soon enough, so we have no choice but to end your employment as of right now," Lillian said coldly.

Judith could barely look at the faces on the board members. She felt her blood start to heat up and felt sick to her stomach. She was furious, and it was all she could do not to jump across the table and poke Lillian in the eye with her untouched muffin. The only face that made any sense to her belonged to Ed Bagrett, another board member. He looked across the table at her with true sympathy in his eyes. He was an older gentleman in his seventies, a kindred soul who had sided with Judith against Lillian on several issues. But today, he could only shrug his shoulders in resignation. Lillian had obviously pushed the other members hard this morning to vote Judith out.

Lillian asked her to leave immediately, and Ed escorted her out of the conference room and down the hall to pack up her things in a daze. Her assistant, Bitsy, helped her as best as she could, shooting sympathetic looks at Judith the whole time. Then Ed and Bitsy walked her out of the building with a boxload of her possessions.

On her way out, as a last act of rebellion, Judith stopped into the board room and grabbed her box of muffins before they could all be eaten. It was not much to show for ten years of work, but it was the best she could do in a pinch.

Out on the sidewalk, Ed looked embarrassed and said, "Judith, I have to apologize for the way this handled. You know that I always thought you did an excellent job for the museum. I tried to stop Lillian but was simply voted down." He told her to keep in touch, gave her a hug, then turned to go back inside.

Bitsy said, "I'm so sorry. I have to run. The board is waiting for me. But you shouldn't drive home yet. Please tell me that you'll go right down to St. John's Coffeehouse and calm down before you drive home." She hurriedly whispered to Judith that she would call her as soon as she could and tell her what she knew.

And that was that. Ten years down the drain.

Judith stumbled her way to her car and placed the box of her possessions and the rest of the muffins inside. Then she made her way down the street towards the coffeehouse. Her phone rang. It was Bitsy calling on her cell.

"Listen, I'm calling from the bathroom," Bitsy whispered in the small, tiled room, so none of the board members could overhear. "Oh Judith, I'm so sorry. The board got here early, and I just knew something was up. So I listened at the conference room door when Thomas wasn't looking. I was terrified this was going to happen. I tried to call you, but you didn't pick up your phone. Lillian called for a vote early this morning. I think some of the members voted against letting you go. Ed did, for sure. But, of course, Lillian steamrolled right over them, and the vote passed."

Judith hesitated, but only for a moment. She was not used to talking to Bitsy as a comrade, but as an employee under her managerial status. Their relationship had been friendly but very professional. And now, Bitsy was talking to her like a friend—and a pitying friend at that. Judith did not know how to deal with it. She hated pity. It just added to how horrible she was feeling at the moment. She felt her world slipping out from under her feet, and she burst out with, "Bitsy, I can't believe what just happened! I think I'm in shock. They let me go. And what in God's name are they going to do without a manager?"

There was a pause, then with sad exasperation Bitsy said, "Judith, they do have a manager. That's the other dirty side of all this. They are just calling the job by another name. All they did was change the title to 'director.' That's it. They obviously did that to help prevent you from bringing some kind of lawsuit."

"Director?" Judith said ironically. "Wow! That's a much more prestigious-sounding title than manager. I would have liked that . . . what am I saying? Who cares what they call it? I can't believe they did this to me. I've been there ten years."

"I know. It's just terrible. OK, you didn't reach your quota this time—so what? You've always hit your goals before, and you probably could do it next time. Obviously, they raised it just so you would have trouble getting there. Something's not right. And you know, now that I think about it, it's probably just a matter of time before they dump me too."

"What do you mean, Bitsy?"

"You know what I mean—out with the old and in with the new. We're both in our sixties, Judith. Employers want the younger people now. People think that being young automatically makes them better at a job. You and I know it's just not true. It's terrifying. I can't even imagine how you must feel!"

"I know. I'm just sick. What in the world am I going to do for money? I really need that job. I could lose my house! And why did this happen? I'm not that old. Hell, I'm younger than some of the board members. How can they discriminate against one of their own kind? That's like a double sin, don't you think? And I'm reliable, creative, knowledgeable, and I know how to get people to open their wallets for contributions. I mean, I know that older generations must be replaced by younger ones sooner or later, but there's a time and a place—and this isn't it. I was still going strong, and dammit, I was good at that job. And not to mention when replacements do have to happen, shouldn't there be some humanity in the way it's handled? What's the matter with those people?"

"Judith, you were good at your job. Not to mention . . . well, I never told you this before, but I think you're just a cool human being too," blurted Bitsy.

"Thanks, Bitsy," Judith said, surprised. After a moment's hesitation she said, "I think you are very cool too. Sorry I never said that before. And let's face it, no one will ever say that about Thomas." Judith laughed, but her anger cut her off. "I can't believe they replaced me with that little snake. You know, he makes my skin actually crawl. Smarmy—that's it. That's the word that comes to mind as soon as you see him."

"You're so right. And you know how he is around Lillian. He flatters, and postures, and brags, and she just fawns all over him. He's thirty or so years younger than we are, Judith. Do they think there's magic in youth? It's not a given that if you're young, you'll be better at doing something."

"That's right. Does he even have an art background? Or a marketing degree? He's a business major of some kind, isn't he?"

"Yep—and that's one of the things that Lillian likes about him. She convinced the board that he will make the museum more money, that it will be more successful."

Judith actually snorted. "That's ridiculous. I always got them their money, until this last event, and that was their fault. We don't even know what Thomas can do because he never does anything. It's one thing to have studied business, and it's quite another to put on a successful fundraising event. I mean, how creative is Thomas? People want creativity served up at fundraisers right along with their wine and cheese. I'd like to see him beat our idea last year at that fundraiser of having live artists camouflaged into the art displays. Of course, I had to fight Lillian tooth and nail to let that idea fly."

"I know, that was just an amazing night," agreed Bitsy. "But the board said, or rather Lillian said, that they liked the idea of getting new out-of-town artists in the door, not just local artists. She said that a new director, like Thomas, could pull that off, that they needed new blood in their art and in their director."

Judith gasped. "You're kidding me, right? Bringing in fabulous artists from out of the area is a great idea. It was also *my* idea! Thomas heard me say it, too. But almost every time I suggested that very thing to the board, I only got pushback. Like, brick-wall pushback. Lillian always told me that we had to support the locals. I managed to win a few of those battles with the help of Ed and bring in a couple of outside exhibits, but they were few and far between. And while I agree that we should support our local talent, I always thought there was room for other talent as well. Bringing in new artistic talent would inspire everyone—our local artists as well as the patrons."

"That *was* your idea. I remember you mentioning it several times to the board. Lillian said Thomas suggested it, and it was like she couldn't hear it until the idea came from his mouth. I'm telling you, new blood is the motto of the day."

"Oh my God. I'll give them new blood all right, but it might be theirs! When I think of how cooperative, how diplomatic and team spirited I tried to be with those people . . . you may not know this, Bitsy, but that wasn't easy for me. All I wanted to do was be creative with ideas for the events and then let loose with it. But I reeled it in for the sake of compromise with their conservative notions. Seriously, I could just spit nails. I guess I should have taken a page from Thomas' book and learned to perfect arrogance—and that smirk!" Judith felt her blood rush while all the rage and frustration from the job she had felt for so many years rose up right there on the street and hit hazardous levels. Her voice rose dangerously, "I'm telling you I could just scream!"

And then, amazingly, she did. She screamed. Her anger boiled over, and she lost it right there on the streets of beautiful, downtown Covington, in broad daylight. No one was more surprised than Bitsy—except maybe Judith herself.

A few people on the street stopped cold and looked at her questioningly, and thank goodness they did. It was just enough to give her back a modicum of self-control. "I have to go, Bitsy," Judith mumbled into her phone and hung up. People were staring, so she knew she had to cover her actions before they called the Sheriff, or an ambulance, or whoever it was that got called for crazy people. So, wild-eyed and red in the face, she pointed vaguely in the direction of some nearby bushes and shouted, "Bees! Watch out!"

She hurried straight into St. John's Coffeehouse to escape the worried looks that were divided between staring at her and looking around warily for flying insects. She had to get caffeine and think.

It's one thing to make way for a new generation, but it's an entirely different thing to be shoved aside and made to feel that nothing you do has value.

—Judith

CHAPTER 2

While she stood in line waiting for coffee, the front door swung open, and in walked a grey-haired woman a few years older than Judith. She was short, maybe five-foot two, plump, and wore a bright, flowery shift and a funny little straw hat on her head. Her face was lined and plain-looking, yet somehow she was not plain at all. Judith noticed the woman mostly because of her twinkling, blue eyes, the cherubic expression on her round face, and because she was looking right at Judith with a beaming smile. The woman made her way over to a table near the door and joined three other women in that same age-range. They began talking in low voices mixed with outbursts of laughter. They were all unquestionably looking over at Judith.

Still wretchedly angry and hurt, Judith did not care one whit if they were laughing at her for whatever reason. She had other, much worse things to worry about. She decided not to drink her coffee in the cafe. She was too upset to sit in a crowded, noisy place, so she resolved to just head home. She paid for her black coffee, tipped the barista, chose not to punch the cardboard man in the face, and made her way between tables toward the door. Nearly there, she felt a sudden tug on the sleeve of her shirt from a table she was passing. Startled and already on edge, Judith almost spilled her coffee. She turned toward the tug, privately cringing inside lest she run into an acquaintance in her present state of mind.

But instead of someone she knew, she found herself looking into the twinkly blue eyes of the same woman with the funny straw hat.

"Hello, dear. I'm Bea—short for Beatrice. Beatrice Walker," said Straw Hat. "And you can just imagine my surprise when I heard you yelling my name outside. You shouted 'Bea's!' remember? It really threw me for a loop." She chuckled, "Of course, then I thought, no-way could she be talking about me. She must be talking about the insect.' I mean, I'm a Bea, but I almost never sting anyone." The other women chuckled and smiled at Judith.

While Bea still had her hand on Judith's arm, she pulled her a little closer, laughing cheerfully. Judith, confused, did not say anything at first. She did not understand what the other woman was talking about, and then it slowly dawned on her that the woman was joking. She smiled a little, but it probably looked more like a grimace, considering her state of mind. She hesitated to answer because she was not sure what the woman wanted, and, even more, she was not sure how to walk away without being too rude. Then she remembered that she had screamed outside. It was something about bees attacking to cover up her crazy outburst. Red-faced, she muttered to the women something like, "Yeah. Lots of bees out there today."

"You know, that's a funny thing," Bea continued, still smiling. "I didn't see a single bee out front. I guess some days those insects can just pick out one person to bother. Trouble is like that sometimes, wouldn't you say? Some days, it just seems to single out and pick on one person in particular."

Judith stared at her and thought, "*What the heck is she talking about? Does she know something about me?*" She did not see how that was possible, so she simply said, "You may have something there. I'd better be careful." She shook her head and tried to turn away toward the door.

But Bea was still hanging onto Judith's shirt. She was strong for such a little woman. Bea pulled her a little closer yet to their table. "Let me introduce you to some friends, dear. These are people who have been chased by trouble a time or two themselves." She laughed softly.

Bea pointed to each woman in turn as she introduced them, "Dear, these are my closest friends. This is Lola, Dawn, and Helen—and you already know me. Most people around here do. Now you must sit down, dear. Why are you hovering over our table like that? It makes everyone so uncomfortable. Here. Here's your chair. Sit down and tell us your name." Bea chuckled and pushed a chair out with her chubby little foot.

Judith was so surprised at the woman's odd but charming insistence and smiling eyes that she found herself plunked down into a chair before she had a chance to finish her thought. *"Could this day get any weirder?"* Shaking her head with that thought, she muttered an introduction, "I'm Judith—Judith Lafferty."

The woman across from her, the one named Lola, smiled broadly. She was of medium height, rangy-thin, and dressed more like she was spending the day in the woods rather than having coffee with friends in a nice little cafe. She wore a beat-up T-shirt that had seen many washings, old, greenish-colored jeans, and rubber boots.

Her outfit caught Judith's attention. *"Wait—is she actually wearing camouflage pants? What's that all about?"*

Lola's hair was reddish brown with grey at the temples, and it was pulled up around a face full of an impressive number of freckles. She had on a Celtic cross hung on a piece of leather around her neck, and no makeup. She was slouched back in her chair with one foot on the seat. But when Judith sat down, she looked at her carefully, sat up straight, and said, "Hey, I know you!"

"That's just great," thought Judith. *"This is going to turn into more than a quick introduction."* She knew how these things went in the South. The woman probably thought she had seen Judith before, so now she was about to hear where the woman went to school for every single grade ever attended, who her relatives were, and what neighborhoods they all lived in. She knew it well—the expected start of conversation between all southern women. Judith did not have the energy for all of that right now. All she wanted to do was leave.

"I live right across the street from you," said Lola, smiling.

Judith was shocked. "You do?" she asked. She was embarrassed and flustered and looked closer at Lola. The woman did look somewhat familiar. Unlike many southern women, Judith was not overly friendly with her neighbors. She liked to keep them at a certain distance, the way she did everyone else. That way, she would not be expected to entertain or attend dreadful little holiday cocktail parties. *"I do enough of that at work,"* she thought and then sadly added, *"I did that at work."*

Lola said, "Yeah, I've lived there for quite a while now. I'm Lola Trahan. I live in that little grey house across the street on the corner."

Judith then vaguely remembered seeing a woman around Lola's age in front of that house a couple of times. She had probably ducked inside at the time so she would not have to say hello.

Lola went on coolly, "Yeah, I've waved to you a couple of times, but, undoubtedly, you didn't see me, right?" There was a wicked little smirk set among those freckles.

Judith blushed. *"Dammit. Why does karma never let anything slide?"* She shrugged apologetically and said, "Yeah, sorry—always so busy at work. You know how it is." The word "work" stabbed her in the heart again. It suddenly made her realize how often she used the "work excuse" in her life.

"By the way, I also created the Living Art exhibit at the Covington Art Museum. Maybe you've seen it?" Lola asked slyly.

"Oh! That's you?" Judith was doubly embarrassed, but Bitsy always had dealings with Lola on Mondays which was Judith's day off. "Well, I love that exhibit." Judith did not go into any more detail than that. What was the point? She did not work there anymore.

Then the woman to Judith's right introduced herself as Dawn Berard. She was a large, well-dressed woman around sixty, who had obviously just come from her favorite blow-dry salon. Her nails were a perfect light coral, her clothes an exquisite navy and white fabric in a classic cut, and her shoes looked expensive. Real expensive. She also looked like she might be best friends with a dermatologist. She had no wrinkles, no crow's feet, and plumped up lips.

Dawn wore an open, frankly assessing, confident look and sat straight in her chair. She was the only one of the women texting constantly on her phone which was obviously a permanent accessory. Judith guessed she was a successful businesswoman of some sort, an executive type. Her name sounded familiar to Judith, but she was afraid to ask and find out that Dawn, no doubt, lived across the street from her too.

Dawn went on to explain, "My husband and I own Berard Accounting." She gave Judith a friendly but no-nonsense look. "What is it you do, Judith?"

Without warning, Judith choked up. It hit her so unexpectedly that she almost could not breathe. Her face reddened, and tears sprung to her eyes. She could not believe her own reactions but also could not seem to control them after her shocking morning. She tried to swallow down her feelings and struggled to gain control. And of course, she was mortified that all this was happening in front of these women.

Meanwhile, the fourth woman at the table introduced herself to Judith. Her name was Helen Hoffmann. While Judith struggled with her feelings, Helen leaned toward her and put her hands on top of Judith's. She was dressed in loose purple pants and a flowing silk tunic which brought out her friendly looking, peaceful eyes. Judith thought while struggling, *"Now what? Why is she touching me?"* She could not help but notice the woman's kind, brown eyes. She immediately dubbed them "old-soul eyes" then thought, *"Oh of course, she's probably my age—so definitely an old soul!"* She almost chuckled but started coughing instead, trying not to cry in front of complete strangers.

"Don't worry, Judith. I'm a bodyworker. I can feel your energy," said Helen. "And it needs some work. You're as tight as a drum. Well, we can fix that right up, and we'll all hold you in the light of healing." Helen started to reach over to massage Judith shoulders, and that seemed to break Judith's spell.

"No!" said Judith, rising suddenly from her chair and breaking contact from Helen's gentle touch. "My energy is fine. It's fantastic, in fact."

Bea leaned forward, whispering up at Judith while batting her sweet eyes, "I think you're in trouble, aren't you, dear? It's OK. It really is. You're safe with this group. We've all been through stuff, and we always help each other."

That did it for Judith. She looked around the table at the four women and saw only friendly, open faces and just could not take it. She did not want to be rude, but she was too proud to sit and be ministered to. Today was not that day. She needed to be alone—now. She turned to go, forgetting her coffee on the table and nearly running into the jumble of chair legs as she stumbled toward the door. "I'm fine. Really. Nice to meet y'all, but I do have to get going—sorry." She just made it outside when the hot tears let loose.

"A bowl of my Mama's gumbo and a little wine will solve any problem you've got," said every Gumbeaux Sistah, ever.

CHAPTER 3

Judith drove home shakily. It was a relief that she only lived four blocks away from the coffeehouse. Once inside the front door, she set down her purse and box of belongings from the museum and just stood there in the middle of the living room.

As always, she felt a measure of comfort from being in her home, surrounded by her own things. Her paintings hung on every wall, and beautiful throw rugs added to the warm and inviting atmosphere. Every room was different. The bathrooms had a New Orleans jazz theme with piano and saxophone paintings. Her bedroom was boho-chic and colorful. The office was jam-packed with organized art items and a messy, well-used desk. Her studio was well-stocked with art supplies, but was not used nearly enough as far as Judith was concerned. Old painted canvases leaned against one wall along with new ones waiting for Judith to have time to put some paint on their surfaces. Her kitchen was decorated as if it was an old, Italian cantina—full of kitchen antiques and bright window shades. Obviously, she had eclectic taste and loved to be surrounded by color. One look at her house outside with its yellow, white, and blue trim, and inside with its colorful paintings, and you knew an artist lived there—even if that artist did not get to paint very often. Her cottage was small, but interesting, and it usually made her happy.

But today she felt empty and scared and did not know which way to turn. She glanced into a hand-painted mirror hung over a worn, wooden desk in the living room. She almost did not recognize herself. Of course, she was still sixty years old, five-foot seven, blonde with hazel eyes and a trim figure. She was not what you would call beautiful, but she had always turned heads because there was something interesting about her lean, high-cheekboned face and intelligent eyes. She had long ago decided that she would never fight with her emerging wrinkles except to apply the best lotions available on her budget. She liked her crow's feet. She also liked the parentheses around her mouth. She laughingly told her children that they made her look like Mick Jagger. *"And how bad could that be?"* she thought. She considered her clothes as another art form, and preferred loose, unique outfits in nice fabrics—either brightly colored or in a stark black and white. They made her feel like an artist even if she did not have time to be one. Now, looking in the mirror, she saw a woman with haunted eyes, biting at her lips nervously.

Judith paced the floor, fighting her rising anxiety. Then she did what she always did when she was upset. After changing into some old clothes, she moved into the bathroom and began cleaning obsessively. She scrubbed the bathtub, trying to wipe away the fear that was overtaking her. Then she wet-mopped the kitchen floor, hoping to eliminate the deep sadness that was overwhelming her. After that, she still did not know what to do. She was so angry that she found it hard to think. The unfairness of the day's events made her want to call a lawyer, hire a hit man, or find a nunnery. They all seemed like viable ideas amidst the muddy thoughts in her head.

She needed to think but could not manage it at the moment. She also wished that she could talk to someone but could not think of anyone to call. Over the past few years, she had done a pretty solid job of isolating herself. She had spent many years, after her kids were grown and gone, nursing an itchy foot. Travel had been her first love back then. So once the kids were out of the house, she saved up some money and then made it her business to go look around to see what was out there. She could not stay put in one place very long and moved from one city to another, taking temporary jobs and seeing the sights. With all that moving going on, it had become a habit to keep to herself in every new town. Having inherited a slightly suspicious streak from her mother, who had had a rough childhood growing up in New York, Judith had learned to always question other people's motives.

But it was not suspicion that made Judith keep to herself while she was moving around the country. It was just easier that way when it came time to leave. Things were less complicated. Relationships were problematic and to be avoided. After a while, keeping to herself became a habit, one that she preserved even when moving to Covington ten years ago. She knew people by sight and professionally through the art museum, but she was not close enough to anyone to call and talk over things when she was in this kind of trouble. But, of course, she had never been in this kind of trouble before, so she had not even realized it was a problem. She could really use a friend right about now but did not have a clue what that would even look like anymore.

There was Bitsy at work, but they were not close, and that was Judith's fault. Bitsy had been lovely to work with all these years, but Judith had kept her at arm's length out of habit. She was the boss and Bitsy, her assistant. Judith would feel very foolish trying to confide in Bitsy after all this time. She was lucky that Bitsy was loyal enough to her as a boss to make that phone call this morning after the board meeting to check on her.

As that woman from the coffeehouse had pointed out to her that morning, the one named Lola, she had not bothered to make friends with her neighbors. Or anyone else for that matter. And she was not associated with a local church, so she would not feel right calling on a priest or pastor at this point.

She thought about calling her last ex-husband, but that idea was laughable. He lived out in California and had a new family with new kids, and even grandkids, and problems of his own. Besides, she had not talked to him going on three years, she realized. That was a closed door now.

There had not been a man in her life in years. Judith had been too busy for a relationship, and besides, she felt mostly annoyed by men these days. It all seemed like a silly phase that she was well and truly over. Men had proved to be complicated issues in the past and completely ignored issues in the present. So, now she was alone. Various men had come and gone. She had even married a couple of them, but she truly did not mind being alone—maybe ninety-seven percent of the time. The three percent she did mind included some Saturday mornings when she would have liked company to go exploring the city. That three percent also included when a hurricane was furiously heading for her small town because it was frightening, and who wants to be alone and frightened? Nobody. And it definitely included the occasional Friday night when a man might go well with a fine dinner and good red wine.

But mostly, she was one of those rare and perhaps blessed souls who are able to make their way through life without the constant need to be shored-up by companionship, or dependents, or love.

Until today it had not been a problem.

She thought of her four children—three daughters and a son. Of all the people in the world, she loved talking to them the most. They were spread all over the United States with their jobs and families, and she talked to each of them about once a week. They were her lifeline, but she hated to worry them. She did not want to burden them with this huge problem she was facing.

Of course, her children were aware of her isolation and anti-social ways. Judith was not always aware of how much they worried about her. The only time that it did register was when they teased her. If she was on the phone with one of them, and the doorbell rang, they would give her a hard time by saying things like, "Mom, it's OK. Please don't kill whoever is at the door. It's probably just a Girl Scout selling cookies." That, at least, made her laugh, but it also made her more aware of her alienating ways which grew worse every year.

She was not able to stop the downward spiral. It was growing in strength, branching out in new directions and manifesting in new ways. These days she disliked going anywhere with anyone if she did not drive herself. This was because she felt she always needed to have an escape route in case she was forced into uncomfortable social situations. And she always needed to sit near a doorway or exit in restaurants and movie theaters. It was not claustrophobia. It was the need to have the ability to escape. She believed that she was good at hiding these new behaviors. She was not aware that they had been noted and worried over by all of her children.

In spite of her social anxiety, at work she had become quite adept at dealing with the public. She managed to be very good at her job, all the while eluding any close relationships. She spoke professionally to any and all contacts and got by just fine. She was such a hard worker that her lack of friendliness was overlooked. She was the first to show up when a job needed doing and the last to leave. Then she always went straight home even when invited to join some of the board members or Bitsy when they went out for coffee or cocktails together.

And she had ended up here, in this position, in this moment. As she stood in the middle of her beautiful little house, she had never felt more alone in her life.

She was in trouble. She had no job, no visible means of support. That would prove disastrous if she did not find work right away. She had a little bit of savings, but nowhere near enough to retire, or even be out of work for more than a few months. She had to find work and at her age, regardless of her abilities, she knew it was not going to be easy. It had been hard enough getting a good job ten years ago when she first applied to the museum. She had been lucky then. She was not feeling particularly lucky anymore.

She stood frozen with panic in her living room for a very long time. Then she took off her clothes, got into bed, and decided that even though it was not yet noon, the day had gone on long enough. She hoped for a better one tomorrow. How could it be worse?

If a young person burns out and changes jobs, they say it was time for that person to move on to their next challenge. If a mature person does that same thing, they say it's because they are old and used up.

—Bea

CHAPTER 4

The following morning, Judith found herself cleaning out the insides of bathroom cabinets which might not have been cleaned well for years. She had not showered that morning, but instead had gotten up, filled herself to the brim with coffee, slipped into a pair of rubber gloves, and started scrubbing every domestic surface within reach. Cleaning helped her think, and she needed a clear head to face her coming challenge. Her phone was switched off, but unfortunately, so was her mind. She was not coming up with any ideas to help with her predicament. She just needed to have faith that she would. Meanwhile, she would just clean.

At three P.M., she found herself in the living room, feet up on the coffee table, sweaty, dirty, and exhausted. Then the doorbell rang. In her mind, she could hear her kids saying to her, "Don't kill whoever it is, Mom. It's probably just the mail lady delivering the mail, as she does every day. You need the mail, Mom. Please don't hurt the nice lady."

She chuckled in spite of herself, and went to greet the mail lady, who had seen Judith looking this bad a time or two in the past from doing chores around the house. So Judith was not worried about her appearance when she swung open the front door. Before she could get it completely open, a hand carrying a coffee cup appeared around the corner and came dangerously close to poking her in the eye.

"Hello, dear," came a cheerful voice from the other side of the door. "You forgot your coffee yesterday, so we decided to bring it to you."

Judith peered around the coffee cup and was completely shocked to find the four women from the coffeehouse yesterday standing on her front steps. Stunned, she sputtered, "What the . . . ?"

"Special delivery!" yelled Lola, with a huge grin on her freckled face.

"You followed me home?" said a stunned Judith in shock and embarrassment over her appearance. She did not want to be rude, but this was above and beyond weird. She thought, *Have they been stalking me? That's so creepy!*" She deeply regretted opening the door.

"Don't be ridiculous," said Dawn sarcastically, checking her phone as she talked. "Nobody has time for stalking anymore. Now we just follow people around. That's different, right?"

"What?" thought Judith. She found herself wondering who the heck these women really were. They looked harmless enough, but she was suddenly filled with doubt, and a little bit of fear.

Helen gave Dawn an exasperated look and explained, "Don't mind her, Judith. She's teasing. We didn't follow you. We know where you live. Lola lives right across the street, remember?"

Lola added with a smirk, "Don't tell me you forgot that already."

"No, I didn't—sorry." Judith took hold of the cup and was surprised to find that it was cold and somewhat used-looking. A thought occurred to her and she asked, astonished, "Wait—is this actually the same coffee from yesterday?"

"Yes, dear," said Bea, smiling brightly. "We took good care of it for you."

"Uh—thank you?" Judith did not know whether to laugh or be scared. Then she decided it did not matter at this point. She shook her head wearily. "You know, it's been such a weird couple of days, nothing should surprise me now. I don't even know what I'm saying anymore."

"We know, dear," sympathized Bea. "We could tell you were having a hard day yesterday."

"That's an understatement," said Judith grimly.

"So we decided to come by and do two favors for you today to cheer you up," Bea said. "First, we've returned your coffee. Of course, we know you don't really want this old coffee, so we're going straight on to favor number two." She turned to Lola, "Is everything ready at your place?"

"Yep, all ready," answered Lola.

"OK then, let's go," said Bea.

"Uh, OK," said Judith, puzzled. "Thanks for stopping by and for the coffee." She started to close the door.

"No, you don't understand," said Dawn, smiling. "You're coming with us." She reached out and tugged firmly on Judith's shirt, forcing her out onto the front steps.

"Wait, what is this?" asked Judith. "Are you kidnapping me?"

"Obviously," answered Dawn. "But don't sweat it. This is our second favor to you. We are going to take you right across to Lola's place where I guarantee you there is plenty of wine and the second-best gumbo in the world."

"Watch it," growled Lola. "Second best, my ass! My mom's recipe is the world's best, and you know it. It's the same recipe she made for my brothers and me for a million years, and it doesn't come any finer."

Dawn was quick to retort in a serious voice, "Well, I believe I speak for the multitudes when I say that my mother's recipe is far superior." She looked down her nose playfully at Lola.

"Listen, you two," chimed in Helen happily, "My family's recipe served workers in the French Quarter at our family's diner during the turn of the century. And not this last century either—the one before that. People stood in line for it."

"Yes, dears, and my mother's gumbo puts them *all* to shame," said Bea with a twinkle. "You see how this works, Judith? We don't agree on whose mother's gumbo is the best, but we do agree that we all love gumbo. And wine! Now let's go. You're coming with us." She reached out, took Judith by the elbow, and pulled her out the door.

"But I'm an absolute mess! I can't go out like this," Judith exclaimed, appalled at her appearance. Plus, she could not but help feel her hackles starting to rise at being ordered about by this tiny woman who she hardly knew. She wanted very much to say, "Don't tell me what to do!" She wondered why the other women put up with it.

Dawn interrupted her thoughts as she looked Judith up and down, "Yes, you are a mess, girl. What in the world have you been doing all day? But you're already out the door, so that's that." She whispered to Judith as they walked down the sidewalk, "You'll find that it's really best, and so much easier, not to argue with Bea. We call her the Velvet Hammer. She won't ever stop beating you into submission until you do the right thing. But she does it so softly that you don't even know what hit you. Just know that her heart is pure gold and so are her intentions. So, let's just move along."

Judith stared at her and thought, *"What in the world have I gotten myself into now?"*

They escorted Judith across the street to the little grey house on the corner. A sense of agitation grew inside her with each step. Just before they reached Lola's front door, Judith thought, *"Have I stepped into another dimension? What is going on here?"* Confusion and hysteria overtook her suddenly and without even really knowing what she was saying, she blurted out, "My mother's gumbo recipe will make y'all weep with shame!"

The women burst out laughing, and Bea said, "Atta girl!" as they all trooped inside.

CHAPTER 5

Lola's house was over a hundred years old, as many of the houses in the neighborhood were. It was a charming, well-cared-for wooden structure with an inviting porch The whole thing was solid as a rock. Judith's own cottage was the same age and style, but Judith had never gotten around to doing much with the landscaping, especially in her backyard. She laughingly told her kids that it was a bog garden, but it was really more of just a bog. Judith could not help admiring Lola's beautiful, old-fashioned front yard garden, complete with roses and a sundial on the side of the porch. She also got a quick peek at the backyard and was filled with awe and garden envy. Her face must have shown her amazement because Dawn leaned over and said, "Don't you hate her? It's the most gorgeous garden in town. Wait 'till you see."

Lola ushered them into the kitchen, as southern women friends were wont to do. A huge, old dining table filled up one half of the large room, inviting good friends and times.

Lola hustled a large pot from the refrigerator and plopped it on her six-burner stove. "I cooked this gumbo for us yesterday so all the flavors would meld overnight and just be ever-so-much more amazing than yours, Dawn," said Lola with a laugh. Next, she produced a large, heavy-bottom pot and began cooking the rice.

"My mom's recipe doesn't need melding," said Dawn with a wink at Judith. "It is perfect from the moment it's cooked."

"What kind of gumbo couldn't use some old-fashioned melding?" sassed Lola. "Oh wait, I know—bad gumbo."

"OK, here we go," sighed Helen. "You two are making my hair turn a shade whiter."

"Dears," said Bea pointedly, "We have other fish to fry today, so to speak. Or other gumbo to boil, if you will. Judith didn't come over here to listen to your gumbo gab. Why don't we all go in the living room till the rice cooks?" They traipsed into Lola's living room which rocked a purple velvet couch, chic art prints, large, glorious house plants, and an abundance of accessory color. It was a very happy room and reminded Judith of Lola herself with her happy, open face full of freckles.

Helen sat next to Judith on the couch and whispered, "I have a little present for you." She held out her hand and plopped a small vial of mysterious liquid in Judith's open palm.

"Uh-oh. Watch out, Judith," said Dawn from across the room. "Witch Hazel here has some powerful potions."

"There's no witchcraft," Helen said matter-of-factly. "I've spent years studying the properties and potency of essential oils. I order the best from all over the world and even create some of my own blends."

"Actually, people come from all over the South to learn about this stuff from Helen," confirmed Dawn. "She's extremely knowledgeable and holds workshops on it."

Helen continued, "I share a lot of my knowledge in my classes, but this blend is special. I made it for you this morning. It will help you with the shock you've received and will also help you go through the upcoming turbulence."

Judith looked at her questioningly, but Helen went on, "It has a calming mood-boosting effect too. It's chock-full of grapefruit, jasmine, and frankincense."

"Yes, she mixed that up with gold and myrrh and sold it at Christmas to these three wise kings from the East who rode through on camels," laughed Lola.

"Aw, cut it out," Dawn snapped while texting on her phone. "It's too early to let our new friend here know what kind of heretic you are."

Lola laughed merrily and started handing out stemless wine glasses. She poured a chilled white wine into each glass.

Judith took a sip and wondered again what these women knew about her. "Helen, what do you mean? What makes you think I've had a shock?"

"Have you looked in the mirror today, girl?" asked Dawn, rolling her eyes.

"Pay her no mind, dear," said Bea, sitting across from Judith. "It was pretty obvious to us yesterday that you were having a rough time—and still are. We just want you to know that you're safe talking to us. We've all been through the mill, and we've helped each other."

"That's right," said Lola. "Some of us are a real mess!" She laughed and pointed straight at Dawn.

"Never mind her," said Dawn. "But really, we do try to help each other, and what we say here, stays here. We'd like to help you if you feel the need to talk about it."

"And we'd just like to get to know you a little too. You seem like an interesting woman. Besides, we women have to stick together. It's no less true now at our age than it was when we were young. In fact, it may be truer as we get older because some of our troubles, aside from everyday problems, now also include those involving ageism. As we age, some of us lose partners and other family members and don't have people to turn to. People divorce, they die, children move away with jobs and families, and we often find ourselves alone. Who else do we have to turn to for help or support? I, myself, am widowed—as is Helen. Dawn is still married, and Lola is divorced."

"I prefer 'happily single,' if you don't mind," winked Lola. "But that's right. Dawn is still married to Stan, but don't ask me how he puts up with her." She looked at Dawn, "Get off the phone, by the way."

Dawn grunted while she studied her phone for a moment longer. "One second, just have to send this last text." Then she looked up and said, "How about you, Judith? Are you partnered up, so to speak?"

"No, I'm not. I've been divorced . . . well, a couple of times . . . and that was plenty enough for me, thank you. And there are no boyfriends in the picture now, either."

"Do you have children?" asked Dawn.

"Yes, four."

"Goodness! I'll bet that kept you busy! Are they local?"

"No. They're spread to the four winds," answered Judith. "The twins are in California, one daughter is in Ohio, and my son is up in Washington."

"So, there's nobody nearby to help if you get in trouble," said Helen. She turned to Bea, "Your instincts are as strong as ever, Bea. I'm so glad you suggested talking to Judith."

"Tell us a little more about yourself," said Dawn. "Like maybe—where are you from, and what you do for a living."

"Wait," said Bea, "Let me start this off so you'll feel more comfortable. Let's just go around in a circle and share about ourselves, shall we?"

"OK, I'll start," said Lola. "Hi, I'm Lola. I like long walks on the beach, piña coladas, and getting caught in the rain."

"Oh, knock it off," laughed Dawn. "Forgive her, Judith, Lola thinks every interview is a match-dot-com questionnaire. She's our resident slut. I've lost track of all the men she's dated."

"There haven't been *that* many men," retorted Lola. "At least I'm not crazy." She nodded in Dawn's direction. "You wouldn't believe the stunts this woman has pulled."

"Now, dears," said Bea, "We're all crazy here—that's a given. Let's try to stay focused for a minute, OK? Keep going, Lola."

"OK, here goes. I'm Lola Trahan, and I'm from Folsom, Louisiana. I own and work for Fleur de Lis Nursery, where I create unique landscaping and gardens plans."

"Lola is a master gardener . . . among other things," interjected Dawn. "That's why her gardens here make our yards look like we planted weeds intentionally—until I hired her to work on my house, that is. Now my place looks pretty amazing too, if I do say so myself."

"Speak for yourself, Dawn," said Helen. "Lola did a great job on your landscaping, but my place looks just fine thank you."

Dawn conceded, "That's true. Helen's place is great. She grows many of the plants she uses in her oils and tinctures."

Judith watched the other women talk and enjoyed their friendly banter. She started to relax a little. The wine did not hurt, either.

"So, if you have any questions about plants or landscaping, I'm your woman," said Lola with a nod.

"And Helen is our resident swami," said Dawn laughing.

"I thought I was Witch Hazel?" answered Helen.

"Same difference."

Helen continued, "I teach meditation over at the Women's Center and do massage, reiki, Feldenkrais, and give workshops on essential oils."

"She also grows her own organic food," said Lola approvingly. "Go to Helen's sometime for a smoothie that will kick your ass! And let's not forget her magic soup. It'll cure anything! And it's all made with veggies and fruits straight from her garden."

Helen smiled, "I'll have to make you some sometime, Judith."

Then Lola pointed to Dawn, "OK, you go."

"OK, I'm Dawn Berard. My husband and I own Berard Accounting. Our main office is on Main Street in Covington, and we handle many of the big accounts in town such as the hospital, medical clinics, and insurance companies. We have a couple of people in the office that do small business accounts too. So if you need someone to do your books, someone good that is, call us." She whipped out her business card automatically and placed it in Judith's hand. "Bea, your turn."

"OK, I'm Bea Walker. I've been retired for a few years now. I did corporate training in customer service for many years—mostly working with government agencies. Now, I mostly just putter."

Dawn, Lola, and Helen broke into laughter. "Oh yeah right," said Lola. "Just putter—that's all she does!"

"She's always up to something—volunteering, meddling, and chasing us around to keep us in line," laughed Dawn.

"Well, I tend to do a lot of volunteer work for the Women's Shelter. That's true enough." said Bea modestly. "And a few other activities here and there."

Judith looked around at the women wonderingly and said, "You know, it strikes me that y'all are so different. It's a wonder y'all ended up so close, and yet I can tell that you're very good friends."

Lola laughed, "We didn't want to be at first, but Bea made us."

Bea nodded in agreement, and the others grinned.

"I think I get it," said Judith. "You tease each other to death, but I can tell there's genuine affection here."

"Yes, we do tease," said Lola, then laughed. "Some of us do it ad nauseam!"

Helen rolled her eyes, "You got that right!"

For the first time in years, Judith felt a twinge of envy. She thought, "*How lucky they are to have each other. I've forgotten what this feels like. In fact, I can't remember the last time I had a good friend. It has to be twenty years ago! It makes me wonder if things would have been a little different for me if I'd had these kinds of connections in my life.*"

Lola interrupted, "Might as well get used to us, Judith. Once Bea decides to adopt you, it's all over. Once upon a time, all of us were either alone or needed help in some way. Bea picked us up like stray cats—one at a time. And like it or not, you're her newest adoptee," she chuckled.

Judith stared at her and suddenly felt a rush of her social anxiety. She felt as if she was suddenly being held captive. Her heart started to beat quickly, and she glanced toward the door—the way out—and panicked.

Bea saw her expression and said quickly, "Don't listen to them, dear. This is how they tease me and they are silly as gooses. We're all just friends here, and we'd just like to get to know you a little better." She shot a warning look at the other women, and they sobered immediately but still looked at Judith with welcoming eyes.

Judith saw those smiling faces and felt herself start to relax again. She thought, "*I can leave anytime. I live just across the street, for heaven's sake!*"

"Yeah, don't mind us. We're just messing around," said Dawn in a gentle voice. "So tell us, what do you do?"

Judith did not know whether it was the wine, the sympathy, or the stress—or all three—but to her horror, she felt sudden tears spring to her eyes.

"Good Lord, I am so sick of crying!" she thought. She had done more of it since she got fired than she had in the last ten years. It did not help that their friendly overtures toward her reminded her of the deep trouble she was in since losing her job. She wanted nothing more than to bolt to the front door and escape the scrutiny of these wonderful women when she was at her most vulnerable. Vulnerability was not something Judith did well.

"See what you did," whispered Lola to Dawn. Dawn scowled back at her.

"Nobody did anything," said Bea calmly. "Judith's been through a lot. But it's all right, dear. Believe me when I say that we've all been through life's wringer a bit. But I'll tell you something—every one of us has been better off for sharing whatever it was that was wringing us out. You'd be surprised how talking about a thing will make you feel better. We always somehow manage to help each other out. And as we said, what we say in this group stays right here. You can trust us, dear."

"Yeah," said Lola, "Even Dawn." Dawn grimaced.

Judith looked around at the four faces in the room, and something clicked inside her. Their friendship and laughter aside, she felt they were people who did not want to judge her or hold her captive. They wanted only to help. She had never experienced that firsthand before. She had always been suspicious of people's motives toward her. But she felt, for maybe the first time, that they were motivated by good intentions. It almost made her cry harder, with relief this time, which was horrifying. But she said, "It's been kind of a brutal last twenty-four hours for me. I've been through something that happens to people our age often, but it doesn't make it any easier to take. I'm in trouble, but I seriously doubt if there is anything anyone can do to help."

Helen took her hand, "Just cut to the chase and tell us what happened. We'll help you if it's at all possible. You'd be surprised what this group can do. When we work together, we're pretty resourceful."

"Somehow, nothing would surprise me about you people at all," Judith said. "I don't know—something about y'all showing up at my house with day-old coffee, and kidnapping me, was the tip off." A smile broke through, even as her tears were still falling.

Judith looked up at those four beautiful, sympathetic faces and told them everything. She started, not with the firing from her job, but with the years before. She had been alone for so much of that time. She told them how there were three things that had made her life good—her four children, her art, and her job. "But," she said, "None of my kids live close. We talk all the time, and we visit when we can, but that doesn't quite cut it, as you can imagine. And my art has taken a back seat because I've had to give all my time and attention to the art museum where I work . . . worked. That job wasn't easy. Sometimes it was nothing short of a pain in the butt, but I liked it and thought I was good at it. And now that's gone."

She told them about the disrespect she had endured at work and the way Lillian always manipulated the other Board members into getting her way. She explained how, for some reason, Lillian had been out to get her for her for a long time, often making her life hellish.

"But mostly the job was a joy because I loved being around all that beautiful art. And Bitsy, my associate. She was such a big help to me. And, of course, the job paid my bills. But now, in one fell swoop, it has been scooped out from under me." She told them a few details about how Lillian Deslattes had acted and about the opportunistic Thomas McCann replacing her.

"Some of us are familiar with Lillian," sniffed Dawn. "And yes, she's a piece of work all right. My husband and I are friends with Ed Bagrett on the museum board, and we donate every year. I don't go to many museum events, but my husband does, and he has told me that Lillian acts like her title is Queen of Covington."

"I don't know why she wanted to get rid of me so badly," said Judith. "I guess it's just out with the old and in with the new. But why? It just doesn't make sense to me."

"It sounds to me like ageism rearing its ugly head," said Lola. "That kind of bigotry—all bigotry really—makes me so mad. It's demeaning and frustrating. And truly unnecessary."

"The idea that older people can't be fabulous employees is complete B.S.," said Dawn. "I've run into it too. I'm sure we all have."

"Yes, we have, dear," said Bea. "It's a terrible problem in our country. In many other countries, the aged are revered and respected for their experience, knowledge, and wisdom. In our country, they are pushed aside and forgotten. It's all backwards."

Lola chimed in, "And employers think the craziest things about us. They think we can't learn new skills, that we are not creative and can't handle pressure, and that we're slow, and weak, and burned out. I mean—have they seen me?" She laughed. "I'm none of those things. I'm downright awesome, in fact."

"You are, girl," grinned Dawn. "We all are."

"Those are the stereotypes that haunt our age group," said Bea. "Yet studies have shown that they are false. It's like if I said the Millennials are all lazy or Generation Xers are all entitled. It is just not true for any group. It's always on a case-by-case basis. People may do things a little differently, but we all get the job done in our own ways."

"That's right," said Judith. "I don't dislike Thomas McCann because he's young, or entitled, or any of that. I don't like him because he's an ass!"

"No matter how true these things are, the negative attitude against the aging population is a real thing, and prevalent," said Helen. "And it's causing problems right on our own doorsteps."

"The worst part of it is that I feel so stupid about it," Judith said. "I'm in my sixties and have very little savings because the museum didn't pay all that well. Now I'm so afraid I won't find work, I'll lose my house, I'll be on the streets, and I'll end up dying under some dark bridge somewhere like an old troll."

"Hey, we've all been afraid of that dark bridge in one form or another," nodded Helen.

"But you notice, dear, that none of us are actually living under a bridge, right?" asked Bea, laughing. "But we certainly could be. We've helped each other through those dark times. And we'll be damned if you'll end up under some bridge either—not on our watch.

"So, here's my question to y'all—what are we going to do about this?"

"I take it we can't blow up the museum, right?" asked Lola, rolling her eyes. "That would be the easiest thing I can think of."

"No, dear, that's a given," said Bea calmly.

When no one came up with an immediate idea, she said, "OK, it's homework time." She took out a red notebook. "I'll organize it."

"What? You—organize something?" laughed Lola.

"What a surprise," said Dawn drolly, but with a grin. "Here comes the Velvet Hammer!"

"OK, we'll meet back at Judith's place in two days at noon," said Bea.

"My house?" said Judith, alarmed, her social panic immediately kicking in.

"Yes, dear, and at that time everyone needs to bring ideas for how we're going to handle Judith's problem, got it?"

"Get used to it," whispered Helen to Judith. "That's how this group rolls. You'll see."

Dawn said, "I've already got an idea for Judith in mind, but I need a day or two to research it."

"That's great, Dawn. I can't wait to hear all about it." Bea turned to Judith and said very seriously, "And dear, we'll be needing some of *your* mom's gumbo when we get there."

Judith's mouth fell open in surprise, but after a moment she managed to nod and say, "OK. I can do that."

"Atta girl," said Bea approvingly. She stood up and said to Lola, "Now how about that gumbo? Is it ready, Lola?"

"Ready and waiting, Chief," grinned Lola. She got up, and they all headed to the kitchen where Lola handed out bowls of hot, steaming gumbo to four hungry women.

"Oh my God. This is so good," said Helen.

Dawn found herself smiling, "Yes, definitely the second best in the whole world."

"Just so you know, Judith, that's the best compliment you can get from one of these women when it comes to gumbo," explained Helen.

Judith found herself happy and hungry for the first time in days. She felt a twinge of possibility in the air. Smiling at the other women around the table as they enjoyed their amazing meal, she asked, "Do all y'all make gumbo as good as this? I hope so because this is fantastic."

"Oh, we do, we do," they all answered, laughing.

"Then I think you should call yourselves the Gumbo Sisters!" she laughed.

"Wait—I love that!" said Lola. "Shoot we should make some T-shirts up." The others agreed, laughing.

"OK," said Dawn. "But in honor of my Breaux Bridge, Louisiana background, let's give it a Cajun twist. Let's spell it G-U-M-B-E-A-U-X Sisters!"

"Of course!" said Lola. "And let's jazz it up a little further—and we can spell 'sisters'—S-I-S-T-A-H-S."

"Perfect!" agreed Helen. "I can't believe we didn't think of this sooner."

Judith laughed, "Then your group could go on tour doing cooking shows across America. I'm sure y'all will end up being social media stars."

"Hold it. What do you mean 'your group?'" Lola asked Judith. Then to the other women she said, "She still doesn't get it. Tell her, Bea."

Bea looked up smiling from her gumbo and said calmly, "You're one of us now, dear."

"Like it or not!" laughed Lola.

Dawn added, "Yes, you are now officially our sister. Our Gumbeaux Sistah, in fact!"

Oddly, Judith did not panic at all.

No woman is an island. You must be at least an isthmus with one arm reaching out towards others.

—Bea

CHAPTER 6

As three o'clock drew near on Thursday afternoon, Judith thought about the four women she was expecting at her house. She was very aware that she did not really know them very well. A fleeting thought occurred to her that they might be a group of con women, cheating unsuspecting victims out of bowls of gumbo. She let that thought hang around for about one second, then laughed at herself out loud, *"Oh no, I'm not getting paranoid in my old age. Not me!"*

The doorbell rang at exactly three. Judith opened the door to find the very prompt Bea standing on her porch. Helen, Lola, and Dawn, texting away on her phone, were close behind her on the front sidewalk. Helen carried fresh-baked cornbread to go with the gumbo.

"There is gumbo, right dear?" inquired Bea seriously.

"Yep, there sure is. Please, come in," said Judith laughing, thinking that if they were gumbo con women, they were sure serious about their business.

Lola said loudly from the porch, "I hope you're not one of those people who eats potato salad with your gumbo. I could never get into it, but Dawn has to have it."

True to those words, Dawn carried in a small, plastic bowl of potato salad. "I didn't know if you would want this or not, but I brought some extra for you, just in case. I'm usually the only one who eats it this way. We're from Breaux Bridge, and my people all love it like this. I don't usually bother bringing it for anyone else because they haven't learned the fine art of mixing the two dishes. It's a killer combination."

Lola laughed, "Killer is right—it will make you want to die. It's a total waste of perfectly good gumbo."

Dawn sniffed, "Many find that it enhances the flavor—not wastes it."

Helen winked at Judith, "We have to go through this all the time." She turned to Lola and Dawn, laughing, "Now, kids, please stop bickering."

Bea ignored the argument and changed the subject in her own quirky, efficient way, "So speaking of art, Judith, these paintings on the walls are exquisite. Are they all yours?"

"Were we speaking of art?" asked Dawn with a little smile.

"If Bea says we were, then we were," nodded Lola with a grin.

Judith smiled too. "To answer your question, yes, they are my work, and I'm so glad you like them. I used to paint all the time, but I haven't created but a few pieces over the last ten years. The Art Museum takes up all my time." She grimaced, "Well . . . took up all my time."

"Well, that's why we're here today—to talk about all that—and to eat gumbo too, of course," smiled Bea. "But first, why don't you show us around, dear?"

Judith led them through her little, hundred-year-old shotgun house. Louisiana houses built in this era were constructed with the rooms attached one after another with no halls. The joke was that a person could shoot a shotgun in through the front door and have it go straight out the back door without hitting any walls—thus the name. Judith's mostly-unused studio was the very last room of the house.

The women were very complimentary about her decorating and her paintings, especially Dawn, who had an eye for artwork and was a bit of a collector. "Are any of your paintings for sale? Shoot, I'd buy two or three of these if they are—they're fabulous."

"It seems you have a common theme in many of your paintings," Bea said. "You've painted several groups of women who are obviously friends in different settings. To me, they tell a story of women supporting women. I love that, dear."

"You know, I've been painting these women for years. I'm not even sure why. I'm very drawn to the subject. I think of the work as inspirational art for women. And Dawn, these are not for sale right now. Sorry, but they are kind of my favorites. But if I don't get another job soon—please ask me again."

"Oh I will, even if you do get a job," laughed Dawn. Then she asked the other women, "Don't these paintings remind you of our little group? And the one with the palm trees in the background reminds me our girlfriends' weekend at the condo in Florida last year!" She smiled, remembering. "That was such a great time." Then back to Judith, "Maybe you'll paint a painting for me one of these days."

Lola piped up, "Do the women in the paintings have a name?"

"You mean actual names like Vicki, Betty, and Cindy?" asked Judith, puzzled.

Lola laughed out loud, "No, but that's funny. No, I meant as a group. Because if they don't, I have one for you. They are the original Gumbeaux Sistahs! Your paintings were created as a premonition to finding your way into our little group."

"Wow—now that's an interesting idea," said Helen. "Has some merit, I'd say."

"I love the idea," said Judith. "Hmmm . . . Gumbeaux Sistahs paintings. It makes me like the work even more."

"Me too," said Dawn. Helen and Bea agreed.

"Speaking of your job, we need to get down to business," said Bea. "Judith, is that gumbo ready?"

"Yes. Let's eat in the dining room. Everybody, come on into the kitchen and serve yourself," said Judith as she led them back to the kitchen.

After everyone was seated and began eating, appreciative noises could be heard around the table. Lola was the first to say, "Well, Judith, you're a true Gumbeaux Sistah. This is just amazing. It's your mom's recipe, right?"

"Yes, when she made gumbo it was almost like she was conjuring up a witch's brew," explained Judith. "She was secretive about the ingredients, and it took a long time to make."

"Isn't it funny how everyone's gumbo tastes completely different? There are so many variations. It can be made with seafood, chicken, sausage, venison, and God knows what else. Some people like okra gumbo. Some like a dark roux and some light. Some people like potato salad with it, and some people don't like to ruin it," laughed Lola, looking meaningfully at Dawn.

"That's right. And some people make it SOOO much better than others, if you know what I mean," answered Dawn, looking right at Lola. She turned to Judith, "But sistah, you nailed it."

"Thank you for the amazing meal, Judith. It was inspired. I think it's time we all got down to work, shall we?" asked Bea, although it was not really a question. "Does everyone have their assignments completed for Judith?"

Helen said, "I'll go first because there's something I want to do right now in Judith's house. I thought we should all start with a healing, so we're going to smudge your house first and get rid of the bad energy from your recent experience."

She pulled out a wad of dried, tied-together plant matter from a big, purple drawstring bag. "This is silver sage," she said, "I picked it in the back hills of Carmel Valley, California last summer. It only grows in hot, dry places, so I can't find it anywhere in Louisiana and have to hold onto it for special occasions. This is one of them." Next she produced a lighter and lit the end of the sage, holding it over a small pottery dish to catch ashes. She told each woman to hold still while she let the fragrant smoke waft over each of them, all the while saying prayers for their well-being and safety.

Judith had seen this type of ceremony before, and she knew that Helen had the best of intentions in mind and appreciated what she was trying to do. Then Helen walked through the house with the burning sage saying prayers for healing and love.

Judith liked the ceremonial aspect of it, and thought that it certainly could not hurt. She had been in such a tailspin since she had been fired. Truth is, she felt a little better when Helen was finished. Maybe it was from just knowing that a good person like Helen cared about her well-being.

"Nice," said Lola, nodding her head at her friend.

"Well done, dear," said Bea.

"Thanks, Helen," said Judith. "I think it helped. I've been so down the last few days. I've thought about selling the place and moving out west to stay with my daughter and her family. I'm just not sure what to do now. Of course, I've been checking online for job openings, and I have to say, it's looking a little bleak."

"That's why we smudged," said Helen, with a little knowing smile. "Wanting to be with your family is natural and a phase of what you're going through. But it's only a phase—or it could only be a phase. The sooner we elevate the energy of this place, the better off you'll feel about moving onto the next phase. OK, that's all I have of my homework for now, but I'll check in later to see if there's more I can do."

"What Helen said was right, Judith," said Dawn, slapping her hand on the table. "It's only a phase to want to run away. It's way too soon to talk about giving up, though. There's plenty of hope yet."

"Hell no, you can't give up. We're just getting started," said Lola.

"That's right, dear," said Bea. "As Dylan Thomas said, 'Do not go gentle into that good night.' You're sixty and close to retiring. From what you said, however, you don't have the means to retire. But you're not old. And even if you were, I think you have plenty of ass-kicking still inside you. That's why we're here. So, let's get going."

"Yes, time to kick ass!" yelled Lola.

Judith smiled at them all, "You women are really amazing. I wish I'd known you when I was younger."

"Now is exact right time for us to be here with each other," said Bea. "And there's something else you should know, dear. These assignments and ideas that we bring to you are not set in stone, so you don't have to stress over them. Often when we do this, we'll start with one idea, and that might lead to something completely different, and often amazing. That's the cool part. You just have to be open to the experience."

"I'm open," said Judith, nodding, surprising herself because she truly meant it.

"With that said, I'm next," said Lola, her eyes shining. "So, here's what I propose. What happened to you at the Art Museum was flat-out ageism—pure and simple. It's evil, unnecessary, hurtful, and truly ignorant. And it has all the earmarks of an issue that my activist friends and I would picket against. So, we're going to treat it as such. We're going to have a rally! I believe you said that the museum board meets on Mondays, right?"

Judith nodded.

"OK, I'll get my activist buddies and show up with signs on Monday, and we'll picket the outside sidewalk of the museum. You will have to make a sign—we all will . . ." said Lola enthusiastically.

"Wait, what!?" said Judith in shock. "Can we do that? Is that legal? I don't want to get arrested."

"She didn't tell you this, but Lola is also a lawyer," said Dawn, nodding.

"What? Really?" asked Judith. "A master gardener and a lawyer? What an unusual combination of skills."

"I also play the sax, but that's another story," said Lola, grinning.

"Sheesh!" said Judith. "You must have a superhero costume on under those clothes. By the way, I play some ukulele. In fact, I'm in a little band called the All Ukulele Band. We're a small group of women who play around town—sometimes at the Farmer's Market on Saturday morning. Maybe we could play together some day."

"I would love that. I don't get to practice near as much as I'd like. And about the lawyer thing—I don't practice law full-time because of my landscaping business, as you know. But I'm associated with my family's law firm, and I'll tell you, my law degree comes in really handy sometimes. So, with these signs we can send some very clear messages to the museum. They should say things like—NO AGEISM! GIVE JUDITH'S JOB BACK! WE WANT JUDITH! COVINGTON ART MUSEUM DISCRIMINATES"

"Wow!" said Judith. "I wasn't expecting that."

"What have you got to lose?" asked Lola, raising her eyebrows.

"Nothing, I guess."

"That's the spirit," laughed Lola. "Just stay open to the idea. This all sounds strange, but I've done it a bunch of times. It may just lead to something good."

"Is this legal, Lola?" ask Judith.

"She doesn't care," laughed Dawn.

Lola giggled as well, "Yes, in fact, it is as long as we're peaceful, truthful, and leave if the police kick us out."

"Police?" asked Judith, her eyes wide.

"Not to worry. This is not my first picket—we'll be fine. Trust me," nodded Lola.

"OK, I'm in," said Judith with trepidation. She wondered what the heck she was getting herself into. First she was fired, then she was hanging around with a bunch of crazy women, then possibly thrown in jail. She shook her head in amazement at herself.

"OK, we'll meet at St. John's Coffeehouse at nine-thirty Monday morning," said Lola. She rubbed her hands together. "This ought to shake things up."

"I'll warn Bitsy, my old assistant, that we're coming so she won't have a heart attack," said Judith.

"This ought to be good," said Dawn with relish. "Of course, we'll all be there to help."

"Yes, count on us, dear. We wouldn't miss it," said Bea.

"Fantastic. OK, don't forget to bring a sign. Makes us look legit," said Lola.

"OK," said Dawn, "Now it's time for my homework assignment. Y'all are going to love this. So you know how the art museum relies on donations from community businesses to keep its doors open? Well, guess which accounting firm always makes a sizable donation at the museum's annual spring event. Which, by the way, is always just lovely. Judith, I assume you are the one who was responsible for it, right?"

"Bitsy and I did it together," nodded Judith.

"Well, last year with those huge displays of dragonfly-themed art for spring—I just loved it! But I digress. So, my firm always contributes generously to the art museum—but we sure don't have to, if you catch my drift," crowed Dawn.

Judith gasped, "Oh my God! You're *that* accounting firm! Of course, I've met your husband before, but not you. He's always the one who delivers the check, usually to Ed Bagrett, so I didn't put two and two together. "

"That's all right, but I'm thinking that Lillian Deslattes will feel a financial pinch in her butt if she doesn't do right by you."

"That's blackmail," said Lola "Good—I like it!"

"That is actually quite good," nodded Bea.

"I know!" laughed Dawn. "So, I'll give Lillian a call in the morning and tell her our new conditions on that donation. We've never asked any conditions before, but today's a new day. I don't think it's asking too much after all we've done for them."

"It's worth a try, that's for sure," said Helen, nodding, "Very creative of you, Dawn."

"Man, I wish I could listen in on that conversation," said Lola gleefully. "Lillian's going to have a coronary!"

"Keep us posted after you talk to Lillian. I can't wait to hear how it turns out," said Bea. The others agreed. "OK then, we've heard from the three of you. Now I know this is a bit unusual, but I'd like to hold off on my idea until after Dawn talks to Lillian and after Lola's rally, if it comes to that. But please plan on spending a little time with me the following morning, if you could."

"I'll clear a little more space on the old calendar," said Dawn, hauling out her ever-present phone. Helen and Lola agreed to do the same.

"Of course I'll be there," said Judith.

"Well that settles it then—first Dawn's call, and if that doesn't work, then we'll do Lola's picketing, and then we meet again. But first, a little more gumbo is in order."

"Maybe a lot more," grinned Lola.

CHAPTER 7

The following morning, Dawn stood in her beautiful, remodeled kitchen. The radio was playing softly in the background, and a fresh cup of hot coffee was in her hand. She had an important task to perform that morning but took a moment to get ready for the day with her daily coffee ritual.

She was dressed, as usual, in a one of her classic work outfits, accessorized by expensive gold jewelry. This particular outfit had been on a mannequin in Columbia Street Marketplace just last week. Whenever Dawn walked into the store, the owner made it her business to show Dawn all the latest arrivals that would complement someone with Dawn's large frame. And since Dawn was a striking woman, with her dark eyes and high color, the owner found it delightful to help Dawn show off fashionable items to her advantage. Dawn was excellent advertising for the store.

It was not a secret that Dawn liked nice things—clothes, condos, hotels, food, boats, makeup, and cars. She was of the *"More is more!"* school of thought.

The radio in the kitchen was playing one of her old favorites: *Can't Get Enough of Your Love, Babe* by Barry White. She found herself humming along to the soulful tune as she sipped her coffee. She thought back for a moment to a time when the song was new, and Dawn did not have the lifestyle she did now. Far from it.

1974—Breaux Bridge, Louisiana: Dawn sang and danced around the tiny bedroom she shared with her little sister, Trinity. A new Barry White song was playing on the radio, and it was quickly becoming a favorite.

"I love that smooth, deep voice of his," she told her sister. "I mean who can resist that? I think I'm half in love with him!" They laughed over it together. Her sister was much younger, but the girls were close.

While she sang, Dawn dressed carefully for her job at the Bridge Burger House in the small, country town of Breaux Bridge, Louisiana. It was a quiet place on Bayou Teche, deep in Cajun country. Dawn's tiny house was set on a sparsely-populated, dirt road near the refinery.

That morning she pulled her dark, thick hair back in a slick ponytail, and her uniform was freshly pressed. She fitted it over her tall frame with ease.

Not for the first time, Dawn thought, *"Thank God they gave us uniforms. It's hard enough to find something to wear for school, much less for work."*

Her eye caught on a little green dress with white piping hanging by a hook on the closet door. The dress belonged to Trinity now, but had once belonged to Dawn.

Dawn grimaced, *"It's a good thing that the other two kids in our family are boys, or they would probably end up wearing that hand-me-down too."*

She had received the dress, already a reject from another little girl's closet, from their church after Dawn's mother had died from breast cancer when she was twelve. Her mother had been very active in the church. When she became ill, the church ladies helped out the family by supplementing food items and donating clothes. At her mom's request, they had also gathered small sewing and alteration jobs for Dawn's mother to do, so that she could help supplement the family's small income. Her mom was able to keep up with the work for a little while, but after a few months, she had to stop. Then the family had to rely solely on her dad's small paycheck from his maintenance job at the refinery. It was a job he was lucky to land.

He was a good man and a hard worker, but he was limited by a lack of education and a bad knee injury from his old high school football days. At that point, the kids quickly learned what it meant to be hungry.

When she was alive, their mother had made sure that she and the kids attended St. Peter's Church every Sunday. Their father had not been interested in the church services, so he never joined them. Then, after her mom was gone, Dawn made sure that her siblings still filed into Mass on Sunday mornings. They took their usual pew in one of the back rows. Being the oldest, she did her best to make sure her brothers and sisters were clean, wore their best, old clothes, and behaved themselves in church.

Because it was the only dress she owned, Dawn always wore that same little, green dress to church. For that and other reasons, Dawn dreaded each and every Sunday. She knelt down and kept her eyes straight ahead in church so she would not see other little girls, together with their mothers and fathers, dressed up in adorable little ruffled dresses. It was one of many humiliations that Dawn never forgot. The poverty. The pity. The cruelty. But she still insisted they attend church in memory of their mother. That, and because of the boxes of donuts offered after the service to the congregation, including five hungry boys and girls.

For a couple of years, things only got worse for Dawn's family. As she grew into her teens, the taunts about their poverty from the other kids at school haunted her. They called Dawn "Rag Doll" after a song by Frankie Valli, about a poor girl dressed in rags. She suffered a lot of teasing in town, as did her brothers and sisters. She had even gotten in several fights because of all the bullying. It served to make Dawn tough in her body and words, and she used both to cut down her adversaries. It taught her not to back down from trouble. People learned to think twice before starting trouble with her.

When Dawn turned fifteen, she got hired by the Bridge Burger Joint to run a register and help with serving when things got busy. Her family's financial strain eased up a tiny bit. She contributed to the family food budget, and her boss let her bring home the leftover french fries at night. She also helped to dress her siblings with clothes bought at the local Goodwill store and from Kmart on special occasions.

Then, in Dawn's sophomore year, she received the biggest break of her young life. Her math teacher, Mrs. Wandell, looked at Dawn, and instead of the tough, stubborn, young girl in her class, she saw a smart, young woman with potential. She invited Dawn to stay after class one day to discuss her grades, and ended up forging a friendship that lasted for many years. Mrs. Wandell took Dawn to task, taught her how to study, and gave her extra time tutoring when she needed it to advance. Dawn, in turn, took her new skills home to her younger brothers and sisters and taught them to study—when she could get them to hold still long enough. Everyone's grades improved. In effect, one excellent teacher's efforts affected an entire family that was sorely in need of some attention.

Dawn and her family were thrilled when Mrs. Wandell helped Dawn to get into Louisiana State University with a full-ride scholarship. Dawn decided to major in the one thing that had eluded her family her entire life—money. She graduated with honors with a degree in accounting, and her entire family showed up at her graduation, driven there by Mrs. Wandell. Dawn's people took up most of a whole row at the ceremony, and there were a great deal of joyful tears and pride flowing for their girl that day.

She felt like the world was opening up to her at last—even more so because of the handsome Dan Berard, a fellow accounting major, who she began dating in her third year at LSU. Dan was from New Orleans, but had dreams of a small Louisiana town lifestyle. He set his sights on Covington, Louisiana, a beautiful little city with several smaller towns surrounding it. It was an area large enough to support a new accounting firm quite well.

He and Dawn settled down there after their wedding. Over the years, they grew their business, the size of their family by having two kids, their wealth by leaps and bounds, and their standing in the community. Dawn was able to help her family back in Breaux Bridge and made sure that each one of her siblings got a chance to go to college, just as she had. She was proud of them, and proud of herself that she had been able to offer them the same kind of help that her teacher had offered her. They had all been extended a real chance at a future, and they were all smart enough to grab it and hold on for dear life.

Once she and Dan had reached a certain economic level, Dawn made sure to look the part with grooming, clothes, regular dermatology visits with Botox injections, and something called the vampire treatment that made her skin glow. Her nails were perfect, and so was her hair. She even managed to soften her strong country accent, and worked on refining an uptown New Orleans accent as best as she could. She was proud of her Cajun roots, but thought that a less pronounced accent might open doors for her and Dan, especially when dealing with accounts for business not in the South. Of course, if she had two glasses of wine, or hung around with Lola long enough, her new accent went straight out the window. She wanted Dan to be proud of her, and she never wanted to feel poor or deprived again.

Dawn thought back on how she and Dan had grown their business. They had worked long hours, networked, and given back to the community. Little by little, they grew to be a thriving presence in the city. They took on bigger and bigger accounts, such as the hospital and insurance companies. They also added dozens of small-business accounts without in-house accounting departments. Their company's reputation was solid.

Thinking of Judith for a second and her problems made Dawn think of the many moments of discrimination she herself had suffered as a woman in business. There were times during client meetings that the other parties, mostly men, but sometimes even women, would direct comments only to Dan and not to her, the woman. There were times when other parties would refuse to meet with Dawn without Dan being present. But Dawn was strong in more ways than one, and soon people grew to know her business savvy and respected her. Dan did not have to win them over in this way, but Dawn often did. She could see it happening in new clients still, especially now that she was getting older. Now she dealt with sexism and ageism. But she had accumulated plenty of business acumen and let them know it soon enough.

So far, Dawn's life had not been without its ups and downs but was fairly smooth sailing after marrying Dan and developing their business. They were quite happy in their marriage, even blissfully happy at times. There was, however, one particularly miserable point in their history. Four years ago, Dan decided to sleep with a young minister named Joyce from their church where Dan was on the council. It was a poor decision.

CHAPTER 8

Dawn took a sip of her coffee and remembered that day well. It was one of the most painful days of her life, and even now the memory caused her to close her eyes with a dull stab to her heart.

But, as hard as it was, it was also the day Dawn had met two very unusual new friends.

Dawn was hurt, angry, and stressed-out the morning when a friend from church took her aside at one of their women's networking breakfasts and told her about Dan's infidelity. She was completely stunned at first. She simply could not believe it. She had always trusted Dan. True, he was a very good-looking man, and women often noticed him. But he had always been faithful as far as Dawn knew. She knew the young female minister in question and did not quite get the attraction at first. Looks-wise, Joyce Flanders was no temptress. But to Dawn, that only made things worse, because if Dan had not been tempted so much by the woman's looks, then he might have been tempted by something more substantial—something more dangerous to their marriage. It broke her heart.

Dawn immediately left the breakfast, went home, packed her bags, and left again by noon. She went straight to the beautiful new Southern Hotel in downtown Covington and took a luxury suite. She left Dan a note which only said, "I've left and you know why."

She told her grown daughters, and everyone else, that Dan and she were remodeling the house. While Dan held down the fort at home and kept an eye on the contractors, she was camping out in luxury. Of course, there was no remodel. There was nothing but pain. Dawn cried till she could not cry anymore that afternoon.

Dan found out where she was staying and called three or four times, but Dawn hung up every time. He left messages telling her that it was all a mistake, that it had not meant anything, that he loved her and wanted her to come home. He sounded miserable and sincere, but she could not stand the sound of his voice.

Dawn fell asleep fully clothed on the big bed, awakening in the early evening. She got out of bed, washed her face, and put on fresh makeup and a nice dress. Then she went downstairs for a light dinner in the hotel restaurant. The hotel bar was bustling with Friday evening patrons, so she stopped in there for a before-dinner martini. She said hello to people she knew, as it was a popular after-work watering hole. She thought proudly that she was holding things together pretty well, and that she was being her usual charming and friendly self.

But when she left the bar and walked down the hall to the restaurant, she found herself suddenly frozen in place. She was simply immobile with the pain of her heartbreak. To her horror, tears came streaming down her face. Dawn finally ducked out a side door and ended up back by the deserted, palm tree lined swimming pool. There she found a corner where she could try and get a hold of herself before having to go back inside.

"At least," she thought, *"There's no one out here right now."*

At that moment, from right behind a large hedge, out strolled Bea and Helen, arm in arm.

"Hello, dear," said Bea, her blue eyes twinkling in the fading light.

Startled by their presence at first, Dawn stared at them for a moment with tears still streaming down her face. She recovered momentarily and swiped at the wetness with a napkin. She managed a smile for the two women, trying to be polite. She assumed they would say their greetings and then go on their way.

———※———

Standing at her kitchen sink, Dawn chuckled as she remembered the first time meeting her friends. She smiled with affection and admiration. *"Those two were like super-glue that day. I couldn't get rid of them—and thank goodness for that!"*

———※———

Seeing Dawn in tears, Helen and Bea dug in stubbornly. They stood near Dawn's poolside table, chatting for the longest time. Dawn dropped several hints that she would like to be alone, but they refused to acknowledge them. Then, much to Dawn's horror, they sat down and made themselves at home at her table, still chattering away. They began to ask her questions about her life—what she did for a living and if she was married. There was something about the two women that, even though they were complete strangers, they were somehow able to draw Dawn out, little by little. She ended up telling these two odd little women what was eating her up inside. She needed to tell someone.

After her story, Dawn said, "Dan and I are finished, of course. Oh, he says he's sorry and that it was a mistake, but really—who is he kidding? A mistake? A typo is a mistake. Dropping mustard on the kitchen floor is a damn mistake. But screwing the church's young music minister, and then calling it a mistake is not just a mistake. That's pure B.S.!" Dawn was furious, crying and half-laughing at the same time.

Helen nodded. "At least you haven't lost your sense of humor. But I sure don't blame you for being angry." Then she turned to Bea, "Don't you have some gumbo at your place? I'll bet our new friend here could use a hot meal and some company."

"Yes, indeed," agreed Bea. They immediately invited Dawn to dinner at Bea's and much to her surprise, she accepted. There was something about these two women that was comforting. She felt safe with them, and it seemed so much better than going back to her lonely hotel room, luxury suite or not.

Off they went and enjoyed some gumbo at Bea's house. It was Bea's mother's gumbo recipe, and it was, of course, fabulous. It was so good that Dawn almost did not miss having her usual side of potato salad. For that reason alone, she had to admit it was first-class gumbo.

After dinner, they sat in Bea's living room, shared a bottle of wine, and talked. Bea was never one to sit idly by in any situation, so she had to ask Dawn, "Well I know it's awfully soon to ask, since all this just happened, but do you have any type of plan about how to handle all this mess? Or maybe you have just a next step in mind at least?"

"No," replied Dawn. "I honestly don't, except to keep working and living at the hotel for now."

"Well, you can't stay there forever," said Helen, and then suggested, "So if you don't have a plan, the very least we can do is help you make one—if you'd like."

Dawn squinted her eyes with skepticism but said she was open to the idea. "What have I got to lose?"

"Atta girl!" said Bea, and forged ahead. "The best way to go about any plan is to first figure out what you want. Now, I know that sometimes it's not easy to know, and often people just ignore what they want while they are taking care of other people in their lives. Let's just say that Helen and I, at this point in our lives, have learned not to ignore it. Going after what we want and helping each other get it is something we take very seriously."

"That sounds wonderful, but also wonderfully oversimplified," said Dawn, narrowing her eyes with skepticism. "For instance, sometimes circumstances and emotions get in the way of knowing what you want, much less getting it."

"That's so true, dear," said Bea. "But it's still a place to start. So . . . shall we?"

"Look, I really have to ask you two something first," said Dawn in her typically honest fashion. "Why are you doing this? I mean, I can tell that you are two very nice women, and very smart. But I can't figure out why you are trying to help me."

"It's like this, dear. Helen and I have both had full lives, and we've both been through a lot—a lot more than you'd ever dream of, actually. Neither one of us had people we could turn to when times got tough, at least not close enough that we felt comfortable asking for help. Neither one of us has children, and even if we did, we wouldn't have wanted to burden them with problems. And there just wasn't anyone else. Then we realized that a lot of people are in this boat. We've come to recognize the signs of people who just need someone to talk to. When we met each other, we were total strangers—just like we are to you right now. But a light went on at that time, and we realized that it didn't matter if we were strangers. Our instincts told us that we could still help each other, and so we became each other's support. A second family, if you will."

"And besides, we discovered that we both loved gumbo," laughed Helen.

"Well, who doesn't?" said Dawn, shrugging.

"We disagree on whose mom's gumbo recipe is best, but of course my mom is the clear winner. She's Italian, after all. We just cook everything better," smiled Helen.

"Oh, here we go," laughed Bea.

"But we do agree that both of our gumbo recipes are pretty darned good," said Helen.

"This *is* really good," admitted Dawn.

"Do you cook, Dawn? More specifically, can you make gumbo?" asked Helen hopefully.

"Of course, but we always have a potato salad side with it where I come from."

"That's a bit of a sacrilege where I come from," laughed Helen. "But of course, if you want to bring your own, no one will mind."

Bea hesitated then said gently, "Dawn, when we saw you crying by the pool tonight, we knew we had to ask if you needed some help. I hope you don't mind, but I'm awfully glad we did now."

Dawn looked at her and smiled sadly, "I'm glad too. Thanks, both of you."

"OK then," said Bea, taking charge as usual. "Let's focus on getting back to the plan, so you can figure out what it is you want to do. What is it that you'd like to see happen?"

"Well, when it comes to Dan, I'd like to kill him slowly, maybe coat him in honey and bury him in a giant red ant pile. The ants and the alligators can fight it out over the spoils," said Dawn, half-crying again.

Helen could not resist a giggle, "Remind me not to mess with you, Dawn."

"Vengeance is mine, sayeth the Dawn," laughed Bea. Then she added, "I see you have a creative evil streak, my friend. Not saying that's all bad, but let's work around it for now. Let's try this—what is the best ending to all this that would make you the happiest?"

"Honestly? I miss my husband. I would really like to kill him, but the truth is, he's always been a really good man and my best friend. He's never cheated before, I don't think. I know the man, and I think it's possible that he may have had confused feelings and was attracted to this younger woman. But I also know he loves me very much," she paused to think.

"Keep going, Dawn. How would the best ending look?" asked Bea.

"Well, if I'm being truly honest, I would like my husband back, but too much has happened for that to happen. I couldn't take him back just like that. I admit that I'm not above wanting to teach Dan a lesson—maybe even getting a little revenge for the pain he's putting me through."

"What do you mean?" asked Helen.

"Here's what I mean," said Dawn, narrowing her eyes with sudden focus. "I hate the idea that he thinks maybe he can hurt me and our marriage and just come back like it never happened.

Meanwhile, I will suffer for years after this, even if it's quietly—although that's not really my style. I'm kind of loud, most of the time." She laughed then continued, "I just don't think that I could ever forget what he did. Or forgive him, unless I made sure he knew how it felt."

"Go on," urged Bea.

Dawn thought, and then a spark came into her hazel eyes. "Actually. . . I may just have a plan after all." She smiled at the two women. "OK, here's what I'm thinking. Let's say I agree to meet him for dinner—maybe Friday— to talk things over. And it might seem cruel but . . . well, what the hell . . . a girl's gotta do what a girl's gotta do. I'll tell him at dinner that I'll be staying at the hotel for three more weeks. Now here's the good part—I'll tell him that . . ." she stopped and grinned. "Yes, I'll tell him that he will need to get in touch with contractors and remodel our kitchen during that time. I've been wanting a new countertop and backsplash for a while now!"

Helen threw her head back and laughed, "Boy, you are good!"

Dawn continued, this time with a dark tone. "I will also tell him that during those three weeks, I will be unfaithful to him. Just once."

At this Bea and Helen's eyes widened. "Oh my," said Bea.

Dawn went on, "He won't know when it will happen, but it will." The look on her face was somehow gleeful and dangerous. "Then at the end of that three week period, if he'd still like to come back, I'll explore the options. That will be my plan. My deal. I think I can live with that."

"Whoa! Nope, I'm never, ever going to cross you, girl!" said Helen, wide-eyed.

"What do you think the outcome will be—what will he say to that?" asked Bea.

"I don't know, honestly," said Dawn. "This is completely new ground for us. But the thing is—I really do mean it. If he wants this marriage, he will have to live through the next three weeks knowing that I've been unfaithful. Just like I'm living through the same thing right now. It won't be easy for him. Our marriage might just break for good. But it's the only way I can think of that I can live with right now."

"And if he can't deal with it?"

"Then we split the house, the business, and everything else. I've come from nothing, and I've had to start over in my life. So I'm not afraid of having nothing. I would hate it, but I'm not afraid of it. I know how to do it. I'm afraid of losing Dan but more afraid of not being able to live with myself. I would feel weak and abused if I just take him back. And one thing I'm not—is weak." Her voice was steady and held a resolve.

"I can believe that. I admire you," said Bea.

"And it looks like you've made up your mind," said Helen gently, then smiled slightly. "And you may just get a new kitchen out of all this."

"So, OK, in two days, it will be Friday," said Bea. "You have a couple of days to think about it, and that's important. Would you like to get together again next week for cocktails just to check in and talk?"

"Yes, I think I'd like that," smiled Dawn. She looked at the two women, her two new friends, and what she felt was true gratitude that she had met them.

After two days of thinking, crying, and ultimately affirming her resolve, Dawn met Dan for dinner Friday night. She dressed carefully in a form-fitting, black cocktail dress and heels. Of course, she had gotten her hair and nails done, and was extra careful with her makeup. She felt she was setting the stage for a dramatic play, which she was.

When she walked into the restaurant of her hotel, she could see that her efforts had the desired effect on her husband.

"You look beautiful, Dawn," he said carefully and contritely as they sat down. Dawn could see he would be on his best behavior for this meeting. She knew full well how charming her husband could be, but her mind was made up. The waiter appeared right away and handed them their menus. Dan was surprised when Dawn handed hers right back and asked the waiter, "Can you just bring me a Ketel One martini and two olives?"

Dan asked for a Sazerac, and when the waiter left, Dan asked, "What about dinner, Dawn? I hear they have an amazing poached oyster with fennel cream entrée that you'd probably love."

Dawn was glad to see that Dan had done his homework on the hotel menu beforehand, but said, "Yes, I do love it. I actually had it here last night, and it's spectacular. But dinner is not really why I'm here, Dan. I have something to say to you, and you may not feel like eating afterwards. Not sure I will either, to tell you the truth."

Their drinks were delivered while Dan looked very uncomfortable, waiting to hear what Dawn had to say. Dawn took a huge gulp to firm up her decision. "Here's the deal, Dan. I don't know why you chose to go outside our marriage . . ."

Dan started to say, "I'm so sorry, Dawn, but it was just a crazy situation. I didn't mean for it to happen. She and her husband are going through a rough patch, and she came to me for help, and I just felt so sorry for her. One thing led to another . . ." But Dawn interrupted him.

"Let me finish. Maybe one day I might like to hear the ending of that story, but tonight is not really that night. You've put me through hell, Dan. That's just the truth of it. You know my family. We're tough, and we're not exactly a forgiving group. Once you've harmed us, it's hard for us to forget. My Uncle Gill is still in jail because someone criticized the kind of car he drove. Of course, I know that's crazy, and I'm not crazy, but I don't take things lightly either. You chose to hurt me and our marriage. You chose to test us. But I have a test of my own."

Dan was looking more uneasy by the minute.

"My plan is this—I'm staying at the Southern Hotel for the next three weeks."

Dan looked crestfallen, "Honey, you know I'm sorry. Please come home. I was so hoping you'd come home with me tonight."

"Three weeks, like I said. During that time please have contractors come in and install a new countertop and backsplash in the kitchen. I'll text you about what I want in there. You'd better do that right away so they can fit you into that three-week time frame."

Dan's mouth fell open, and he started to protest then thought better of it. He finally said, "OK, if that is what it will take to bring you home."

Dawn continued, "Well, great, but I'm not finished. I'm staying at this hotel where, downstairs, our little town has its most popular and sophisticated cocktail bar. There are lots of locals just dropping in for a cocktail after work, lots of business meetings that go on here, and lots of out-of-towners staying here. Here's the thing—and this is the part you really won't like—sometime during the next three weeks, I will sleep with someone in this hotel. Someone who is not my husband. It might be someone from out of town, or it could be someone local. Maybe someone we both know from work or even—our church."

Dan looked panicked, like he might even begin to cry.

Dawn went on, "You won't know when it will happen, and you won't ever know who it will be. Then, after three weeks is over, I will come home to our house. If you are still there, and I have a new kitchen, then we can talk about forgiveness and putting our marriage back together. If you are not there, I will understand. It takes a great deal of strength to hold up under this kind of insult. I've always been strong. You know that. Let's see if you are strong too. I will understand if you leave." Then she added, "But you've always been a good man—and somewhat wise. We'll just have to see now how wise you are."

"You can't be serious!" said Dan, appalled.

"Actually, I am," said Dawn calmly. She drank down the remainder of her martini and stood up. "Well, I think that covers it. If it makes any difference to you at this point, I hope you make it. I really do. I'll be home on Friday in three weeks. Goodnight, Dan. I'm going to leave now."

Dawn knew her husband's face like she knew her own. She had never seen it register the level of shock that it held now. When she walked out of the restaurant, she thought sadly, but with a measure of satisfaction, "*That man should know better than to mess with a Robichaux girl.*"

During the next three weeks, Dawn had dinner with Bea and Helen twice and solidified their friendship and mutual love of gumbo. She told them that one night, about a week after she had met Dan for dinner, she had discovered him having a drink in the Southern Hotel bar, obviously stalking her. He had looked pale and several pounds thinner. Dawn felt sorry for him, but was determined to see her plan through. It was the hardest three weeks of her life. Dan's too.

Three weeks to the day after their dinner, Dawn pulled into her driveway late Friday evening. She smiled when she saw that the lights were on all over the house. She walked in the front door and found dinner and lit candles waiting for her on the dining room table. As a bonus, there was a big pot of gumbo on the stove that Dan had actually made himself. A bowl of fresh flowers sat on the new countertop.

The only thing he said when Dawn walked in was, "Welcome home, Dawn. I've missed you like crazy, and yes, I'll always be strong for you." He never asked her about her three weeks, and she never told him about it either.

He took her to bed that night. The marriage was too fractured to fix at this point, so they decided instead to say "the hell with it," and completely start over.

Dawn had never loved him more. And she kept in touch with her new friends, Bea and Helen. They often met for coffee at St. John's Coffeehouse and got together occasionally at each other's houses for gumbo.

Bea had raised an eyebrow when Dawn first told them her plan. "Are you ready to take that risk, dear?"

Dawn answered, "No, but yes. Sometimes you just have to draw a line in the sand."

"We know exactly what you mean," said Helen. "And so you have."

Over cocktails one night, after the three weeks were up, Helen could not resist asking, "Well, it's all over with now, Dawn. You drew your line in the sand, and apparently it was the right thing to do. But are you ever going to tell us what happened during those three weeks?"

Dawn smiled slyly at them both, then continued to sip her martini.

"I guess not," laughed Helen. "Shoot."

They never asked again, and she never did tell.

You are under no obligation to be crazy when you join this group. We can teach you everything you need to know.

—Dawn

CHAPTER 9

Dawn mused over that period in her life and instantly felt so grateful for her sisters—her Gumbeaux Sistahs. Her thoughts turned to her newest sistah, Judith, and how much she needed help now. With that in mind, she picked up her phone, dialed the art museum, and asked for Lillian Deslattes. She was transferred to the conference room where Lillian sat, going over some notes.

"Lillian? Dawn Berard here. How have you been?"

"Excellent," said Lillian. "How nice to hear from you. How is Dan?"

"We're both fine, thanks," answered Dawn crisply. "But I need to discuss something disturbing that has come to my attention. It's about Judith Lafferty."

"Oh?" said Lillian, suddenly alert.

"Yes. You probably aren't aware of this, but Judith is a great friend of mine—a lovely woman. She's smart and capable."

"Really? No, I didn't know that. But honestly, I'm afraid that has not been my experience," said Lillian carefully.

Dawn said in a super sweet voice, "Oh dear. Well, I'm sure there's a big misunderstanding. She's such a dear friend, such a professional, too. Those events she put on every year were nothing short of enchanting. They made the museum contributors, like Dan and me, want to just throw our checkbooks at her. Might I suggest that you take another look and reconsider your opinion?"

Lillian gave a short bark of a laugh and said with a bit of chill in her voice, "Well, I can see why you'd want to throw something at her. Listen Dawn, there was no misunderstanding. Maybe you don't know her as well you think. The woman is incompetent."

"You mean the woman who put on the fundraisers for the art museum for the last ten years and did so with great success? The one who raised so much money last year that the museum was able to get Barry Bishop's paintings on the wall for the fall show?"

"Yes. But you have no idea . . ." started Lillian hurriedly.

"But I do have a very good idea, Lillian," cutting her off. "I know that Berard Accounting is one of your top sponsors for many of those events. Judith has always stayed in the background when it came to those events, and you, of course, always take credit for everything. But we both know, and so does everyone else, who the real credit goes to, don't we?" Dawn's tone was pure ice now.

Lillian said pointedly, "Dawn, what do you want? I'm not sure why you're taking up my time with in-house museum matters that don't really concern you. It's my job to look out for the welfare of this organization. And if there is dead wood, or incompetency, or staff that needs to make room for new blood, it's my job to make sure that happens."

"I'll tell you what I want, Lillian. I want the board to reinstate Judith as manager of the art museum. She was fired in an unprofessional, and probably illegal, manner."

Lillian was on high alert now, "There was nothing illegal about it. She didn't make fundraising quotas, and we had to let her go. So, what you're asking is not going to happen. I know what's best for the museum." She was so used to having people do what she demanded that it did not occur to her that someone would dare question her.

"Do you? I wonder if the rest of the board agrees with you."

"They will back me up, as usual." Lillian's voice was the epitome of confidence.

"I wonder if they will if Berard Accounting pulls their sponsorship," said Dawn archly.

Lillian gasped and backtracked, "Seriously, Dawn? This matter is museum board business, and we are handling it in a manner that is best for the organization. You wouldn't want to do something that would hurt the museum, would you? You and Dan have always been loyal contributors to what is a beloved local institution. Think about what you are saying."

"I am. Neither of us wants to hurt the museum. So, of course, with your reputation of being so easy to work with, I know you'll reconsider, right?" said Dawn sarcastically.

"No, I won't. I can't. The museum needs for her to be gone, and I'll thank you to stay out of museum business."

"OK, thank you. You've been very helpful. I just needed to see where you stood before moving forward."

"Moving forward? Just what are you up? I hope you're not going to do anything rash."

"Wait and see. Enjoy your afternoon, Lillian." Dawn hung up with a fast-beating heart but still wearing a smile. "That was kind of fun," she laughed. "That woman has always driven me crazy."

She picked up her phone and texted her Gumbeaux Sistahs. *"Emergency coffee meeting—Sat. morning—tomorrow—9AM St. John's Coffeehouse"*.

—m—

The next morning, Judith walked the four blocks to St. John's Coffeehouse to meet her new friends. They were already waiting for her at a table with her coffee order, a skinny-vanilla latte. Bea had texted her on her way to ask what she planned to order. The place was crowded, and they did not want to waste time. When Judith walked up, the sistahs were chatting, and Dawn was busy texting.

"OK, put down the phone and tell us what's up," said Lola.

Dawn finished her text and looked up, grinning, "OK Sistahs, here's what's happening." She told them all about her phone call with Lillian Deslattes. "What an awful woman!"

Lola cracked up, but Bea gave her a warning look.

"Seriously, she sure has it in for you, Judith," said Dawn. "What did you ever do to her?"

"I wish I knew!" said Judith, shaking her head. "Mostly I just tried to get my job done and stay out of her way. I don't know—maybe that was it. Maybe I should have been in her face more. Maybe she respects confrontation."

Dawn maintained, "Somehow, I don't think so. She wants you out, and she wants this young man in, but I wonder why. She said something about you not making new quotas. But as you told us already, she had raised those quotas just for the event. Again, I wonder why. She also mentioned that sometimes we need to make room for new blood. Do you think it's truly just a case of ageism?"

"Could be. Man, I hate that! Whatever happened to 'If it ain't broke, don't fix it?'" asked Lola. "Judith did a great job there."

"What's shocking is that Lillian herself is so ageist. She's close to our age, isn't she?" asked Dawn.

"I don't think you can assume that older people wouldn't be ageist," said Bea. "They have been subjected to an exclusionary culture all their lives, just as much as younger people. Unless they challenge it on their own, they can fall victim to that type of thinking too. Plenty of them unthinkingly accept second-class status as 'just the way things are.'"

"Thank God we're enlightened," said Helen with a smirk.

"Well, at least I am," laughed Lola.

"You've had too much coffee, obviously," grinned Dawn, and then said seriously, "So, am I right to think that it's time to move to part two of our plans for Judith?" She looked around and found four heads nodding in agreement. "OK Lola, that means you're up."

Lola sat up abruptly in her chair, suddenly all fiery energy, "OK y'all, it's time to picket. I love a good picket, don't you? So, we all should bring signs and friends to meet Monday morning at St. John's at nine-thirty. We'll catch the board when they open for the day. Dawn, can you call the press?"

"On it," said Dawn, making notes on her phone.

"I can't believe you're doing all this for me," said Judith, looking around frankly. "I guess I still don't quite understand. I only hope that I can return the favor someday."

"It's because you're our Gumbeaux Sistah, girl. I mean, who else is going to do it?" laughed Helen.

"Well, that's my point," said Judith. "Most people would not do anything at all."

"That's exactly why we have to be sistahs," said Bea, standing up. "And don't worry about returning the favor—because you will, I promise." Helen, Lola, and Dawn hooted with laughter.

"Watch out, Judith," said Lola. "Bea will put you to work before you can even put your hat on."

"That's what sistahs do," smiled Bea. "We stick together and make things happen."

"Well, let's go do it again!" said Lola happily.

CHAPTER 10

L illian Deslattes hung up the phone with Dawn and sat in the conference room of the art museum going over their conversation. She was furious but also worried that Dawn would go through with her threat. But she thought, *"I'll be damned if Dawn Berard is going to tell me what to do."* It was time for Judith Lafferty to leave the museum for so many reasons, some of which were known only to Lillian. *"And you'd think that after ten years at the same job, she'd step aside and let new blood take over."* Thomas to be exact.

"It's just time," she thought. Of course, it wasn't an easy thing to go through—to just step aside and let new people take over. But it happened to everyone sooner or later. Even to her. After all she had been through, she knew better than anyone when it was time for a person to move on from a position when their time was up. Sometimes you had to be the instigator, and sometimes you had to be the recipient of the bad news. But the instigator is the bringer of change, and that was sometimes necessary.

The Covington Art Museum was quiet at that time of day, and Lillian was left alone with her thoughts and memories. Her heart grew heavy with old mixed feelings. They were a strange combination of pride, love, and deep sadness, all jumbled up together.

She got up, walked to the conference room door, and looked straight out of the museum's front windows just in time to see her husband, Jack, getting out of his car. She had been waiting for him to pick her up so they could go to lunch. She did not know why he had not simply texted her to come out, but that was all right. Jack was very social and liked to come in and say hello to whoever was around.

She habitually glanced at a nearby mirror to check her hair and makeup. She could not help but feeling a little proud of her own reflection. She saw a woman who, after all these years, had kept her size six figure by sheer willpower alone. Her blue eyes shone out of a pretty, but aging pale face with dark, almost-black hair. She knew she was still attractive at fifty-nine. Her eyes drew back to Jack getting ready to walk into the front door, and worry lines crossed her forehead. Those lines were often there these days when she thought of her husband.

Lillian looked past her husband, and her eye caught on a *For Rent* sign on the building across the street from the museum. It made her breath hitch. A real estate sign could always make her both smile and wince at the same time. So many of her life's memories revolved around real estate—and her family. The memories were like life itself, both wonderful and terribly sad.

1985—Covington, Louisiana

"Oh my God, Jack—we did it! It's ours." said twenty-four-year-old Lillian, sitting in the passenger seat of their Ford Taurus. It was a Saturday morning, and she was wearing jeans, a stylish, white, long shirt and white Keds. Her black hair was tied back in a scarf, and she looked young, fresh, and full of excitement. Jack sat next to her, also dressed in jeans with his longish brown hair and black sunglasses. They were eating sausage sandwiches from a local fast food joint and sitting in front of a commercially zoned building in downtown Covington. The building still had a *For Lease* sign in front of it, but it was solidly spoken for at this point—by Lillian and Jack Deslattes. They had signed the rental agreement the day before and were so excited about it that they decided to have breakfast sitting in front of their soon-to-open, new business—the Magnolia Real Estate Co.

They had named the company after Jack's mom's favorite flower, since she loaned them money to help kick off their new venture.

"It's all ours, alright, Lilly. And it's a miracle," said Jack with a huge grin on his handsome face. "And one day soon, we won't have to eat any more sausage sandwiches. We can have eggs Benedict, or caviar on toast, or whatever it is rich people eat for breakfast." He poked her in the ribs. "But you'll sneak out with me once in a while for fast food, won't you? I kind of like these things."

She laughed and threw her arms around him. "Jack, you make everything fun. Let's spend our lives making lots of money and having lots of fun doing it."

And it was exactly that—fun and exciting for many years. They were successful beyond their dreams, handling real estate all over St. Tammany Parish and beyond. They designed and built a beautiful home on the Tchefuncte River where they raised their two children, Gwendolyn and Larry.

When the kids finished college and came into the business, one at a time, she and Jack had been thrilled and proud. Their kids had done well at Magnolia Real Estate, and before long they became the top sellers consistently in the company. Lillian had doted on those kids.

—⚊⚊—

"*Over-doted, I guess,*" she thought grimly, staring out the front window of the museum. Then she shook her head. "*No, what happened was a natural progression. It's the way life is. Changes happen.*" The first change came when Jack had health problems and retired in his mid-fifties. His diet was never very good before his heart attack, but it sure improved after that. He cut out red meat, certainly sausage sandwiches, and most alcohol. Then he took up golf and soon became a fanatic. She watched him come up the front steps now of the museum, and admired his slim physique and healthy tan, something you would have never seen on Jack before his heart turned on him.

His retirement had been hard on Lillian. She missed his presence around the office and being able to discuss real estate deals in detail like they once did. But she and the kids had it all under control. It was a well-oiled machine by that time, so Jack never looked back. Eventually, Lillian made the kids full partners in the firm and all went just fine for a while. Both kids enjoyed going to real estate conventions, something Lillian and Jack had rarely attended, which proved to be well-worth the firm's money. Their kids learned about new innovations in the business and implemented new software programs and technology improvements. Social media was embraced and managed by her daughter. Lillian was impressed with the new additions and spent many hours learning the programs to stay current. She had to admit that the new regimen made operating the business much easier in the long run, and it showed in their bottom line.

But after a while, things began to change again. Gwendolyn started making remarks to Lillian such as, "I'll bet you'd love to be playing golf with dad right now, wouldn't you?" Then both kids began to make unilateral decisions about the business behind her back. At first, she found it astonishing. It hurt her feelings and made her boiling mad. She confronted them about it, but they always had an excuse, such as, "Mom, you were out showing that property, and we needed to make this decision or we would lose the deal." So she shoved the hard feelings aside, little by little, always making excuses for their behavior because they were her children. She was proud that they were so sharp and decisive.

Then, eventually, she was no longer consulted about anything by the kids. It became a partnership in name only. Ageism was in full force. She found herself making excuses for it, then not fighting back, then falling into complacency. She thought, *"If they keep pushing me away, they might just push me straight into some kind of assisted living home before I'm sixty!"*

She tried to talk to Jack about it, but he was so happy being retired that he tried to get her to retire too. Her words fell on deaf ears. Well-tanned, golf ears.

After so much pressure from both sides, she considered retirement. She loved her job, loved the company, and was not really ready for it, but apparently it was the right thing to do. *The older must make way for the young. That's the way of nature, isn't it?"* she thought. It did not matter that she was still sharp as a tack and able to finagle a deal with the best of them.

So, one day she let go. The children and Jack threw her a big retirement party, but they were the only ones celebrating.

Afterwards, Lillian drifted and did not know what to do with herself. She tried golf with Jack, but truly loathed the game. She did volunteer work, but it was just not for her. What Lillian still loved was the chase, the deal making. She found herself growing bitter toward her family over the years for having forced her into the situation. She did not know how to deal with the bitterness except to turn and inflict it on other people. She became harsher—and manipulative. After all, she had learned every trick in the book about how to deal with the public through her real estate business, so she knew when to be charming and when to come down hard like a brick. People slowly began to be wary of her as she grew into the role of a hard woman who always got her way. While it did not exactly make Lillian happy, it made her powerful.

She discovered that she had an avid interest and fascination for art. She studied up on it and even began collecting some paintings for her home. Eventually, she pushed and bullied her way onto several art-related boards, including the New Orleans Museum of Art board. Years later, when the Covington Art Museum opened, she found a position on that board, since it was closer to home. The Covington museum was impressed with her credentials coming from the fabulous New Orleans Museum of Art.

Lillian knew how to wield her power, and she carved out her own little world at the museum where she felt strong. Cruel and strong. The other board members began to fear her. Each of them at some time or other had experienced her sarcastic, wicked tongue.

Ed Bagrett, one of the Covington Museum's board members, once suggested that the entire board be allowed to judge art for intake, and not just the small Intake Committee headed by Lillian. Lillian asked him sweetly what kind of experience he had had as a curator. Lillian, herself, did have experience from the New Orleans Museum of Art. Ed replied that his experience came from being an avid art collector, and also because he was an artist himself, as were several others on the board.

"Seriously, Ed? So, let me get this straight. Your answer is— no experience, right?" retorted Lillian with cold finality. "Please just stick with what you know. This is obviously not your wheelhouse."

Very few board members had the nerve to cross or challenge her viper tongue.

Lillian grew more formidable with the years, but her bitterness and power caused a greater rift between her and her family. She often feigned a busy schedule when family events came up so they spent less and less time together. There was a hidden, deep resentment that had never healed in her heart.

Then about a year ago, something changed again. This time with Jack, and the tenuous ties she had with her husband were all but severed. Lillian did not want to believe it, but all the signs were there. She suspected an affair.

She could not prove anything, but Jack was acting strangely. He started coming around the museum more and more, which was unusual. He said he was stopping by to see if Lillian needed any help. A few times over the years, the museum board had asked Jack to make minor repairs in the museum since he was handy, available, and happy to help. Plus, it saved the museum money. Still, it puzzled Lillian. Why was he around so often? It certainly was not to see her. Something did not feel right. She knew Jack had a lot of free time, but she also knew he had usually rather spend that time on the links. Then, one afternoon, she saw Jack hanging out in the doorway of the museum front office talking to Judith Lafferty, and it struck her like a hammer on an anvil.

Her breath caught in her lungs, and tears stung her eyes. *"Oh my God—no!"* she thought. She stood there trying not to cry for a minute, but soon enough her tough nature came out. She silently walked closer to the two of them so she could hear their conversation.

They were discussing the beautiful new garden window installation. It was designed by a local landscaper, Lola Trahan. The designer had turned a beautiful, hundred-year-old bay window into a living work of art. They had had a grand reveal for the window, and people stopped into the museum to see the window as often as they came to see the art on the walls.

Jack had been asking about the installation and how often it needed to be maintained.

"That's weird," thought Lillian. *"Why the sudden interest in sculpture gardening?"* Jack was a garden fanatic, but he usually stuck with his vegetable garden. They enjoyed cucumbers, tomatoes, and many other fresh vegetables that went with his new healthy lifestyle, thanks to Jack's labors in the garden.

She heard Judith say that the landscaper came in once a week on Mondays for maintenance, but Judith seldom saw her because that was her day off. Jack and Judith talked about how beautiful the garden was. He told her about his gardening and surplus of tomatoes at home and offered to bring her some.

Lillian backed slowly away from their conversation with her radar at full alert. She walked slowly into the room where the Living Art Installation stood. She could not help but admire it herself—it was unique and beautiful. Lola Trahan, the creator of the garden, had outdone herself. Bitsy was in charge of dealing with the garden upkeep and was doing a great job. Lillian had never told Judith or Bitsy this, but before the big reveal, she had secretly removed Lola Trahan's name from list of invitees. So when the reveal night came along, Lola was not there. And there stood Lillian, front and center, taking credit and accepting praise for the installation.

She stared at the garden now, her thoughts still on Jack. The conversation she had just overheard seemed innocuous enough with Jack offering to bring Judith some tomatoes, but Lillian was far from convinced that nothing was going on. She felt it in her very bones that Jack was up to something.

She sighed and thought, *"Thank God I have Thomas."*

CHAPTER 11

Judith sat in front of her easel, poised with a brush over a canvas she had started earlier that afternoon. For the first time in six months, she had found time to paint. She had almost forgotten what a pleasure it was. This painting featured a group of women, side by side, laughing, playing, singing, playing the ukulele, and giving support to each other. She smiled as she added details to the painting, bringing out the women's personalities.

She could not help being a little distracted. Aside from the all-consuming fact that she had just lost a job that she really needed, she had also just received a text from Lola. The message had gone out to all the sistahs, and said, *"Remember Picket Line on Monday 9:30AM. Bring your anti-ageism signs. Geaux G.S.!"*

Judith's first reaction had been to shiver in anticipation. She had never picketed before and was not sure what to expect. She assumed it was like she had seen on the TV news where people walked up and down, chanting some kind of slogan. *"But what would our slogan be?"* she wondered. One popped into her head: "LILLIAN & THOMAS—GO DROP IN A HOLE." She smiled wickedly and thought, *I'd pay good money to hear that chanted outside of the museum."*

Or maybe, she thought, the chant should be, "AGEISM & SEXISM IN THE WORKPLACE ARE AGAINST THE LAW." That was getting closer. She bet that Lola had some good ideas. Lola was making signs for both of them. She knew that Lola's signs would say something about anti-ageism, and the other would say, "REHIRE JUDITH!"

Lola seemed to know all about discrimination, picketing, and the law. It was impressive having an activist-lawyer friend, and it was certainly coming in handy. Judith trusted her to keep them out of jail. That was the last thing she needed right now.

She thought about being rehired by the museum, if that was at all possible. Dare she hope? She did not know what else to do but hope, actually. What would she do if she did not get her job back? Just in case, she had begun brushing off her ten-year-old resume, and would start job-hunting, if the sistahs efforts did not pay off.

Judith had boned up on the statistics of women her age being hired in a tight job market, which this certainly was. It seemed bleak. Workers in their sixties get thirty-five percent fewer call-backs from employers than those in their twenties and thirties. Because of this, people in her age bracket who were out of work were often forced into early Social Security. This hurt the amount of monthly benefits they could receive. And it also hurt everyone else paying the cost of Social Security. Too many people on Social Security threatened its very existence. People were living longer and being forced into early retirement when they could work longer and not tax the system as much.

Judith realized that she was fighting against, not just an illegal act, but a whole culture as well. "How in the world do you fight that?" she thought out loud. "If I could prove ageism, I could bring a lawsuit, I guess."

However, Lola did not think she had a very good case. Lillian had never actually said in front of witnesses that Judith was too old for the job. She had only implied it with her comments to the board. She called Judith's last event "a worn-out idea." She even went so far as to ask if Judith herself was tired in front of other board members under the guise of concern. But Judith knew what she was saying.

"Seriously, who does Lillian think she's fooling? With her face lifts, liposuction, dyed black hair—which is never a good idea on anyone— she's not fooling anyone. She's probably as old as I am. She just has a lot more money, so she can look better." Actually, Judith did not judge Lillian for her face lifts or liposuction. She was just astonished that

Lillian was trying to use her groomed-up looks to make Judith seem older and out of date.

For one older person to age-discriminate against another was the ultimate insult and the height of B.S. to Judith. Yet, once again, it came down to cultural norms that needed to change.

It seemed to Judith that you heard so much about people pushing back about racism, sexism, and discrimination against the LGBTQ community, but not enough about ageism. Yes, people get older, and that was an irrefutable fact. But when someone her age is capable of doing a job, they should be judged on their merits, not their age. Being judged on something other than merit is the common denominator of all discrimination.

Lola told her that discrimination lawsuits were growing in number but lagged way behind the other discrimination suits. This was supposedly because they were harder to prove, as it was in her case. *"But that doesn't mean we have to give up,"* she thought. "It *doesn't mean we should shut up either."* Judith was suddenly struck by the idea that being around the sistahs was motivating her to think differently—to think about taking action. That made her smile to herself—at her new daring and attitude. She shook her head in wonder.

Do not go gentle into that good night.

—Dylan Thomas

Hell no, kick some ass first.

—Lola

CHAPTER 12

Lola was in her element, standing in her kitchen surrounded by budding new plants and flowers in full bloom. In the center of the room was a huge, old farm table. She had pulled it out of her mom and dad's kitchen years ago, when they had bought a replacement. She had called "dibs" on it before any of her brothers could grab it. Now she was the proud owner of the table where her family had eaten many meals together—laughing, talking, arguing, and joking, as her loud family was apt to do even to this day.

Her parent's kitchen was still the Trahan family meeting place. All three of her brothers and she were grown now. But often on a Saturday morning, there were liable to be three or four members of the family meeting there for coffee or a quick breakfast. It was a sure thing on holidays that they would all be in the kitchen, along with their wives and children too.

But the old table now belonged to Lola. She loved to sit there, coffee in hand, working on projects and thinking up ideas.

She was taking a break from today's project: i.e., making Judith's protest signs. She took her old saxophone out of its case and ran some practice riffs just for the sheer pleasure of it. It had a mellow, hollow sound she loved which always reminded her of her dad. He played the sax himself, and Lola and he had spent many evenings sitting on her parents' back porch playing the old Louisiana blues tunes they both loved. It felt so good to play now. Judith had talked about her ukulele band, and it had reminded Lola that she hadn't made any music in a while. While she played, her eyes lingered on the protest signs she had put together so far.

Lola had protested so many things in the past that nowadays she could recycle the protests signs by simply turning them around backwards and writing some new protest on the reverse side.

As a lawyer, she thought the protest was a good tactic on Judith's part. She knew the uphill climb it could be to win age discrimination cases, even when you had strong proof on your side. Lola thought the best move was to threaten the museum with bad press. Then they would negotiate for Judith's cause with the idea that if she threatened legal action, the museum might back down or at least meet them halfway. No one wanted to deal with lawyers if they did not have to. They might be willing to deal with Lola and her list of demands which were mostly concerned with getting Judith's job back.

The demands would come under her family law firm name, Trahan & Associates, run by two of her brothers and their employees. They represented the family nursery business as well as other corporate entities in legal matters.

Her grandfather had started Trahan Nurseries in Bush, Louisiana, along with his wife, Lola's grandmother, and their son— Lola's father. They grew the business over the years into a master nursery business, with growers all over the South. They supplied wholesale plants and flowers to other nurseries, landscapers, flower shops, and grocery stores east of the Mississippi. They also ran three large retail stores under the Trahan Nursery name, which were mostly run by her cousins. It was truly a family business.

Lola's glance went to a nearby bookcase which held a treasured photo of her father in his forties. He was standing and smiling next to his parents in front of their first nursery. A blown up, framed version of that same photo hung in every branch of the Trahan nurseries. She thought fondly of her dad who, in his eighties now, still came into the nursery almost every day to check on things. It was a habit of sixty years that he had no intention of breaking as long as he was still breathing. His presence was always welcome. He was a beloved figure by his employees and customers alike. That photo always made Lola smile and shake her head at all the wonderful memories she had of him.

CHAPTER 13

1977—Bush, Louisiana

Lola arrived at her dad's nursery office at lunchtime on the pretext that she was delivering a ham and cheese sandwich to him. She really needed to talk to him, and she knew it was a good time to catch him—right after the morning customer rush. She opened his office door, stuck the lunch bag inside, and said loudly, "Guess whose daughter loves him and comes bearing food!"

When she then stuck her head past the door, Lola saw her father grinning up at her from his desk, "I guess that would be me—your lucky old dad. Come on in."

Lola hugged her dad and drew out two thick sandwiches with homemade pickles from her mom's pantry. She had a thermos of sweet tea to go with it.

"Wow this is wonderful! How did you know I was craving a ham and cheese?"

"Intuition and genius, I guess. And the fact that it's what you eat for lunch every single day," she laughed. "But it comes with a price. I need to talk."

"OK kid, what's up?" he said. It was same way he had started many a conversation with his only daughter for as long as Lola could remember. Whether they were working at the nursery together, or out fishing on the lake, or even when they were both just sitting on the back porch listening to the locusts' call many an evening, Lola and her dad could talk to each other. Lola was also very close to her mother, but when it came to a good old heart-to-heart, her dad was her go-to guy.

"It's time for me to declare a major at school, and I just can't decide what to choose," she sighed. "I'm going crazy here. Can you help me figure this out?"

Her dad took a bite of his sandwich and looked seriously at his daughter, "This is one of those decisions you have to make yourself, Lola girl, but let me just say this—and it's the same advice I gave your brothers. They too wanted to have this conversation, but I have to admit that they weren't smart enough to bring me lunch when we had it."

Lola smiled affectionately at him and waited.

"As you know, your brothers both chose to go into law school, even though our business is, of course, nurseries. I advised them to do that, but the choice was ultimately theirs. Now they've started Trahan & Associates law firm and represent our business as well as other corporations. And they do very well for themselves, as you know."

"Our business needs looking after on so many levels, but as lawyers, they could represent many of our needs that I couldn't. And here's the thing, if our little nursery empire ever goes under, the boys would still have a strong business to support their families."

She listened attentively to her father as he went on, "I know you love the plant side of this business. I also know how smart you are—how capable you are. You could do anything. Of that I have no doubt. But why not follow in some of those proven footsteps too? You could get yourself a law degree, and get a secondary degree in horticulture, or biology. It would take you a little longer, but that way you'd be ready for anything that might come your way. Even if you never entered the family law firm officially, having a 'cocktail knowledge of the law,'" he stopped and smiled teasingly, "It still would help you in every business you might start."

Lola took those words to heart and did exactly what her father suggested. It was practical and suited her interests perfectly. After law school, she ended up working at both Trahan Nurseries and Trahan & Associates law firm, learning both sides of the growing business.

She loved learning about growing beautiful, healthy plants—how to care for them, sell them, and market them. She also loved being able to contribute to the legal side of things that helped her family. Her negotiating skills grew and helped add to the family wealth. Lola's range of experience in the business became vast.

Her father's teasing remark about the "cocktail knowledge of the law" had cracked Lola up back then, but she found that her legal knowledge came in handy quite often. It was especially handy with the activism projects she took on, such as protesting against local fracking, marching for women's rights, and campaigning for her favorite candidates. She had learned to draw her law degree like a sword at times and wield it appropriately, most often with good results.

Lola certainly hoped for good results at the picket line for Judith's benefit. Earlier, she had drafted a list of the demands they wanted from the art museum at the demonstration. Then, she had jumped on the phone and rounded up warm bodies to show up Monday morning. Between her contacts and those of Bea, Dawn, and Helen, they should have enough folks for a decent demonstration.

She finished practicing her sax, quickly finished up her picket signs, and then went into the bathroom to freshen up. She took her curly red hair out of its scrunchy and fluffed it around her shoulders. A pair of crazy blue eyes peered back at her from a face full of freckles in the mirror. She had resented those freckles when she was younger, but as she grew older, she learned to love the way her red hair and freckles set her apart. She was rangy-thin and of medium height, standing about five-foot five. Her size made her seem even feistier than she was, if that were possible. Wrinkles showed themselves at the corners of her eyes and mouth, and it did not seem to matter on her unusual face which always drew attention. She was pretty in an odd way, and she was not above using it to her advantage, especially when it came to men.

She thought of the string of men that had come in and out of her life. There were quite a few, if truth be told. Faces floated by in her mind, but she stopped with a lurch when she thought of the only one that had really mattered—Bud Broussard.

———⚭———

1987—Bush, Louisiana

Bud Broussard owned one of the big nurseries in New Orleans and bought wholesale from her family's business. Lola was twenty-eight, out of law school, and working as a lawyer and as manager of one of the Trahan nurseries when Bud drove up to the nursery office in Bush one day to talk to Lola's father. His motive was to try and negotiate better prices on the bulk orders for his business. Her father immediately and happily walked him straight into Lola's office and said to her with a wink, "Lola, this is Bud Broussard. I know you two have talked on the phone, but Bud is here in person to discuss business with you." When it came to negotiating, her dad was tough, but Lola was nothing short of a little iron fist. Bud recovered from his surprise at the hand-off and immediately turned on the charm. Little did he know what he would end up bargaining for that afternoon.

Also, little did he know that the minute he stepped out of his old red truck in jeans and a T-shirt, Lola had spied him and sized him up. His clothes and truck gave him a country vibe, but Lola recognized Bud Broussard through online pictures and knew through the grapevine that he was a savvy businessman. She watched him approach the front office door, cool, tall, tan, lean, and sexy with a smile. Lola waited for him like a cat at a mouse hole.

By the time he left their two-hour-long, flirtatious meeting which included a couple of Abita beers each, they had negotiated a minimum discount to keep him happy and a promise that he would increase the size of his orders to keep her happy. But Bud was already happy. He had Lola's phone number and dinner plans for that Friday night.

Bud and she dated for a tumultuous three months. They did not always agree on politics and current issues, so they pretty much fought steadily for the entire time—in between bouts of passionate loving. Both were stubborn and neither minded a good argument or two. Both were interested in local and world issues, but Dan was satisfied to talk about the world's problems and do what he could locally, and Lola wanted to go out and see the world firsthand. Bud was proud and down-to-earth with strong values, sometimes to the point where he put up an immovable wall of self-righteousness.

During those times, Lola would tell him, laughingly, "Lighten up already, Bud. John Wayne already has your job."

And he would say, imitating the Duke, "Well, little lady, you can't change the stripes on this tiger."

She would roll her eyes then tackle him in a big hug. She was petite, and he was so tall and strong that they stood out wherever they went. They were both beautiful, and they loved each other fiercely— and it showed. They were the local "Hollywood Couple," for sure.

But Hollywood marriages can breed friction just like any other. Their relationship just did not hold against all their differences, and pretty soon, they both realized it. Bud had a business and was based in New Orleans. He had strong family ties there too. Lola, of course, had a strong family too, but in Bush. On top of that, Lola was headstrong and wanted to travel and did not have the same obligations he did. Lola helped run the business, but Bud *was* his business. She wanted to be free, not bogged down with too many ties. She kept telling him that they were young and could go and do anything they wanted, anywhere in the world. They could teach school in impoverished countries, or bring running water to small villages in Africa. She was constantly talking and dreaming about organizations they could join and see the world, helping out at the same time.

Bud wanted kids. Lola did not.

Lola wanted the world.

Their first year of marriage was bumpy, but it came and went. After the second rough year, they were worn out. The arguing and disagreeing never seemed to stop. One Saturday morning, Lola came into the kitchen with some travel brochures she wanted to show Bud. She found him sitting at the table.

When she walked in, it struck her that she had never seen him look so despondent before. He glanced at the brochures and shook his head. She knew what he was going to say before he opened his mouth, "Babe, we just keep coming back to the same issues. What it comes down to is, basically, we really don't want the same things." He paused, then sad sadly, "This is never going to work, is it?" It was really a statement, not a question. She could see weariness and tears in his brown eyes.

She felt a knife go through her heart. She looked into his handsome face and felt so much love. But the truth was she was tired too. The marriage was grinding up the both of them. This was the moment. She could have lied, and she could have fought for him. But she knew he was right. If they had met at an other time or place, they might have had a chance. But Lola could not stop. She was young and full of energy, ambition, and dreams. The world was a big playground waiting for her to join the games. She needed to fly and the freedom to do it. She truly loved Bud, but she was never going to be happy staying put in one place at this point in her life.

So, it tore open her heart, but she left and went as far away as she could get. Lola joined the Peace Corps, who welcomed her with open arms with her law degree and knowledge of horticulture. She was sent to Guatemala and the Dominican Republic. She worked in small sectors with education, agriculture, and health officials, and found it unbelievably rewarding. Then, after her two-year stint in the Corps, she drifted out to California and then through West Virginia and up into New York, feeling out the culture of her own country.

At one point when she was in California, she had heard that Bud had remarried and had two little boys—twins. It broke yet another piece of her heart, but she was also happy for him. It was what he wanted, and she wanted nothing but happiness for her old John Wayne.

Eventually, Lola moved back to Louisiana. As they say "Anyone born in Louisiana who leaves always comes back."

Once back in town, Lola continued to help part time at the family law firm, but she also started her own business. Fleur de Lis Landscaping was born. The business offered Lola as a specialty landscape designer, and had a side line of plant design and care in hotels and office buildings. Most recently she was delighted to acquire the account of the Southern Hotel in Covington which showed off enormous flower arrangements in the lobby and huge pots of plants all over its grounds.

Lola happily settled into her new life and occasionally let her mind drift back over all the adventures she had had over the years—including romantic ones. She probably knew way more men than was her fair share. She was not promiscuous, but Lola did what Lola wanted to do. Always did and always will.

Then over a year ago, she had taken things a little too far and crossed a line. She found herself having a fling with a married man. Normally, that would never have happened—it was one area where she would have normally avoided. But Lola had met the man at a time when she was feeling particularly down on herself. She did not usually feel lonely, but after a few meaningless flings in a row with men that she felt nothing for, she had hit the bottom. She felt terrible about the fling and cut it off after only one night. But it had also made her wonder if one day she would ever settle down. She was almost sixty now and entrenched into her life back in Louisiana. She thought that maybe it was time for a change.

She was still as open to men as she had ever been, but found herself wanting the company of a good man, not just sexually, but in every way. She wanted to have someone to wake up with on the weekends and go off exploring for the day. She wanted a great companion, not just an occasional lover whenever Lola got in a frisky mood, which truth be told, was often. It was time for a change.

—◆—

Her eyes came into focus in the bathroom mirror as she got herself ready to go. She laughed out loud for a moment at her memories and said to herself, "OK yes, I do get frisky once in a while but certainly not as often as Dawn would have everyone believe!"

Thinking of Dawn reminded her of how she had come to know, love, and be part of the Gumbeaux Sistahs. The memory always brought a smile to Lola's sunny face.

CHAPTER 14

2017—Covington, LA

One afternoon, Lola was making her regular rounds at the hotel and was out by the pool attending to several groups of big, potted, tropical plants. She had a magical touch with plants because she was privy to the Trahan family secrets, which included several exclusive plant-growing solutions concocted by her grandfather and perfected by her dad. Lola knew her business well. She also had the taste to match clients with the right landscaping and plant arrangement suggestions. Word about her services was getting around, especially after she landed the Southern Hotel account.

There were two groups of guests nearby while she worked, and she did her best not to disturb them. One was a group of three women in their sixties. The other was a group of young men in their twenties who appeared to be drinking heavily and growing more boisterous by the minute.

Lola ignored them all and went about her business, trimming and feeding plants and watering them with the hotel hose. Truth be told, Lola was trying to hurry through her work that day because she did not like the energy coming off the young male group—as much as she usually liked testosterone. She just did not like it when it turned aggressive and ugly. She sensed that this group was a bit threatening, and then knew it for certain when their remarks started to be directed her way.

She kept her back to them, but distinctly heard things like, "Hey Brad, your girlfriend over there is getting pretty close. I think she wants your body," followed by snorts of laughter.

Lola moved further away, and a little while later, even though Lola was nowhere near them, she heard louder laughter and remarks. "She wants it, alright! Actually, she's got a pretty good body herself. Come on over here, baby!" Lola moved closer to the group of three older women, who seemed to be in a mild disagreement of some sort.

The largest woman of the three women was saying, "Bea, I'm not going to get her in trouble!"

The one obviously named Bea said, "It's not the way to solve every problem, dear."

Lola tuned them out so she could concentrate on the young men and know what they were up to. She usually knew when to fight and when to be cool, but she was starting to do a slow burn. She did not want to say anything because she wanted to keep the hotel job— it was a sweet deal, easy money, and brought in referrals.

After a few more inciting remarks, including some that were starting to be downright crude amid raucous laughter at her expense, Lola started to put the hose away and pack up.

"I'll just come back another time," she thought, gritting her teeth with anger.

Then to her surprise, the large woman from the nearby group walked up to her and asked to borrow her hose for a moment. Meanwhile, the other two women moved inside the hotel lobby and stood watching through a large window. "Don't worry, I'll bring it right back," said the woman.

With the running hose in hand, the woman walked closer to the group of young men. They immediately turned their drunken remarks to her, "Oh no, here comes another one! Hey lady, you got a boyfriend? My friend Brad here needs a lap dance."

The woman smiled calmly at the young men and said, "Good evening, boys," giving them a chance to make nice.

One of them, the one named Brad, snarled, "What do you want? Bring back the other one—now her I'd do. But not you, grandma.

You just get back to work before you get your ass fired." He laughed with his drunken friends.

Dawn smirked, "Actually, I don't work here. Consequently, no matter what I do, I can't get fired from this place. And to be clear—I don't consider *this* work. This is strictly for pleasure." She lifted the hose and squirted them all as thoroughly as she could, knocking their drinks to the concrete and forcing them to jump to their feet, yelling obscenities.

Lola's mouth fell open in shock as she stood nearby.

Then Dawn dropped the hose, grabbed Lola by the arm, and bee-lined straight it for the lobby. Dawn told Lola to meet her out front, and then headed for the front desk where she immediately asked for the manager who happened to be nearby and asked if he could be of some help.

Dawn told the manager that there was a group of drunk, sopping-wet men in their clothes by the pool who were being rude, insulting, and threatening her and her friends. She said that there was a great deal of broken glass by the pool, also due to their drunken partying.

The owner thanked her and left on the run toward the pool, and Dawn rejoined Bea, Helen, and Lola in front of the hotel.

"I can't believe you did that, Dawn," said Bea disapprovingly, but she was stifling a laugh.

"We'd better get out of here before those guys come looking for us!" said Dawn. They invited Lola to join them for a drink at the bar across the street, and she agreed heartily. Minutes later, they were clinking cocktail glasses together.

After introductions, Lola said, "That was maybe the best thing I've ever seen. I wanted so much to do that, but the Southern Hotel is a sweet gig, and I hated to blow it over a few idiots."

"Bea didn't want us to do it. We were even arguing about it," smiled Dawn.

"Well, honestly, Dawn, you can't solve every problem by squirting people down with a hose," said Bea.

"Well, of course not—but that's only because there's never a hose handy when you need it. But I really wanted to do it—just once," Dawn laughed loudly. "Besides, I never actually touched them. My mom always said you can catch more flies with honey, but you should always carry a can of Raid!"

"Well, I can't thank you enough," smiled Lola.

"We have to watch out for each other, right?" asked Helen.

After much laughter and high-spirited conversation between the women, Helen said, "So, this might seem like an odd question, but let me ask you something, Lola," said Helen, "How do you feel about gumbo?"

Lola answered, "Oh, I love gumbo! My mom makes the best gumbo in the world. You would love it. Maybe I could have y'all over to the house, and I could make her recipe to say thank you. But why do you ask?"

"OK, wait just a second. Before we go any further, let me get this straight right now. *My* mom makes the best gumbo. Hands down. But I would love to taste your mom's too," said Dawn, laughing.

"Hmm," said Lola, catching Dawn's teasing, "Well, we'll just have to see about that. Can y'all come over Thursday?"

"Yes! But I need to know—how do you feel about sides of potato salad with gumbo?" asked Dawn, now suddenly dead serious.

"I think it's a mistake," laughed Lola.

"No biggie," said Dawn. "I'm used to that attitude. But don't be surprised if I bring my own."

On Thursday evening, Lola was ready for her new friends/ heroines with a big pot of her mom's gumbo, white rice, French bread, sweet tea, and lots of wine. Dawn, Bea, and Helen arrived, and the talk, dining, and fun lasted for hours. Lola felt so comfortable with this group. She told them, "I still can't believe you hosed those guys down. Every time I think about it, I crack up."

"Yeah, it's probably a good thing we left right away. I wasn't sure who would end up getting the boot from the hotel—them or us," laughed Dawn. Then she asked, "By the way, aside from your plant care job, do you also design gardens?"

"Oh sure," Lola said, and went on to tell them about her family's long relationship with the plant business in all its forms. She also told them about her legal work at the family business.

"You're a lawyer too? That's so interesting! And ooh, that could come in real handy," said Bea, nodding at the others, "especially if Dawn keeps up with these kinds of antics, and I suspect she will." She winked at Lola, "We may all just end up needing a lawyer."

"Do you threaten to sue your plants if they don't grow?" Helen joked.

They all laughed, but Dawn cut in, "You know I have an idea, Lola." She told her that she and her husband had strong connections with the Covington Art Museum, and that there was a beautiful old bay window at the museum that takes up a whole wall. "For the longest time I've wanted them to do something with that window. I have visions of doing a permanent art installation there using plants. It could be a living art display. I'll bet we could wheedle a budget out of the board for the right project. And if you have a decent portfolio, it might just be the nudge to get it going. Is this something in which you might be interested?"

Lola said excitedly, "Oh yes I would. That sounds like just my kind of project. I'd have to see the space of course, but I'm picturing something already—like creating an indoor rainforest of sorts. It could be so cool."

"I like the way you think," said Dawn grinning, then she took a big spoonful of gumbo. "And your gumbo is absolutely divine. Almost as good as my mom's."

"C'mon, my mom could take your mom any day," laughed Lola.

"Seriously, have you seen my mom?" said Dawn.

The women talked until late that night. When the last person left, Lola felt she had stepped into a situation that felt so natural—like she had been friends with these women her whole life.

Two weeks later, on a Monday morning, Lola found herself in the art museum looking at the old bay window, surrounded by Dawn, Lillian Deslattes, and a couple of the board members. Bitsy was there too and was given the job of contact person for Lola if the project was approved. Afterwards, Lola submitted a proposal that was well received. The following Monday, at the regular board meeting, the project was granted a go and a budget allotted. Lola would create the project and maintain the garden weekly under a one-year contract that she had negotiated herself. After the year was up, they would have to renew the contract year by year. Lola was off and running.

When the new living art garden was done, the art museum used their next big event to reveal it to the public.

Dawn had proved that her judgment was right on target. Lola's garden turned out to be as much of a draw as any fine art exhibit. It served the purpose of bringing in patrons in between exhibits and events as well.

The exhibit brought Lola into the museum for maintenance most Mondays, which was Judith's day off, so they never really saw each other. Bitsy reported on it to Judith, who loved the exhibit, but was happy to have one less responsibility at work to deal with.

Lola laughed, remembering all that had happened that extraordinary year. The exhibit brought many new referrals and tons of jobs, but best of all, it brought her three friends she cherished and could count on for support. Best of all, it brought her Dawn, her new best friend and someone she could joke around with who got her wacky sense of humor. These were priceless gifts in her life.

CHAPTER 15

Finishing up her signs for Judith's picket line, Lola hurried to fix herself up to get ready for what she hoped would be an extraordinary evening.

She did not know what to hope for and was a bit pessimistic. *"If it turns out to be a good night,"* she thought, *"Then it might be good for only one night and then turn out to be a disappointment in the long run."* If it had involved anyone's company but this particular person's, she wouldn't be sweating it at all. But she knew that this guy could bring her great happiness or hell. It could truly go either way.

She still could hardly believe how it happened. Two days before, she was in Mo's Art Supply buying sign-making supplies. She had markers and wooden stakes at home leftover from past campaigns but was picking up some extra poster board and foam core pieces. Suddenly behind her she heard a deep, male voice say, "Uh oh, poster board. I know the signs of a picket line in the making when I see one. Lola-girl, who are you after this time?"

She smiled before she swung around. Thirty-odd years could go by in a blink if it wanted to, but that voice was imprinted into her DNA. She would know it anywhere—Bud.

"Yep," she smiled, "There's a certain nursery business in New Orleans that needs straightening out. We've got pickets on the way."

"Well, I feel sorry for the knucklehead that owns it. He had better change his evil ways right now—he doesn't stand a chance."

Lola grinned, "Hi, Bud. I see you remember old lessons well— don't mess with a Trahan."

"Hi yourself, Lola," he smiled and reached out to give her a big hug.

She moved easily into his big arms that went around her in such a familiar way, *"Damn,"* she thought, *"I remember this man so well."*

He pulled back and looked at her, smiling, "So what are you up to these days? I heard it through the nursery grapevine you moved back to town years ago. And that now you're working for yourself. Is that right?"

"Well, yes. You know me—fingers in many pies. I still help out with legal matters at the family firm, but I branched out to landscaping, design, and corporate plant care. I've been back in Louisiana for a few years. I live in Covington now."

"I should have tried to get in touch to say 'hello,'" he said, tilting his head and making it a question.

"Yeah, you should have," she smiled mischievously.

"Well, you would be impressed, Lola. The business has grown like you wouldn't believe. There's a store in New Orleans, as you know, but now we have one in Mandeville and in Baton Rouge too."

"Wow, hey that's terrific. That must keep you hopping."

"It has for quite a while now. I've got my two sons working with me now. You've never met them, but you would like them. They're just like their old man," he laughed.

"Ha!" she laughed, "Well, that can be taken more ways than one. Remember, I know you pretty well—the good sides and the bad."

"What bad sides?" he teased. Then he leaned back, looking at her, "Woman, you look amazing."

"You look good too, Bud. Your wife must take good care of you."

"Ah," he said sadly, "So, you haven't heard. We split a few years back. After all these years of mostly staying together for the boys, we had to give it up so we could enjoy our last roundup, so to speak."

Lola had heard that rumor, but wanted to make sure it was true before she said the wrong thing. "Oh, that's too bad. Seriously.

Divorce sucks, as we both know. I'm so glad you got two amazing kids out of it."

"That's the truth. I was really lucky that way."

She looked at him for a beat, "Well I'd better be going. It was good to see you. It really was."

"Uh, before you run off, Lola . . . how about having dinner for old times' sake? It would be fun to catch up, don't you think? It's been such a long time." He reached for her hand and paused, "Wait . . . is that . . ?"

He stared at right hand—more specifically, the ring on her right hand. It had been his mother's ring that he had given to her before they got married. It was not her wedding ring, but it was a lovely ruby in a simple gold setting. Lola had always worn it on this hand back then, and here it was still. "Yep, it is. What can I say? I always really liked this ring."

His eyes roamed over her quickly, "I see. I'm glad to hear that. I'm glad you still have it."

Lola hesitated, watching him and thought, *"I'll be damned if that old spark isn't still there. I guess some things never change."* She knew he felt it too. But this was the worst kind of trouble if it went badly. Losing Bud the first time was hard enough, and she never forgot the pain it brought. She never wanted to go through that again.

"C'mon," he said, reading her thoughts, "It's just a meal. We can handle that—it might even be fun."

Lola looked up at him, grinning, "OK, I guess we're big kids now—we can handle it. How about tomorrow?"

"You're on. I'll pick you up."

That was two days ago, and Lola had not slept much since. Normally, she was cool and feisty, but her fingernails were showing signs of nervous biting, and her appetite was non-existent. She was genuinely nervous. She put on a long, black summer dress with little strappy sandals and a sheer, pink wrap. It was a look that said "sexy, classy, and modest," all at the same time.

She heard steps on the porch, heard his knock, and swung that door wide open.

You can't solve every problem you have by squirting them with a hose.

—Bea

Of course not. There's never a hose around when you need it.

—Dawn

CHAPTER 16

Thomas McCann sat on the couch in his mid-priced, rented apartment on the edge of the historical district of Covington. He was enjoying a glass of red wine and surveying his possessions, a pastime that sometimes cheered him up and other times could put him in a foul mood. He loved the things he owned. They were quality art pieces that he had acquired over his thirty-three years. The problem was that there were not enough of them. The place seemed sparse to him, and Thomas hated sparse. He loved lavish. He had come from a poor family in Bakersfield, California. His father was a small appliance repairman, and his mother was a waitress in a steakhouse. His mother and he had been very close. She had Thomas when she was over forty, and he was her first and only child. So she protected him from life's mishaps as best she could. His mother was fierce and dominated their family life, and Thomas loved and admired her greatly. When she died, Thomas took it hard.

They had lived in a rusted mobile home on an ugly road with other beat-up mobile home residents. His father lived there still. Growing up, Thomas swore that one day he would have money and nice things and live a life of which he could be proud.

It was the disappointment of his life that, so far, he had not been able to achieve such a lifestyle. It did not help that things had been going well for a while, but then his career had taken a sudden nose dive a couple of years ago. He had to start completely over to try and recover from a complete career disaster.

Before the fall, and right after graduating from California State University with a business degree, he landed a coveted position in

San Diego at a small museum by the ocean. He had always had an interest in fine art and enjoyed being surrounded by great works. He stayed there for several years until he got a shot at a prominent museum in San Francisco where he had always wanted to live. He pictured himself as a big shot in the big city. One day, he hoped to land a job at the San Francisco Museum of Modern Art. His career was on such a projectile.

But Thomas had a setback. An incident. He called them his "little compulsions." He had them often, actually, but this time it caught up with him. Remembering the incident forced Thomas to his feet and over to his etagere. He unlocked and opened the glass doors and reached in for the small, hand-cast, bronze dresser mirror sitting on one of the glass shelves. Both guilt and pleasure filled him as he caressed the flowing lines of the old piece.

Glancing in the hand mirror, he felt pleased as usual with his appearance. He was tall and kept his physique trim by running each morning before work. He had dark, well-trimmed hair, dark eyes and lashes, and full lips. It all added up to a sensuousness women appreciated. His looks had served him well in his career and personal life.

The mirror was extraordinarily beautiful in his hand, and it reminded him of the exceptional exhibit of which it had been a part. The exhibit had been some choice works by art deco artist—Erté. Thomas had been so proud of being able to help curate the exhibit, which was on loan from a museum in Chicago. The show was well-received, and Thomas had put the whole thing together himself, placing each piece lovingly into the display to its best effect. He had made a point of such hands-on care so he would get much of the credit for the display success. That would have given him another notch in his belt toward that San Francisco job to which he aspired. That was his first mistake. It gave him a notch all right, but it was a big mistake to do the project on his own. He should have known better. The solo work offered no checks and balances on his behavior. When it was time to pack up and return the pieces to Chicago, it was Thomas, once again, who made sure that each valuable object was packed to perfection for its return. That was his second mistake. When the pieces arrived in Chicago and inventory taken, one piece was missing—a treasured, handmade, one-of-a-kind mirror.

Although there was no proof, as the piece was never recovered, there was one obvious person to blame—the person who packed up the items and signed the shipping roster.

Thomas was quietly let go, as to not draw bad publicity to the museum. He found himself in the big city, but not as a big shot. In fact, his shot was gone.

He had stored the mirror in a rented storage facility along with several other treasures he had acquired over the years from museums, galleries, and even private parties to which he had been invited. Visiting the storage unit often helped him deal with his "little compulsion." He knew he had a problem, but he felt he could not very well talk to anyone about it without landing in jail for theft. He was in trouble. And he was in debt. His love of lavishness and the good life drove him to live a life mostly on credit. He was drowning in it. And now he needed a job—badly.

Luckily, he had heard about an upcoming Museum Curator's Conference being held at the San Francisco Convention Center. He thought it would be an excellent place for job opportunities all over the country, so he signed up to attend.

With newly printed business cards and a beautifully tailored suit, Thomas wandered around the conference, meeting as many people as he could. He kept an eye out in case his boss from the last job showed up. That would prove awkward at best. He saw a couple of people who might know about him being fired but managed to avoid them. The job search was not going to be easy, but he already knew that. Still, the convention seemed like his best shot. He was not sure how he was going to deal with a potential employee checking his references, but he figured he would deal with it as the problem arose. He relied a lot on his considerable personal charm and looks.

Museum positions in his field were coveted and hard to come by, and he had to be careful about who he approached. His idea was to apply to a small museum, out of state where he was unknown. He would start at the bottom again, but still be in the game, and work his way back up, erasing his past references on his resume and adding fresh ones.

However, at the end of the first conference day, he felt mildly discouraged. The realization had come home to him just how hard his career search was going to be. Deciding that he could really use a drink, he made his way to the hotel bar and ordered a gin and tonic. He settled into his seat to reflect on his meager options. After just a couple of sips, he overheard female voices from the table right behind him. It sounded like a mature woman's voice talking to a younger woman, "I don't envy what you are going through up in the Cleveland Museum, Marie. It must be terribly stressful looking after a venue of that size."

"It's a crazy business we're in, Lillian," said the younger woman, "but you know we both love it, right?"

"So true, so true. Our little museum in Covington, Louisiana, has its challenges too. There's nothing I'd like better than to see our current manager get the boot. She makes my job a nightmare."

"The wrong manager can make everyone's job hard," agreed the younger woman. "When I was hired, I took the place of a gentleman who was clearly losing his marbles. But everyone was terrified of him. It took a while, but the board finally saw the light. They showed him the door, which opened it wide for me, thank God." She laughed.

"I'm happy for you, Marie."

"Well, hang in there, Lillian. I wish we could see each other more than just once a year at this convention. Will I see you at the morning session tomorrow?"

"Sure, I'll look for you. I'll be the one with two fists full of coffee," Lillian laughed gaily.

The younger woman walked back into the main lobby, and the older one, Lillian, stayed to finish her martini.

Thomas' thoughts were spinning. *"A small museum in a little city in Louisiana? That's a nice long way from San Francisco."*

He glanced in the mirror over the bar and was able to see the woman still sitting there. She was older and probably had had a lot of work done on her face. But honestly, they had done a good job. She was pretty in an Elizabeth Taylor kind of way—dark hair and eyes and pale skin. She had kept her figure too. He admired her taste in obviously expensive, well-cut clothes. He smelled money and made up his mind. "*Really, why not?*"

Turning his chair toward her, he said, "Lillian, I hope you won't hold it against me, but I couldn't help but overhear your conversation."

Lillian looked up at the attractive young man, eyed him from head to toe. With lightning speed, she thought of all the things that were going on in her life, including her failing marriage and family life. There were so many things she needed, not the least of which was the need to feel like an attractive woman again. She weighed several decisions at once and settled on one. Then she said slowly with a smile, "I might hold it against you, but then I might not. It all depends."

Thomas gave her his best, sexy smile back, "I think we might be able to help each other out."

She invited him to join her at her table.

CHAPTER 17

At nine-thirty A.M. on Monday morning, the Gumbeaux Sistahs and a large group of picketers composed of friends, family, and Lola's activist group, met at St. John's Coffeehouse. They coffee'd up, formed a line, and marched down to the art museum with Lola in the lead. Their signs were held high and said variations on "AGEISM IS DISCRIMINATION!" and, "TALENT HAS NO AGE LIMIT" and, directly to the point, "BRING BACK JUDITH!"

Dawn had called the local newspaper and TV station. They came out and half-heartedly took pictures of the picketers marching along Columbia St.

As planned, they arrived at the entrance to the museum just as Thomas and Bitsy were arriving for work. Thomas was dressed as usual in a beautifully tailored suit as if he were an old-time, southern gentleman, which he certainly was not. When he saw the picketers, his mouth fell open, and a couple of ungentlemanly expletives escaped his lips. He told Bitsy to hurry up with her key and get the door open. Then, standing in the doorway, he said to the crowd, "Are you people serious?"

"Better get the board down here—now," growled Lola.

He slipped inside ahead of Bitsy who turned back before closing the door and gave the crowd the thumbs up sign and a cute grin.

"OK," yelled Lola, "Most of you know the drill. The law says we can picket on the city sidewalk, but we can't block access to the museum or other businesses. So, let's form a line and leave an opening for people to go in and out of the door."

The picketers lined up behind Lola, who yelled, "OK, here's our chant—it's the simple call-and-answer kind. Judith and I will call and the rest of you answer, got it?"

The crowd agreed enthusiastically, and Lola continued, "OK, we'll say, 'What do we want?' and you say, 'No ageism!' Then we'll say, 'When do we want it?' and you say, 'Now!' Got it? OK, try to speak clearly when you say 'No ageism,' or else no one will know why the heck we're here. If cars drive by and honk, wave, smile, and show them your signs. If they honk and give you the finger, then just wave and ignore them. Don't retaliate in any way. The only trouble we want is with the art museum today. And Dawn, this means you," She laughed.

Dawn shook her sign menacingly with a grin, and Helen, standing next to her, laughed.

The picketers began marching in a circle in front of the museum. After a minute, Lola's attention was drawn to her right hand holding the picket sign. Something seemed like it was missing, and it kept distracting her. Then it struck her. The ring that Bud had given her was not on her hand. For just a moment, she panicked. She had always loved that ring, and since their date the other night, it was all the more important to her. She tried to think back to when she last saw it. Sometimes when she worked a landscaping job, she absent-mindedly took off her jewelry and placed it nearby where she was working. Then she realized that she had last noticed the ring yesterday on her way to take care of the living art garden at the museum. Chances were good she had lost it there. She would ask Bitsy about it as soon as she could. Right now, she had a picket to run.

After about fifteen minutes, Lillian Deslattes and several other board members approached the museum one at a time. They entered without saying a word to the picketers, but Ed flashed Judith a little smile, and Lillian's glance held a death threat. Lola tried to get them to engage with her, especially Lillian, but she was ignored. After ten more minutes of chanting, Lillian re-emerged from the building and demanded, "OK, what is all this about—what do you people want? Lola Trahan, what are you up to?"

Lola said loudly for everyone to hear, "I'm from Trahan Law Firm, and I represent your former employee, Judith Lafferty." She motioned to Judith to step closer.

Lillian looked at Judith and said snidely, "Well, I'm surprised to see you here. You don't work here anymore, remember?" Then she turned back to Lola, "And wait—you're a lawyer? I thought you were a gardener?"

"In fact, I'm both," Lola said, all business-like. "Here is a list of our demands. It's short and sweet. Top of the list is that you cease discriminatory practices in your business. Second on the list is that you reinstate Judith Lafferty as the manager of the museum. She was let go because of those discriminatory practices. It's called ageism, and it's against the law. Our lawyers are prepared to bring the case to court, if necessary, if our demands are not met."

Without saying another word, Lillian took the list from Lola, and simply went right back inside.

Dawn said, "She's so awful, Lola. Makes me wish I had a garden hose to squirt her with, know what I mean?"

The picketers started chanting again, and Lillian came back outside after about fifteen minutes, no doubt having conferred with her lawyer and the other board members.

At Lola's urging, the picketers grew loud while Lillian stared at them, list in hand. Then she spoke, and everyone quieted and strained to listen. "The board and I have studied your demands, and let me make myself perfectly clear here, they are completely ridiculous. Your charges are false, and you have no proof of anything. You're just making things up. Judith Lafferty was let go due to incompetency at her job. Period. We do not discriminate in our practice here, and we will not reinstate her job. She can go be incompetent somewhere else. And as for your lawyers, well, our lawyers say you have no case, and you know it. So, there is our answer to your demands. Now, we have business to attend to, and we have no time for this. Som go home." She turned crisply on her expensive heels and went back inside.

The group continued to picket and then disbanded around noon, since no one from the board came out to talk to them again. After thanking all the people who showed up to help, Lola, Judith, Dawn, Bea, and Helen conferred.

"I think I can kiss that job goodbye for good," said Judith downheartedly. "I'm grateful that everyone tried today, but I don't think it got us anywhere."

"It was pretty anti-climactic," admitted Dawn, talking and texting on her phone at the same time. "A couple of press people showed up for about half a minute, but it was hard to get them excited about what we were trying to do."

"We're not beaten yet," said Lola, trying to be positive. "What we need is to get some food in us and then regroup. Dawn, how about you get off the phone for a minute, and let's figure out what to do."

The plan was for Dawn to drive them all to Bea's house, which was just a few blocks away, to talk things over and enjoy some gumbo—of course.

"My mom's gumbo is better than your mom's,"
said every Gumbeaux Sistah, ever.

CHAPTER 18

The sistahs got in Dawn's big SUV for the ride over to Bea's. When everyone was seated, Dawn said, "On the way over, I want to make a quick stop because I want to show y'all something up the street. It'll only take a minute."

They drove up Columbia Street and took a right on Boston Street. They had to pass by the Southern Hotel on their way, and just as they did, the hotel front doors swung open, and a wedding party burst outside carrying white umbrellas. They were followed by guests waving a sea of white handkerchiefs. A brass band played lively New Orleans music while the group danced their way to the next building, obviously on their way to the banquet hall next door for their wedding reception.

"Oh! Look, a Second Line," said Helen. She rolled down her window, and waved at the parading group.

"Can we stop and join them?" asked Lola. "I mean, who can resist a Second Line?" Whenever Lola saw a Second Line, she always joined in the festivities. They were especially fun when she was down in the French Quarter with visitors from out of town. Sometimes a Second Line would spring up, seemingly from out of nowhere. To the surprise, and often the confusion, of her visitors, Lola would simply join the back of the line of merrymakers for a few blocks, waiving a handkerchief or napkin, dancing down the middle of the street. She made sure that her visitors did the same and then afterwards, amid much laughter, she would tell them all about the tradition. She explained that Second Lines started with old time Jazz funerals. The front of the line, or First Line of people in the moving group of mourners, would be the funeral party along with a traditional jazz band. They would move slowly and respectfully up the street, honoring the deceased. The people in the group after the main party were the Second Line. Anyone could join in that line and move down the street with the music and funeral. The tradition evolved into more of a moving block party. Weddings held Second Lines, along with parties and other celebrations. Often, there was no special particular event at all to commemorate except the pure joy of being alive in Louisiana.

The sistahs were debating whether or not to join in when Bea reminded them of the gumbo waiting for them at her house, and that settled it.

Dawn drove on, turned at the next block, and stopped the car, putting them right up the street from the art museum.

"What is this?" asked Helen, confused. "We're almost back where we started."

Dawn rolled down the driver's window and pointed out a building on their left. "I had to go around the corner to get here, but I just wanted you girls to see this cute little building. Isn't it the sweetest little venue? I'm thinking about getting into a real estate deal with it and wanted to find out what y'all thought of the place." The structure she pointed out was on a corner, right next door to a gift shop and up the street from a popular restaurant, Mattina Bella's.

"What kind of business is in there?" asked Helen.

"It used to be a bath shop, but it's empty now. It's a cute place though, right?" asked Dawn.

"Yeah, it's super cute, all right," said Lola. "But let's get a move on to Bea's place. I'm starving, and we have stuff to talk about. Tell us about the real estate deal while you're driving."

"It's just a new project," said Dawn vaguely. "I'll tell you about it later. Let's go eat."

They arrived at Bea's house and pulled into the driveway of the old craftsman-style house. Bea had added an attached garage years ago, and she used her remote to open the garage door. It was the entrance Bea always used to get into the house. The women piled out of the car, traipsed through the garage, and entered her kitchen.

Bea's kitchen was a combination of old-fashioned coziness and super-modern appliances. She liked to cook, and it showed. Pots and herbs hung from the ceiling, and a heavy wooden table sat off to one side, doubling as an island. Warm gumbo was on the stove waiting for them. Bea got out some bread, butter, and sweet tea, and Dawn brought out her potato salad from her huge Louis Vuitton bag, which cracked Lola up.

"You're the only woman I know who would dare carry greasy food like that in such an expensive bag," grinned Lola.

"It's just a purse," laughed Dawn, "but potato salad is sacred."

They helped themselves to Bea's mom's recipe, and for a few minutes, the only sounds that were heard were groans of pure gastronomic pleasure.

"So," said Judith finally, getting to the bottom of her bowl, "Looks like we're probably not going to get anything out of our demands except a clearer picture of where we stand, which can be a good thing. I'm out, and Thomas is in. Lillian is not budging an inch. They're obviously not going to rehire me, but at least now I know."

"You're right, I'm afraid. It doesn't look great as far as the museum rehiring you. They must have a good lawyer because they didn't even flinch at our demand letter," Lola agreed glumly.

"Well, I say let them keep that old job," said Dawn gaily, surprising everyone.

"Easy for you to say," said Lola, exasperated. "It's not so easy for Judith though."

"Wait a minute. Do you have something up your sleeve, dear?" asked Bea, looking at Dawn suspiciously. "You have that look in your eyes."

"Maybe," said Dawn, swallowing the last of her gumbo and grinning widely. "In fact, what I have in mind is pure genius. It's better even than my usual brand of genius. You're gonna love it."

"Spill it, Dawn. What have you been up to?" grinned Lola.

"I have no idea what you're going to say, but I am definitely curious," admitted Judith.

"OK, here it is. First—let's face it, Lillian Deslattes is a first-class bee-otch if there ever was one. It was worth a shot to try, but I think we all knew that she'd never back down to some picketers and a demand letter. She probably eats letters from lawyers for lunch," Dawn said, shaking her head.

"Go on," urged Helen.

"OK. So, you know how I showed y'all that sweet little building on the way over here?"

They all nodded expectantly.

"Well," she laughed, "there's a method to my madness."

"That's debatable," mumbled Lola.

"OK, so picture this, sistahs. What if Judith opened her own place—her own gallery and gift shop one block up the street from the museum?" She finished with her mouth and eyes wide open, waiting for their shocked response.

"What?" yelped Judith, her own eyes wide with shock.

"Wait, hear me out. You already know a lot about what sells inside a gallery because the museum reserves a small portion of the gallery for small works for sale, right?"

"That's true," began Judith, "but . . ."

"And you've been saying how you could not create your own art for years because of having to give one hundred percent of your time to that job, right?"

"Well, yes, but . . ."

"Then why would you want that job back?" asked Dawn, throwing up her hands triumphantly.

"Uh, money?" chimed in Lola sarcastically.

"Dawn, I really do appreciate your idea and your faith in me, but opening a gallery would take every penny I've got and then some. It would be a terrible risk for me," said Judith, shaking her head emphatically, her anxiety flaring.

"No wait, you can't let this opportunity pass you by," enthused Dawn, digging in her purse and coming up with a stack of papers.

"Look, I've got the lease agreement here right now for you to sign. All you need is a pen!"

Bea started to say, "Dawn, I think . . ."

But Judith interrupted, "What?" She came to her feet in a flash. "Ok, now just wait a minute. This is going too far. It's all way too much. I don't know what to think about y'all. Honestly, you seem to be taking over my life suddenly, and now you're pushing me to sign some real estate deal? When I'm broke, jobless, and not in a very good place, you want me to go further into debt? I mean, I appreciate all the gumbo, and the picketing, and phone calls, and I realize y'all mean well, but now I just don't know what to think. Actually, I do. I think I'd better go."

She picked up her purse and hurried out the garage door, walking quickly up the street for six blocks to the safety and sanity of her own home.

"Nice going, Dawn," said Lola.

CHAPTER 19

The next morning, Judith slept late. She had woken up at her usual early time, but then turned over and went right back to sleep when she remembered all the trouble her waking life held. On top of it all, after running out on the sistahs yesterday, she was back to being friendless. She was miserable and could not think of a single thing that could motivate her to get out of bed.

Until the doorbell rang. She ignored it and rolled over. *"It's probably the UPS driver. They will just have to leave whatever it is at the door,"* she thought.

The bell rang again. And again insistently. "Oh come on!" she yelled. "What are you delivering—solid gold?" But she struggled up out of bed and wrapped a robe around herself, smoothing her hair down. "There'd better be an armored car sitting at the curb when I open this door," she grumbled.

Before she could get the door completely open, a hand carrying a coffee cup appeared around the corner and came dangerously close to poking her in the eye.

"Hello, dear," came a cheerful voice from the other side of the door. "We brought you this—and it's nice and hot this time."

Judith peered around the cup and the door, and was shocked to find the sistahs standing on her front steps. Stunned, she sputtered, "What . . . again?"

On her front porch stood Bea, Lola, and Helen—all carrying coffee and picket signs that said things like, "WE LOVE YOU, JUDITH!" and, "WE'RE NOT REALLY WEIRDOS!" Standing a little apart from the others stood Dawn with a sheepish grin, carrying her sign that said "I'M AN IDIOT!"

"Lola made my sign," she said.

"Dear, can we come in? We're sorry we freaked you out," asked Bea.

"We're so sorry," echoed Lola, and Helen added, "Please, let us in so we can explain."

Judith looked at the apologetic crew and rolled her eyes, but she was secretly relieved to see them. "Well, this trick worked once before—and I guess it's gonna work again. Come on in. But this doesn't mean I'm signing my life away on any papers."

The sistahs trouped in and sat down in Judith's living room.

"Thanks for the coffee," said Judith. "You do realize that every time my doorbell rings from now on, I'm going to think it's y'all bringing coffee, or picket signs, or God-knows what else."

The sistahs all laughed, a bit carefully. They knew they were not out of the woods yet.

Dawn started, "Judith, I have something important to tell you. Can I explain what that was all about yesterday?"

"Sure, I guess so," said Judith in an unhappy tone. She was not anxious to relive the events of the day before.

"Look, I didn't mean that you should sign those papers and go into business by yourself. I know you're not in any position to do something like that. What I meant was that you should get a partner to help with the money and everything—kind of an investor-partner, if you will."

"Oh please, who in their right mind would be willing to partner with me?"

"Well, me, of course," explained Dawn.

Lola laughed, "She said 'in her right mind,' Dawn."

Dawn ignored her, "Picture it, Judith—you and me as partners. We could open the Gumbeaux Sistahs Gallery! All of us could help out in the store, and that way, you could work part time at the gallery and get back to painting too."

They all stared at Judith, waiting, and Helen said encouragingly, "Dawn explained everything to us, and seriously, this might just work."

"Didn't I tell you this was genius?" said Dawn.

Judith felt a little glimmer of excitement filling her heart. She hardly dared to allow it to creep in, but she could not help it, "Dawn, you make it sounds so good, but could we actually pull off something like this?"

"I think we'll do more than pull it off. I think we'll kill it."

"If we could make this work, I would absolutely love it." Judith's brain started spinning with ideas, "And you know we could do workshops and offer ukulele lessons too. And part of it could be a gift shop to help with small sales in between the sales of the big paintings."

"That's the spirit!" Dawn was so excited she was practically jumping up and down. Judith was not far behind her.

"And we could do special events like the museum does. I'm pretty good at that, if I do say so myself," enthused Judith.

"Oh yes, ma'am—we sure could." They grabbed each other by the shoulders and were now genuinely dancing.

The other women watched their crazy antics, laughing.

Helen spoke up, "Oooh, can I sell my essential oil products in one little bitty corner?"

"Are you a Gumbeaux Sistah?" asked Dawn, and Helen nodded. "Well then, of course you can. We'll sell all sorts of wonderful things, and we won't be limited in the types of products we carry, like the museum is."

"Good point," agreed Judith.

"You know . . . did I see a little bay window in that building?" asked Lola.

"Yes, you did. What are you thinking?" asked Dawn.

"Well, I don't see any reason why I can't do another living art garden, this time for the Gumbeaux Sistahs Gallery. It's a huge draw for the museum. Why don't we do one too?"

"My God! That's a fantastic idea. And that ought to get Lillian's goat—two birds, one stone," laughed Dawn.

"Actually, I think my maintenance contract on the museum garden is up for renewal next month," said Lola.

"Are you thinking what I think you're thinking?" asked Dawn. "You could walk away from their garden maintenance next month, and see how well they do without you. They don't appreciate you enough anyway. Lillian takes all the credit for your beautiful installment."

"Oh, but I hate for you to turn down work at the museum because of this, Lola," said Judith.

"Are you kidding? It would give me great pleasure to stick it to that Deslattes woman. For a whole year she's been a pain in my ass. She didn't even invite me to the reveal party at the museum, and then she tried to claim all the credit for the garden herself. It was outrageous! Besides, I'm going to keep a bar stocked in the back room at the new gallery. It will give us a place to hang out on Friday nights."

"Oh my God, y'all make this sound like so much fun," said Judith with hope in her heart for the first time in so long.

"We're going to have a blast," grinned Helen. "And, of course, we'll help you fix up and run the place to give you time to paint, or whatever you need."

"Can we really do this, do you think?" asked Judith, afraid to hope.

"One thing you'll both need is a business plan," said Bea, seriously. "So, now it's time for me to bring out my homework for you. I've been holding back so I can offer something of value to you, but I needed to see what you needed first. And it's time. I've done a ton of workshops and coaching to small businesses on marketing, business plans, budgeting, etc. We could work something up for you very quickly if you decide that this is for you. Maybe you could rent the store before someone else grabs it, and then we could meet at the end of the week and get things rolling," she suggested.

"Oh, things are already rolling," said Dawn, smiling. "Rental property gets grabbed up quickly in that area. So as I mentioned before, I've got the lease agreement right here in my bag."

Lola laughed, "Good Lord, what isn't in that bag?"

Dawn ignored her, "It's all ready for both our signatures, partner."

Judith squeaked out a grateful, "You are amazing, Dawn."

"Too true, too true," said Dawn with a wink.

CHAPTER 20

The next morning, all five of the Gumbeaux Sistahs met the real estate agent at the new property, and Dawn and Judith finalized the lease. The agent left them with the keys to the front door, and the women began to look around and plan excitedly.

"I just can't believe we're actually doing this," laughed Judith, her eyes glowing, "It's wonderful—and completely terrifying."

"This is going to be such a hoot." said Helen.

"Keep in mind, dear, that we will support you and Dawn in any way we can," said Bea. "But I have a strong hunch that you'll do just fine here. It's a great idea, and if you stick to a business plan as best as you can, I don't think you can lose. I've recently read a statistic that small businesses are more likely to be successful when started by people over fifty. Isn't that something? Life experience counts for a lot in this case."

"Judith, I can't believe you're going into business with Dawn," teased Lola, laughing. "Don't you know? That woman's crazy!"

While pulling out her phone to answer a text, Dawn retorted, "Ha! I knew you'd be jealous."

"You know, I think I am," said Lola, nodding. "And get off that phone." She suddenly looked thoughtful, "Would you look at this front window! It's perfect for the new living art installation—even better than I thought because of the light in here. And guess what—for your new going-into-business present, my labor for it is free." She grinned at them hugely.

"Oh no, you don't," said Dawn. "We want to pay you."

"Oh, you will, don't worry," laughed Lola. She handed Dawn and Judith a handful of business cards each. "Invite me to opening night, of course, get me loads of new customers, and we'll call it even. That's more than Lillian Deslattes ever did for me. She did her best to keep my name a secret from potential customers. I think she even told a few of them that she created it. The woman is a power freak. That's no way to treat your artists. Seriously!"

"Oh, we would do all that for you anyway," said Judith happily. "We'll get you loads of customers."

"Look," pointed Helen. "I could put up a shelf in the corner there for my essential oils, and I have the perfect little shelf at home already for its space."

"And I have an old counter in storage," said Dawn, thinking. "It was once in our front office before we remodeled. It would perfect right here."

"And I have several easels at the house that you can have that I've used in training workshops," said Bea.

"Oh! I've got a beautiful old armoire that you could use. It would look cool with gift items on it," offered Lola.

"Wow, it's almost furnished already," said Judith. "And last night, I started on two new, large paintings at the house. And I've been going through some older pieces that I think would be great to open with. Speaking of which, when do you want to open, Dawn?"

"You know, I was over at the art museum checking on their garden this morning," said Lola. "Bitsy and Thomas were going on and on about an event they have coming up on March fifteenth."

"That's three weeks from now," said Helen, checking her phone.

"That's the Spring Fling," said Judith wistfully. "It's a very popular event. I wonder what Thomas has planned. We usually go all out for that event."

"You don't have time to wonder, partner, because that's when we will open our doors. March fifteenth will be opening night! Everyone will be in the neighborhood for the event. We'll just have to do a better job than the museum so they will come to our place. I'm up for a little competition, how about you?" asked Dawn excitedly.

"Yikes!" said Judith. "Three weeks! There are a million things to do."

"We'll help," said Lola. "Dawn's right. That would be the perfect night to do the grand opening so we can steal from the museum's thunder and take advantage of their crowd. Ooh—I have a potter friend named Erika who I'm sure will be happy to fill a table in here with her beautiful pieces to sell that night. Her work is awesome. She's even had a couple of pieces in the New Orleans Museum of Art."

"Awesome," said Dawn, "Can you contact her?"

"I'm on it," said Lola, whipping out her phone.

"You know, my daughter Lizzy makes jewelry in her spare time," said Judith. "It's actually beautiful work. Look, she made this bracelet for me."

"I wondered where you got that—I love it. Can you get her to make us some for opening night?" asked Dawn and added, "Get her to make me one too."

"I'm sure I can," said Judith. "We'll need a display case for jewelry."

"Leave that to me. I'll find us one somewhere," said Dawn, adding, "Listen, can we get together tomorrow morning to talk about everything?"

"I have my band practice in the morning, and I'm meeting Bea in the afternoon to talk more about the business plan. Aren't you coming to that? Otherwise we can meet here tomorrow night?" said Judith.

"Can't make the meeting with Bea in the afternoon. I have to meet with a client," said Dawn. "But you can fill me in later. I can do tomorrow night though—seven P.M., OK?"

"Yep," said Judith happily.

"And by the way, did you say band practice?" asked Dawn.

"Yes, remember I told you about my all-women ukulele band? We practice on Thursday mornings. I know it sounds weird, but we're actually pretty decent, and people always have a good time when we play. Are any of you interested in learning to play?"

"I don't think that's for me, dear. I'll stick with my piano," smiled Bea.

"No thanks, but I've been practicing my sax again lately," said Lola.

"Speaking of practicing, Judith, how's your self-care these days?" asked Helen. "It's important to take care of yourself, especially during times of stress."

"I know you're right, Helen, and thanks for asking. The answer is—it's probably not as good as it could be. There's so much going on."

"OK if I stop by later on this morning? I've made up a batch of my magic soup, and I'll bring you some. It will keep your system on track. It's organic, clean, and tastes pretty great too. Not as good as gumbo, mind you, but it's so good for you. I think you need this right now."

"Magic soup?" smiled Judith. "I like the sound of that. Dawn said you were a witch. Now I will have proof."

"Don't make fun," said Lola seriously. "Helen can fix what ails you, and that soup is delicious. I don't know about magic but . . ."

"Oh no, it's magic all right," said Bea, nodding.

"Ok then—I'm convinced," said Judith. "Come on over."

CHAPTER 21

Lola & Bud

With everything else going on—her regular business, plus the picketing for Judith, and taking care of the garden at the museum, it was a wonder Lola had had a chance to think of Bud at all.

But she did. Oh, she did all right. She thought of him now as she cared for plants at several corporate venues on her usual rounds.

Lola and Bud's date had been what you could call "successful." Another word for it might be—hilarious. Also—romantic.

He had taken her to Del Porto, her favorite Italian restaurant in Covington. She had ordered the Crawfish Cannelloni, a perfect fusion of her favorite food influences—Louisianan and Italian. Bud had ordered the Pasta Primavera. Their wine was served, and then Bud proceeded to remind Lola of their past history together. They really had some fun times before the not-so-fun times set in.

At one point in the evening, Lola was laughing particularly hard over one long-ago afternoon they had spent together. She had almost forgotten about it. A friend of theirs, Tony, had invited them to go duck hunting, of all things, in a local swamp. Tony was a talented craftsman. He carved out his own handmade pirogues, a light, fast-moving little boat for two people, perfect for skimming through the Louisiana backwaters. Neither Lola nor Bud knew anything about duck hunting, but they decided to go because they just wanted to ride in the little boats.

Tony had put Lola in his pirogue for safety, since he was experienced with both the boat and the swamp. Bud was in his own boat. Tony had brought shotguns for all three of them, but Lola had no intention of shooting anything. Neither did Bud, but he did want to shoot the gun once, for the experience of it. He had never shot a shotgun before and was curious about it.

Tony took them deep into the swamp where it was dead-quiet, beautiful, and mysterious. Lola loved sitting in the early morning sun experiencing the stillness of nature. Then Bud said he was going to fire the gun once.

Lola told him, "Bud, nature doesn't need your loud gun shots out here."

But Bud was determined. "I'll just do it once, then I'll be quiet."

So, Bud raised the gun to the side of the pirogue, away from Lola and Tony's boat.

The problem was that the small, light boat could not withstand the recoil from the shotgun firing directly to the side. The whole pirogue, Bud, their lunch, a cooler, and other odds and ends, flipped sideways, rolled over, and dunked everything completely underwater. Bud came right back up, still sitting in the boat and spluttering dirty swamp water.

Tony and Lola were momentarily frozen in surprise. Then, while Bud frantically tried to rescue the cooler and other items, Lola and Tony laughed themselves silly.

Talking over that long ago moment with Bud made Lola laugh so hard in the restaurant, it almost made her choke. Tears formed in her eyes as she got herself under control.

"Bud, stop! You're going to kill me."

They looked at each other and grinned. There's something about laughing that hard with someone that does something to people. Lola was sure there was a scientific explanation or a specific chemical reaction name to explain it. Whatever it was, that kind of shared laughter can burst two willing hearts wide open.

Later in the evening, they decided that they would like to do some more laughing together. "Maybe Sunday evening?" asked Bud.

By mutual consent, they also decided to keep their little get together a secret from family and friends for now. Lola and Bud's breakup years ago had caused them all quite a lot of pain. They did not know if this was a good thing or a one-off, so they decided just to keep it to themselves for now.

But right now, it sure seemed like an awfully good thing.

—⟋⟍—

Lillian and Thomas

Lillian sat in the conference room going over the proposed lineup of talent to display for the next year. Thomas had dropped the list into her hands when she arrived that morning. She groaned as she read it and put her hand to her forehead. "Oh my God, he didn't listen to me at all. He's got artwork in here that is not museum quality at all. It's like he didn't even look at their work. Obviously he's not used to curating, especially with local artists. I told him to check with me or Bitsy before he scheduled anyone. This is going to have to be completely revised."

She remembered the understanding they had come to back at the San Francisco Curators Conference after having spent that first glorious, stolen night together. They made a plan that Lillian would help him move to Louisiana, and set him up as Assistant Manager. All of that went smoothly. She had no trouble selling the idea of hiring him to the museum board, since his prior position was with a notable big city museum.

She thought back wistfully for a moment to when Thomas first arrived in Covington, and there had been a lot of love-making and laughter between them. She showed him to his new office in the museum when he had first arrived.

—⟋⟍—

Lillian helped Thomas carry a few personal items into his office and set them down on his desk. "I'm sorry it's small, but it will have to do until Judith is gone, then you can take over her space."

"It will do just fine for now," he said, closing the door behind them. "Seems like a nice little operation here, Lillian. You've done a great job with this place."

She preened with the compliment and said, "We really do procure some amazing installations for such a small museum. I think you'll be pleasantly surprised at what can be done here."

"I'm sure I will be. You're always surprising me." He moved closer and put his arm around her waist, grinning. "And this little office is perfect for personal meetings with my boss."

He looked around the room and asked, "Oh wait, are there any cameras in here?"

Lillian laughed, "No, we don't have any in the museum yet, although I suppose we should do that one of these day when the budget allows. Once you start working your magic around here, we'll get bigger and better, and then we'll need those cameras, no doubt. But we're such a small city, and up till now we've never had any trouble here at all."

He drew her closer to him and kissed her hard, pushing her against his desk. He whispered, "Well, trouble has just arrived." She laughed and kissed him back passionately.

But there was not much laughter between the two of them now. Since installing him in his position of Director, Lillian had often been irritated with him.

They had a plan and an understanding when he first arrived. That plan was that he would be installed as Assistant Manager to start. Then eventually, he would replace Judith and gain the revised title of Director. Lillian's part of the plan was to arrange it so that Judith could not meet new fundraising quotas for the upcoming events. Then Lillian would have an excuse to kick her to the curb and install Thomas. The scheme would solve Thomas' need for a job and also keep him close for their romantic rendezvous. Meanwhile, Thomas needed to prove himself useful and worthy of the higher position. Lillian was relying on him to help her prove her case, so that he could take over when the time came. But Thomas seemed to have forgotten that part of the bargain. He had done none of it, in fact, and seemed to rely on his good looks and charm and the fact that he was Lillian's boy-toy to keep his position. He was just not pulling his weight.

Lillian was having second thoughts about him—and third, fourth, and fifth thoughts too. She was delighted that Judith was gone, but Thomas was getting harder and harder to motivate to do his job. It was obvious he relied on uncomplaining Bitsy as his assistant for the majority of his duties.

The situation was a constant irritant to her, and their love life had fizzled to a near dead stop because of it. His desire for her was obviously still going strong, but Lillian was disgusted. And disgust is hardly arousing.

She wondered more than once what she would have found if she had actually checked Thomas' work references from his previous jobs. He had been so charming and persuasive and—let's face it— such a young, pleasing lover that all talk about references had gone right out the window. Lillian, frankly, had not completely understood the young man's attraction to her. She was still pretty for her age, but still, there was quite an age difference between them. But Lillian had seen an advantage at having the young man around, and as per usual, sensing any advantage, Lillian grabbed it.

She wondered now about checking those references and whether they would have influenced her decision to hire him at the museum if she had. *"Probably not,"* she thought, knowing herself, *"Probably not."*

It's one thing for younger people to practice ageism. That's bad enough. It's almost worse when older people practice it against each other.

—Judith

CHAPTER 22

Helen arrived around noon with a tureen full of her magic soup. She insisted that Judith, who had not had lunch yet, sit down and let Helen serve them both a bowl.

Judith took a spoonful and said, "Oh my God, Helen. This is so good. It doesn't have to be magic—just tasting this good is good enough for me." She ate another spoonful with an appreciative sigh.

"Oh, it's magic all right—and organic too. It's helped many people I know get their digestion straightened out, which makes people healthier and happier and have a lot more energy. At this stage of our lives, our bodies have been around awhile. We are organic beings and our bodies wear out. But if we take care of the engine, the car will last longer and run well. This stuff will fix you right up. It helps with stress too, which I know you're under right now because stress does all sorts of damage. So, I brought you the recipe. Don't eat it all the time. I wouldn't want you to get sick of it," she laughed.

"I doubt that could ever happen," Judith said seriously.

"Just try to eat it for several meals a week, and it will do the trick. We're getting older and good health makes all the difference in a quality life."

"I won't have any problem with that," said Judith happily, "I might just have another bowl right now."

"You know, it even has helped some people lose weight," said Helen knowingly. "The healthier your body gets, the more you want to take care of it."

"Now you're talking. That kind of information is right up my alley," said Judith ruefully. "I certainly could lose a few."

"You should ask Bea about it," said Helen.

"Did Bea lose some weight with this?"

"Only about thirty pounds," laughed Helen.

"What? I can't even picture that. I mean, that's a lot."

"Oh, it's no secret," said Helen. "Ask her about it sometime. Yep, soup and dancing—that's Bea's secret to weight loss."

"Dancing?" asked Judith incredulously.

"Yep, that part's her story to tell, though. But seriously, ask her."

"I will," said Judith. "You know, I've never asked you, but how did you and Bea get together? You two are the original Gumbeaux Sistahs. I mean, you two knew each other before the others joined in, right? I'd like to hear that story."

"How did we meet? The better question is 'why did we meet?'" Helen was suddenly serious. She closed her eyes for a moment and shook her head. "The answer to that would be—we met because we each needed someone to save us. So we saved each other. Do you really want to hear about it? It's both a sad and happy story."

"Yes, I really do."

"Well, I can tell you my half of the story anyway. If Bea were here, she'd tell you her half too. She shares parts of it so it will help people, but it's still hers to tell.

"So, here's my half. Keep in mind, Judith, some of this story will be hard to hear." Helen reached out and patted Judith's hand, as if comforting her. "OK, so I met Bea ten years ago when I was fifty-seven. At the time I was married to a man named Luke. We'd been together for about two years by then. When Luke and I first met, I was just beginning my studies of the effects nutrition has on our health. I went to school and attended conferences. I read everything I could get my hands on about it. It was a theory that was pretty ahead of its time. I talked to so many women who were suffering from mysterious illnesses that doctors were diagnosing as this and that, and it was apparent that nobody knew what was going on with them. Their current medical solutions to the maladies were just not working. The women suffered bad digestion, fatigue, odd pains, lethargy, and several other symptoms. They were being diagnosed as having MS,

Lyme disease, Celiac disease, Irritable Bowel syndrome, and many other things, when what they really had was poor nutrition. Their bodies were crying for help, and no one knew how to cure them. And I was learning to fix some of them. It was such an amazing period of my life.

"Then came Luke. I'd never been married before him, and I have no children. So, we had a lot of freedom and spent as much time as possible together. He was completely charming and so attentive. He'd surprise me at work a couple of times a week with flowers or other gifts. He took me out to 'show me off,' is what he said. He swept me off my feet, really. I wasn't used to so much attention, and it was quite flattering. Before very long he suggested that we get married, and I was surprised and so happy. He moved into my house because I had the bigger place.

"But as my studies got more intense and exciting, they began to take up more and more of my time. I loved it—the work was so fascinating and still is. But unfortunately, it did not fascinate Luke. He started acting moody around the house. He was busy too because he owned his own auto shop, but he wasn't as busy as I was. He started to resent the time I spent away from him.

"Honestly, I know this sounds like such a cliché, and I'm still so embarrassed that it happened to me. But you just don't see it coming sometimes. You don't think it can happen to you. As you can probably guess, Luke started to get abusive. At first it was in small ways. He started saying ugly things to me—things that made me feel unattractive and useless. He made me question myself constantly.

"Please understand this, Judith, I loved him, or thought I did. But, little by little, he became someone else. It was so confusing. How could a person tell someone they loved her one minute, and then break a heavy ceramic mug over their head the next?"

Judith's mouth fell open. "Oh Helen, no!"

"Well, yes, it happened—that and worse. I was concussed and ended up in the hospital. And guess what—I did the typical stupid thing that some women do. I covered up for him. I didn't tell anyone what he'd done. I kept thinking that it was all a mistake somehow—that he'd just made a big mistake, and it would never happen again.

"But, of course, it did—quite a few times, actually.

"Eventually, I became afraid to leave the house except to go to work. He followed me all the time, and the slightest misstep on my part, or even no misstep at all sometimes, would provoke him. It was as if he thought it was his duty to stop me from living a life of my own. He wanted complete control. I lost all my friends and eventually had to give up my studies too. And, Judith, he hurt me badly. If I hadn't left, he would have killed me.

"Then one night, after his fist had connected with my left eye, I snapped. Or maybe I woke up. Afterwards, he took a shower, and I made a break for it. I walked out of my own house, got in the car, and drove away to Safe House. It's a sanctuary for battered women and children. I finally was able to admit to myself that that is exactly what I was.

"So, you'll never guess who the intake counselor at the Safe House was that night."

"Was it Bea?" guessed Judith. "That's where you met Bea?"

"None other," said Helen, shaking her head at the memory. "And thank God it was. So, you know how Bea is. She's got the biggest heart. She and I connected that night in a way that's never happened to me before. She listened. She heard me. And saw me. I mean the *me* that had been hiding for a long time.

"We called the police and had Luke arrested that same night. Later, we went to trial. Lucky for me, I had a few witnesses at my job that saw my black eyes and broken bones. Bea was a witness for me too. The judge believed me, and my dear old husband, Luke, actually went to prison."

"Oh Helen, that's just horrible. I can't believe that anyone could hurt you. That just makes me so sick. Is that bastard still in jail?"

"Well, no," said Helen, looking at her feet. "He got out a little over a year later. The judge did issue a restraining order against him and said he couldn't come within a hundred feet of me, my house, or my work. But still, he would show up occasionally in different places—always watching me. He would call me on the landline at home and hang up, just to torture me. I changed the number, but he wasn't that easy to get rid of.

"Meanwhile, Bea and I became the best of friends—sisters really. She was in a position where she needed company and a roommate. So, I rented out my house and moved in with her.

"Somehow, Luke found out that I was staying with Bea because he started parking up the street from her house at night for short periods of time. This went on for months. We called the police several times, but he never stayed around long enough for them to catch him. He'd stay just long enough to let me know he was watching. Needless to say, I was not doing well. I was terrified. It's taken me a very long time to be able to even breathe deeply because of that man.

"But Bea saved me. If I had been by myself, I would have lost it. Just having someone to talk to every day was amazing. It took me forever to get up the nerve just to go to the grocery. To make me feel a little safer, Bea went to the sporting goods store one day and bought eight heavy, wooden baseball bats, and put one in every room of her house.

"And Judith, when I say that Bea saved my life, I mean it literally." She paused and got choked up for a moment.

"What do you mean, Helen?" asked Judith. "What are you telling me?"

"It's just that . . . Luke came back one night."

"Oh my God," said Judith, putting a hand over her mouth.

"He apparently waited till Bea had just left the house. I was sitting in Bea's kitchen, watching TV. I always turned it up loud when Bea wasn't home. My hearing is OK, but just not as good as used to be. I didn't hear him. And then, suddenly, he was right behind me. I heard a voice say, "Hello, bitch." Judith, when I tell you my heart froze, please believe me. I couldn't even turn around. I realized right away that he had probably snuck in through the garage door as Bea pulled out. The garage is connected by a door to the kitchen. Sometimes one of us forgets to lock it, coming in and out from the car. He was apparently waiting in the bushes, or nearby, knowing that it was Bea's night to work at the Safe House. As soon as her car pulled out, he snuck in and came after me.

"I tell you, I couldn't move. I could no more call out for help or try to get to another room than I could fly to the moon.

"I heard him coming closer, and he was talking the whole time. He said things like, 'It's time to pay the price, Helen. I don't know what you were thinking. You can't pull this off. You can't make it without me. You're nothing. Just a stupid, old woman that's not worth a shit. Sure, I get mad sometimes, but who wouldn't get mad living with you? Who wouldn't go crazy living with an idiot like you?'

"While he talked, he kept slamming his fist against the countertops. He threw things like the salt and pepper shakers and the tea kettle across the room and slammed a couple of open drawers shut. Each slam sounded like a gunshot to me. He went on and on. Luke always did like the sound of his own voice. I sat there waiting for the first punch, the first shove, the first something. I remember thinking that I knew he wouldn't stop this time. I knew Luke was getting ready to kill me. I waited for the end. And I know this sounds crazy, but I remember that I was thinking that poor Bea was going to come home to a horrible mess in her house. Isn't that the craziest thing?"

"You're a kind person. It doesn't surprise me a bit, honestly. Did he hurt you badly, Helen?"

"No," she said simply. "Bea killed him."

Judith gasped. "What?"

"Well, sort of, she did," said Helen quietly.

"What are you talking about, Helen?"

"When Bea pulled out of the garage, she saw Luke sneak in at the last second. So, Bea didn't close the garage door with the remote, as she normally would. Instead, she pulled the car over in front of a neighbor's house a couple of doors down, grabbed her phone, and called the police. Then she ran back to the house and re-entered through the garage. One of our baseball bats was hidden in the garage, so Bea grabbed it and quietly hurried into the kitchen. Luke was so busy slamming drawers and screaming at me that he'd worked himself up into a kind of crazed frenzy. He didn't even hear her behind him. Bea had noticed that he had taken one of their kitchen knives from the magnetic strip on the wall. When she saw Luke raise the knife, Bea swung that bat as hard as she could and knocked Luke clear across the room. I didn't know she had that much strength. She was getting ready to hit him again, but I spun around, and it distracted her for just a second. In that moment, Luke jumped up and ran into the garage, and back outside. His head was bleeding, and he was stumbling like a drunk. He made it two doors down to his car and managed to get in and start it. Bea and I ran outside to see where he'd gone. Bea was still holding onto the bat when Luke squealed out into the street, got halfway down the block, and slammed into a neighbor's big oak tree."

"Oh my God," said Judith.

"Bea and I watched as, one by one, the neighbors came out of their houses to find out what had happened after hearing the crash. At that moment, the police roared up and went straight to the crash. Bea and I quietly went back into the house and quickly washed off the bat. We cleaned up Lucas's blood and fingerprints in the kitchen, and waited for the police to show up. When they did come, we told them the truth, well, part of it anyway—that Luke had been breaking his restraining order and hanging around the house, looking for me. The police records showed that Bea had called them when she first spotted him outside the house. Luckily for us, Luke had been drinking, a lot, and had left an empty pint bottle in the car. The police found it right away when they searched, and they declared it an alcohol related death. They said he had blunt trauma to the head from his crash into the tree."

"So, Luke was gone," continued Helen. "It was the only way he was going to stop coming after me. He was going to kill me one day or die trying. I doubt that he pictured it being the latter, though. I wish it would have all happened differently, and I'm sorry for all the bad things that happened to him. But Judith, I could finally breathe free. I could finally start to live again.

"And, you know, you don't go through something like that with someone without becoming true sisters. Bea saved my life.

"And next time you see her, ask her how I saved hers too," she smiled shyly.

You can catch more flies with honey, but it helps to carry a big can of Raid.

—Dawn

CHAPTER 23

Judith pulled up across the street from Bea's house on Thursday afternoon. It was in a scenic part of town. Nearby Lee Lane held a dozen adorable little shops that were always busy. Directly across from Bea's house was a shady, picturesque park with an unusual, striking sculpture of four women holding up an iron dome. The next street over held Judith's favorite little British Tea House, where they served high tea with tiny sandwiches and scones. Between the busy venues, finding parking was usually a challenge.

Judith got lucky though, and found a spot right in front of the little park. She crossed the street and walked up the flagstone path to Bea's front door. It opened right away to Bea's apple-friendly, smiling face.

"Hello, dear," Bea said warmly, and hugged Judith like an old friend. Judith had been looking forward to their meeting all day. Not only because they were going to go over a business plan for the new gallery, but also because Bea was somewhat of a mystery to Judith, and she was glad to spend some time with her alone. On the surface, Bea was open and generous. But aside from that, Judith knew very little about her because Bea did not talk about herself very much.

Her home was cozy and sparkling clean. Judith could smell something tantalizing cooking. "I've got cookies for us," Bea said, walking back to the kitchen, leaving Judith in the living room. "Make yourself at home. Coffee?"

But Judith did not answer immediately. Her attention was captured completely by a large bookshelf in the room filled with gleaming silver trophies. She looked closer and saw many couples perched on top of the shiny awards. All the trophies were for dancing.

"Bea, what is all this? Helen said you liked to dance, but I had no idea. When did you do all this dancing?"

"It's still going on," said Bea. "It's a secret vice. I do ballroom, Cajun, zydeco, round dancing, square dancing, even some tap. It's kind of my superpower," she laughed.

"I'm so impressed," said Judith, gawking at all the gleaming silver. "Have you always danced? Did you start as a little girl?"

"Oh no, I started a few years back. It was just after Helen had saved me from a certain suicide attempt of mine," said Bea, nodding, watching Judith closely and waiting to see how she would react. Bea's eyes looked sad, but steady and calm.

Judith's mouth fell open, and she did not know what to say. She could not even talk for a moment. Bea waited patiently. Finally, Judith squeaked out, "What? You, Bea? I just don't believe it. I can't even imagine that."

"Well, you don't have to, but it's quite true, dear. Sad but true. I planned on ending my life, and would have, but Helen saved me. Didn't she tell you? I know she came over for a visit this week."

"No! She said you had a story to tell, but it was up to you if you wanted to share it."

"I want to, dear, if you are ready to hear it. It's kind of sad though. Both sad and happy. It's one of those real stories."

"I would love to hear it, Bea," said Judith sincerely. "You and Helen are always surprising me."

"Well, it's just life, dear. So, my story goes back a little ways to when I met my husband, John Walker, in college at Loyola. He was studying law, and I was a business major. There were women in my major back then, but not that many, so I guess I stood out because of it. But that's not why my John noticed me. Here's what happened. My family lived in the university neighborhood. And even though my family could certainly afford my tuition, my folks were old-school and thought it would be a valuable lesson for me to pay my own way. That was actually possible when our generation was young. So I worked part-time in the university cafeteria doing several jobs, including hauling big, steaming trays of food to the buffet and working the serving line and cash register. John had a paid meal ticket, so he ate most of his meals in the cafeteria. We noticed each other early on, and there was a lot of smiling going on between us for a while. But we were both shy." Bea looked away for a moment, remembering. "We didn't speak one word to each other for a couple of weeks. He told me later that he'd been waiting for the right opportunity and the right amount of nerve, and I had been hoping he'd make the first move. I might still be waiting today if I hadn't decided to force the issue one day," she laughed. "So, I was in the serving line one afternoon when he came in for his usual lunch. We were serving macaroni and cheese with a side of broccoli that day. When he nervously passed me his tray, I gave him just a tiny bit of macaroni and a massive, overflowing serving of broccoli. He took one look at his tray and burst out laughing. He still didn't say anything, but he grinned at me and took his tray to a nearby table. There he proceeded to eat every bit of that pile of food, all the while nodding and smiling at me. After a few minutes, I was able to take a break and joined him at his table. I asked him how he liked his mac and cheese and he told me, laughing, that he was still looking for it.

"I married that boy within the year. We struggled and fought and loved each other so much. I swear we were happy for thirty-five years. It was a marvelous life, it really was. John became a successful contracts lawyer in New Orleans, and I went into corporate business training. We traveled, had wonderful friends, and lots of parties. I couldn't have children as it turned out, but we were very happy anyway.

"Then one day, he just died, Judith. To this day it just kills me to say those words. It's still unbelievable to me. You see, John was so healthy. He watched his diet religiously, and he ran every morning before work. One day, he went out for his usual run down St. Charles Avenue, and died of a heart attack right there on the streetcar line."

"Oh no. That's terrible, Bea. I'm so sorry," said Judith, feeling tears spring to her eyes.

"It was the worst day of my life," said Bea, tears in her own eyes. "He was a lovely man—so good to me. Then after he passed . . . well, let's just say I didn't do very well. Oh, I held on for a few months—barely. For the first couple of weeks, I literally couldn't get off the couch. Friends came around for a while, but their visits dwindled as time went by. My parents were already gone, and my sister lives in Milwaukee. And as I said, John and I had no kids, so I was pretty much alone. Alone with my grief and my memories. And to be honest, my thoughts started to turn to leaving this planet to be with John."

Judith touched Bea's shoulder, overwhelmed with sympathy for her friend.

Bea went on. "Oh, I know it sounds awful, but it seemed perfectly reasonable to me at the time. I completely understand now how people can talk themselves into doing away with themselves. It's a terrible mistake, I know that now, but I can understand it because I almost went there myself. I missed John so much. I missed his company and how he watched out for me in so many little ways. I missed taking care of him. I really missed taking care of someone.

"But before I went through with ending my life, I decided to try one more thing first to help me get through the pain. I volunteered at the women's shelter—the Safe House. Years ago, I was once on their board, so I knew many people there, and they knew me. I ended up taking over for the night intake person a couple of times a week. Sometimes women need to get away from bad situations in the middle of the night. Some even leave while their abuser is in the house, when they are asleep. The shelter will take them in anytime, and someone needs to be there twenty-four seven. It was only my second night on the shift when Helen came in."

"Are you serious?" said Judith, her eyes wide. "Your second night!"

"As serious as I've ever been, dear. She came in, and she looked like hell. She was scared to death, with bruises on her face and arms. I took one look at her, and my heart just went out to her. Poor Helen. It was bad. She had talked to the shelter counselor earlier that week and was told that we had a spot for her, and to come in any time she needed. She was hesitant to leave her home but ended up running away at the last minute. Her husband, Luke, had come home angry about something, and took it out on Helen so that the poor thing could hardly walk. One eye was swollen shut. You would have cried, Judith. She waited till Luke was taking a shower. She had suitcases already packed and hidden in the garage, just in case. It's a good thing she did. She barely got out because he came out of the shower just as she was leaving, and she had to run for it."

"What kind of animal would hit sweet Helen? That bastard!" said Judith, outraged.

"Oh yes, he was a bastard all right, dear. I don't know if you know how these shelters work, but your stay there is temporary. If you don't have a place to go, and Helen didn't, then you work with the counselor who will try to find a place for you to stay and figure out your next steps."

"I worked the following two nights at the shelter because I wanted to stay and help Helen. I spent most of my shift talking to her. She had no place to go and needed help. So, I decided to invite her to stay with me for a while. It sounds impulsive and a little dangerous, but I thought it would be good for both of us. She said 'Yes' immediately, which surprised me and kind of made me think it was meant to be. Do you know what I mean?"

Judith nodded.

"So, Helen parked herself in one of my spare bedrooms, and for a while things were a little better. She brought charges against Luke, and the court process was brutal. She succeeded in getting him some jail time, but not nearly enough. She immediately began the process of divorcing him before he got out, and I kept working a couple of nights a week at the shelter. I was retired from corporate training at this point.

"Helen had such a rough time. She tried going back to work for a little while, but she had to stop because once Luke was out of jail, he started following her everywhere even though he wasn't supposed to by order of the court. We just had to take it one day at a time.

"Then came that night—and I believe that you know which one I mean, dear, am I right?"

Judith nodded sadly.

"I'll never forget that kind of fear. Never. It was one of the most terrifying nights of my life. It was also the one that saved me."

"Helen told me what happened—what you did," said Judith.

"Yes, it's all true," said Bea. "Luke had come to hurt Helen. I truly believe he came to kill her. He was an angry man, dear—mad at life, and furious with Helen for divorcing him. We were very wary of him for months. Then one night, I got careless with the garage door, and it almost cost Helen her life. I tell you, Judith, my heart almost froze when I saw him sneaking into my house.

"Later, after Luke was dead, Helen and I were both questioned by the police, of course. We told them that we scared him away from the house, and he took off in the car, obviously very drunk, and ran into the tree. I don't know—maybe the crash killed him, Judith. And maybe I contributed to the head injury that killed him. We'll never know. Helen backed up my story. I don't know if I would have gotten in trouble, since they might have called it self-defense. If they had done an autopsy and determined that his death was caused by a blow to the back of his head, and not from the crash, then I could have been charged or dragged through the courts. Who knows what would have happened. Helen was not about to let that happen to me. She protected me. I had protected her, and she turned right around and protected me.

"Unfortunately, the trauma of the night brought up so many things in my life. I was shaken from the incident and still very depressed with grief. Honestly, I just couldn't quite come up with a reason to keep going, even with Helen in so much need. One night, a few days after Luke's death, I decided that I'd had enough. I had a bottle of pills and a fifth of vodka to keep them company. It was two o'clock in the morning, and Helen was asleep. I sat at the kitchen table in the semi-darkness and laid out all the little pills in a circle on the counter. I had already started on the vodka for courage.

"My plan was to work my way around the circle, swallowing the pills. I was going to come around full circle, and I remember being amused at my ironic little plan. I got two pills down the hatch when the overhead lights went on..."

———

Bea remembered every detail of that night. After she had managed to take two pills from her circle on the counter, the lights came on, and Helen plopped down at the counter across from her.

"Hi, Bea," Helen whispered.

"Hello, dear," Bea said. Then Helen looked into Bea's eyes with the deepest kindness Bea had ever seen.

"It's time to talk," Helen said.

"There's not much to say, really."

"Your little display on the counter here says otherwise."

"Helen," Bea said, "I just can't find any reason to stay here. I've tried. I really have. I'm in too much pain, and besides, I've done pretty much everything I wanted to do here on earth."

"Oh really?" asked Helen.

"Well yes, really." Bea said, meaning it.

Helen thought for a moment, then said, "Bea, when you were a little girl, did you foresee all the wonderful things that would happen to you in this life? I mean, did you know you were going to meet a wonderful man like John? Or live where you've lived? Or have the friends you've had? Or traveled where you've gone? Or have the fantastic career you've had?"

"Well, no. No one knows that ahead of time."

"Exactly," she said. "No one knows the kind of wonderful adventures, loves, and friendships they will have. And you know what? Nothing's changed. You still don't know what adventures will come your way, what love will be in your life, what joy there is to come. You wouldn't have wanted to miss out on your life till now, would you?"

"Oh no. I've had a wonderful life," said Bea.

"And you don't know what's coming," Helen said, "but I guarantee there will be more joy, more love, and more adventures. You just can't miss out on those either."

"What if you're wrong, Helen? What if I used them all up?"

"How can you believe that? My God, if anyone could believe that, it would be me. But I haven't given up, and I found wonderful you. You are such a gift in my life, Bea. I didn't think it was possible. And you've already started on a new adventure. You've brought my friendship into your life. You saved me, and you know what? I love you. So, already—new friendship and new love."

Helen went on, "And here's something else, Bea. I think there are a lot more women like us who need love, friendship, and adventures. Maybe you and I could even help some of them. And, who knows, maybe if we're lucky we might even end up with some great-looking firemen, having mind-bending sex." She smiled.

Bea chuckled, and it was music to Helen's ears.

"So how about we throw all this nonsense out?" she asked, pointing to the pills, "And start looking together for all those things? We could look for people to help out, and for new adventures in our lives. And you know what we're going to start with?"

Bea hesitated and shook her head.

"You'll never guess, so I'll just tell you," she said. "Dancing! We're gonna dance our faces off. Starting this week, we're both signing up for dancing lessons."

—m—

"Helen is amazing," Judith interrupted in awe. "You both are."

"Helen always amazes me. Just when you think you know her, she blows all your preconceived notions about her straight out the window," laughed Bea. "And she was true to her word, too. The very next day we went to our first dancing lesson. Helen hadn't danced for years, but she knew a couple of dance groups that met regularly. We started out with the waltz and Cajun dancing. One group met in a studio, and the other met at the Abita Town Hall.

"And I must tell you, Judith, I loved it. I really did. I was hooked from day one. We went through all these lessons and steps, and then we coupled off and started to really dance. The minute the music started, I got swept away."

"Is Helen a good dancer?" asked Judith.

"Oh yes, Helen's very good," nodded Bea.

"And you must be good too," said Judith, eyeing all the trophies.

"Oh no, dear. I'm actually pretty great," smiled Bea.

Judith laughed, "Maybe you could show me sometime."

"Oh, don't you worry—I will. Dawn and Lola come to watch the dance exhibitions sometimes. And you know, it's amazing what can happen at a dance. People sometimes find themselves in the music," her eyes sparkled.

Judith smiled too. "Well, you were right—that was quite a story. You know, I don't exactly know how to say this, but—thank you for hanging around. I'm so glad I got to know you."

"You too, dear. Well, I've bent your ear for too long today, and we're supposed to be working on your business plan."

They moved to Bea's dining room table and got down to work. With Bea's guidance, Judith made numerous decisions that afternoon that were later confirmed by Dawn when they talked that night. They decided that the name of the new business was officially going to be The Gumbeaux Sistahs Gallery. Their target market was women over forty-five who were looking for a place to shop, hang out with friends, take workshops, share resources, and feel accepted and appreciated. The gallery would sell paintings and artsy gifts, along with Helen's essential oils. Coffee, tea, water, scones, cookies, and croissants would be offered to people, and they could even take some lessons and workshops in the areas of art, music, health, finances, business, and plant care.

"Between all the Gumbeaux Sistahs, we have expertise in every one of those subjects," said Judith, marveling.

They decided that a portion of the gallery could be furnished with tables and chairs for workshops or for people to just have coffee and visit. Bea would handle the PR. Helen, Bea, Lola, and Judith could help take turns running the store during business hours until the business took off, and then they could hire someone permanently. Lola could do the website and help with social media. Dawn and Judith would run the events. Dawn would be responsible for accounting and for getting the word out by mouth to all the business organizations where she was a member. And Judith would fill the walls with glorious paintings to her heart's content.

They put together a full calendar of possible events for the first year. They explored financial needs and goals.

At the end of the whirlwind session, Judith had a very strong picture of her new business and how it could function. She could not wait to tell Dawn.

"I don't know when I've had a more productive afternoon," said Judith. "One thing we left out though. The original Gumbeaux Sistahs, including yourself, will have permanent Gumbeaux Sistah status at this club. Did I say club? Oh my, it feels like a club to me! A club and gallery. This membership entitles you to free snacks and workshops for life."

"Oh, nothing's free, dear," said Bea, shaking her head. "I know, no doubt, we'll all be drawn into working events and workshops as well as our normal offerings. But the thing is—and I believe I speak for us all—we're going to love the gallery every bit as much as you and Dawn will."

Bea got up and looked out the front window. "Judith, as I mentioned, there's one more part to this story. It's time for you to see this."

Judith came to the window, and Bea pointed across the street to a woman sitting on a bench in the corner of the tiny park. "See that bench? We call it the Friendship Bench. Every Thursday afternoon between two and four o'clock, people come and sit on the bench. The rules are—"

"Rules?" asked Judith, puzzled.

"Certainly. The rules are that only one person at a time can sit, and they can't stay more than 20 minutes."

"Why do they sit?" asked Judith, mystified.

"They come and sit for many reasons, dear. Some of them have overwhelming problems and have no one to talk to. Some of them are in real trouble. Some are terribly lonely and just need someone to acknowledge their very existence."

"But who do they talk to?" asked Judith

"Why, me, of course," smiled Bea. "And Helen too. We take turns. Look, there's Helen now." We watched as Helen walked up to the bench and took her place next to the waiting woman.

"How do people find out about the bench?"

"By word of mouth only. We've been doing this for a few years now. It makes us happy because we're helping out some genuinely lovely people. Mind you, we're not therapists and don't pretend to be. We talk about whatever the people want to talk about. It might be their problems, or it might just be their favorite recipes for barbecued shrimp. If there is a problem they are trying to solve, we use our resources, sometimes consulting Dawn and Lola and others. Between the four of us, we know this community pretty well. We just try to be a friend to these people. We'll no doubt consult you from time to time now, too."

"I'll do whatever I can. That may be the most beautiful idea I've ever heard. Every time I turn around, you and the other sistahs amaze me more. How did you come up with this idea?"

"I read an article about a Grandmother's Bench in Zimbabwe where women started something similar. It struck Helen and me as such an easy thing to do, and such a great idea, that we started it right away. First, we spread the word to the women's shelter residents and staff. By word of mouth, the news of the Friendship Bench spread to neighbors and friends of friends. Taking turns on the bench is all very civilized. If two people come at the same time—one can wait in another corner of the park, or in their car, till the bench is free and it's their turn. Sometimes we go out for coffee with people after the bench time is up.

"And here's where you really come in, Judith. When the business opens, I'd like to add one more aspect to The Gumbeaux Sistahs Gallery. I'd like for you to support another Friendship Bench in front of the store. We can install a nice bench under that beautiful little tree in front. Helen and I and several other women that you'll meet have expressed interest in being 'Friends' and can take turns sitting and meeting people there. What do you think?"

"My God, Bea. I love that idea. More and more the gallery sounds like a wonderful place for us and the community."

"And of course, I'm hoping that all those women who come to the bench will become honorary Gumbeaux Sistahs too. Even if they're men," laughed Bea. "I can't wait. It's so exciting. I'm so glad you're doing this—and by the way, Dawn is all for it too. I checked with her already."

"I can't wait either. And I just wanted to tell you something. Thank you so much for finding me," said Judith with sudden tears in her eyes. Then she laughed. "You and that cold cup of coffee may be two of the best things to ever happen to me."

"You are too, Judith. As I always say—so many of us could be the best things to happen to each other, if we would let it happen."

"Well it's going to happen now, isn't it?"

"It already is, dear," smiled Bea.

CHAPTER 24

The board meeting started at ten A.M. the following Monday morning, and at ten after, their conversations were already heated and buzzing. Right off the bat, Lillian had read aloud a second letter of demand, written by Lola Trahan, Attorney at Law. The letter requested severance pay for Judith for a wrongful termination.

When Lillian finished reading, she laughed with a smug look on her face. "So, of course we will be ignoring this nonsense too. She doesn't have a leg to stand on. This is a last-ditch effort by that Trahan woman." Her hawk eyes looked around, daring anyone to disagree. "Does anyone have any objections?"

Board member, Ed Bagrett, spoke up tremulously, "Now hold on. Judith did do a good job for us. Her fundraising skills alone paid for her salary many times over and much of the museum expenses too. And she was let go in such a hasty manner. Don't you think we should consider some token amount at least?"

"A token?" shrilled Lillian. "We are not in the business of tokens. When people don't do their jobs, they don't get tokens. If she had done her job and brought in her quota of new funds at our last event, we wouldn't be in this position and neither would she."

"But didn't you raise the quota at the last minute on her?" asked Ed, a little more bravely.

"That quota raise was long overdue, and you know it, Ed." She waved his objection away with one hand. "I am seriously so happy to have new blood in this museum. Thomas is going to make the Spring Fling the best event we've ever had."

"Is *he* going to be able to make that new quota?" asked Ed pointedly.

"Not at first. That wouldn't be fair since he is new, but we will give him the quota that Judith had last year to start. When he gets his feet wet, we can raise it again," said Lillian airily. "Unless, of course, someone else thinks they can do a better job and take over the job of fund-raising for the Spring Fling?"

That shot the group down. They all knew what a tough job it was. No one dared object. They voted on it, and it passed.

Another board member, Marcy Meyers, spoke up then. "Have y'all seen the new art gallery opening down the street? Well, it's not open yet, and I haven't been inside, but they are super busy down there fixing up the place. I wonder when they plan on opening."

"A new gallery?" asked Lillian, surprised and a little annoyed. She usually had the scoop on all the new goings-on in town before the others. "Well, maybe that will be good for the museum. Maybe people will start to think of our street as 'Artist Row,' and more people will come to visit. We'll have our museum, the Art Association across the street, and the new gallery up the block. Seems like a positive thing to me.

"Meanwhile, we do have one more thing to talk about on the agenda today, and it regards our resident gardener and threatening letter-writing lawyer, Lola Trahan." Lillian waived the demand letter to make her point. "It seems her contract is up on care-taking her living garden installation."

Marcy smiled. "It's so beautiful. I never get tired of looking at it."

Lillian's tone was frosty, "I concur, but while it is pretty, I have no idea why we are paying her so much. We could have two gardens for the amount we're paying her. I myself could make those plants grow like that, and so could any of you. They're just plants, for heaven's sake!"

Marcy and the others looked skeptical.

Lillian went on, "Plus, I'd like to remind you that Miss Trahan has been a world of trouble to us lately—first with the picket line, and then with her demand letters. Keep that in mind. We don't need that kind of trouble. So, here's what I propose. I would like to move that we continue her contract, but offer her a lower price. It will send her a message. Plus, it will save us some money."

CHAPTER 25

While the board met, Bitsy sat at her computer in the museum office. Suddenly, her door flew open, and Lola hurried in carrying an envelope.

"Hi, Bits," said Lola. "Is the board still meeting?"

"Oh, hey," answered Bitsy. "Yep, they're still in there. What's up?"

"I wanted to find out if they would consider giving Judith some severance pay before I made my next move. Do you have any idea which way they are leaning on her pay issue?"

Bitsy snorted, "Are you kidding? Don't bother waiting—it's a non-issue. Lillian will never agree to that—not in a million years. It just threatens her position that Judith was fired for legal reasons."

"Well, I knew that, really, but I had to try," said Lola grim-faced. "But since it's a moot point, I need you to do something for me, Bits."

"Whatcha got?"

"Will you please deliver this envelope to the board—right now?" asked Lola.

"What is it?"

"I'm letting them know that I won't be renewing my contract with the museum for the care of the garden."

Bitsy almost choked. "Oh Lola, is that a good idea? How will the exhibit do without you? I would hate to see anything happen to that beautiful work."

"I would too. And I'll be honest, I don't think it's gonna do very well. My family has secrets to plant care—especially those that need to flourish in certain dark museum corners. But maybe they'll get lucky. I doubt they will, but let Lillian deal with it. It's all on her head anyway. And Bitsy, I know I haven't kept you completely in the loop, but I've just been so busy. I'll catch you up later. But can you just do this for me now?"

"Well, sure," said Bitsy.

"Oh and listen, one other thing. I seem to have lost a ring. It's a ruby and gold vintage design, and it means a lot to me. It's a sentimental thing. I'm not sure what I could have done with it, but I might have misplaced it while working on the garden. Could you kind of look around for it for me?"

"Of course, I'll let you know if it turns up," said Bitsy. "I'll miss seeing you around here on Mondays. I got used to you coming in to take care of the garden all the time."

"Don't worry—I'll see you around town. But I really gotta run now. By the way, I don't envy you having to deliver this letter. If I were you, I'd drop it off and run for the hills. Go to lunch or something. Lillian is about to get her knickers in a twist!" she laughed.

As soon as Lola left, Bitsy carried the envelope to the conference room and knocked. "Sorry to interrupt, everyone, but I was requested to deliver this now and asked that you read it during the meeting. It seemed important, so here it is."

She handed the envelope to Lillian and left quickly. She went straight to her little office, and taking Lola's advice, grabbed her purse and took her coffee break down the street at St. John's. On her way out, she heard the first bellows of Lillian's tirade.

"How dare she!" yelled Lillian.

"But you just said we were paying her too much and that anyone could do this," said Ed calmly.

"That little twerp! Who does she think she is? This is because of Judith—I promise you. But don't worry. I'll just get Bitsy to hire another gardener, pronto, at half the cost. She's not the only gardener in town, for heaven's sake."

Ed, for once, was firm. "I believe that Lola Trahan was a bit more than a gardener, Lillian. Everyone says that she worked magic with that exhibit."

But Lillian completely ignored him. She stuck her head out the door and yelled, "Bitsy! Get in here!"

No answer.

CHAPTER 26

The large back room of the Covington Art Museum was used for storage, intake of new exhibits, and packing and shipping of old exhibits. It also served as a makeshift staff lunchroom.

Thomas sat on one of the old, Fifties-style, green vinyl chairs that matched the aluminum table and served as their dining set. He sipped bitter office-coffee, deep in thought. They were thoughts that would have shocked everybody in town.

All morning, Bitsy and he had been in the middle of readying the outgoing exhibit for return to the Chicago museum where it originated. On the other side of the room, large crates sat containing the incoming exhibit waiting to be unpacked. They contained a California artist's work that Judith had procured. Thomas hoped it would be successful so he could take the credit.

The outgoing exhibit certainly had been a coup, also arranged by Judith. She had curated a collection that surprised everyone by managing to have the Covington museum placed on the exhibit's tour of America. It contained the artwork of an astounding trio of artists—Picasso, Chagall, and Cezanne. The works were not originals but lithographs. But still, they were extremely special because each had been created at their respective original atelier and were numbered. Less expensive copies of the pieces were available for sale at the museum shop, and they had sold quite a few. While the locals adored their own Louisiana artists, to have such classic legends in their little city was truly a marvel. The museum had never had such a success in sales, and it would have been a wonderful month for Judith if Lillian had not raised her fundraising quota so high. Lillian saw that Judith was about to have a successful exhibit and had to do something to make her fail so she could replace her with Thomas. The quota raise was a smart but conniving move.

Thomas took his time with the packing of the old exhibit. He was starting to feel lightheaded, and his heart was racing. He struggled to control himself around Bitsy so she would not see his odd reaction to such beautiful work.

He had always been susceptible to what is known as Stendahl Syndrome, a condition involving symptoms such as rapid heartbeat, shortness of breath, faintness, and confusion. It can happen when an individual is exposed to objects of great beauty, such as phenomenal artwork. Thomas had experienced it many times working at his position in the San Diego museum and once when he visited the De Young Museum in San Francisco. The last time it occurred was on a museum-paid trip to a conference in New York. While there, Thomas visited the Metropolitan Opera House, and stood in front of the giant mural paintings by Marc Chagall. Looking up at the magnificent works, he nearly fell backwards in a faint and had to make his way to a door to breathe fresh air in order to recover.

He felt the symptoms coming on now as he packed and held the work of that very same artist in his own hands. He handled the Chagall litho with great reverence.

Each lithograph was set in a striking, hand-painted, wooden frame which looked like it had come straight out of an old monastery. The frames looked like works of art themselves. Each framed litho was worth many thousands of dollars.

Bitsy and he had worked all morning packing the artwork to museum standards and loading the shipping crates. At lunch time, Bitsy had to run to a doctor's appointment, but she would be back as soon as she could to help finish up.

Thomas had very little time.

For weeks, he had his eye on a small six-by-eight inch Chagall lithograph of a man and woman floating over Paris. The piece was called *Romeo and Juliet*. He loved the colors and composition, but the theme of the people floating over the city and being above all humanity—he truly related to that.

He sat in the back room, staring at the small artwork that he held in his hands. Never had he ever felt his "little compulsions" as strongly as he was feeling them for this piece. Often, when Thomas felt the need to "re-home an object," (a phrase he made up, amusedly, when he moved a valuable object d'art from its rightful owner to his own private collection), the urges were spontaneous. When this artwork first arrived in the museum, the urges he had felt were also immediate and urgent, but he forced himself to be patient. Instead, he had often lingered in front of the lithograph hanging in the museum when no one was watching. He had touched the frame and even the work itself, even though every museum employee in the world knew that was strictly forbidden. But weeks of admiring the piece with patience had given him a plan. He knew a man from his old neighborhood who really should be in jail for forgery crimes, specifically art forgery. This person had been arrested but had never served time due to lack of evidence. Thomas had once loaned him money, and that debt was still outstanding. Until now. Since the artwork was not an original, and a well-known piece, it had been easily copied by his friend, and sent to Thomas at his home.

Now that Bitsy was out of the office, it was time to make a switch, and that's exactly what he did. Once finished, even Thomas had trouble telling the difference between the original and the forged piece. But one was in a frame and ready to be packed and shipped, and the other was in Thomas' desk drawer, hidden in the pages of a large art book. When the coast was clear, Thomas would find an honored place for it in his étagère of stolen goods at his apartment.

He occasionally worried about having the stolen goods at his house on display, but convinced himself that there was actually little risk. No one ever came to his house except Lillian, and she had only been there on a few occasions, and not before calling first. He merely removed the collection to the back of his closet in minutes before Lillian's arrival. But the occasions of Lillian's visits had completely stopped these days.

He grimaced at the thought. He and Lillian were definitely fizzling out, and it bothered him a great deal. Yes, he was tired of her constant bossiness, but at the same time, she excited him in a way he would never understand. But Thomas suspected that she was weary of him and probably still in love with her husband. After all, she had never mentioned divorcing him, and neither had Thomas. He knew she was rethinking her decision about hooking up with him. He would have to be careful that her feelings for him did not spill over into their professional relationship right now. Lillian would get rid of him in a shot, just like she had gotten rid of Judith. He would have to play it smart and hope that he could continue their connection until he could get a job in a big city. He longed so much to reclaim his former glamorous life.

A deep frown crossed his handsome face for a moment. He was thinking of the upcoming Spring Fling, the museum's big fundraising event. With Judith gone, the success of the event now fell on his shoulders and he was worried. He had never overseen an entire event by himself, and he really knew zip about fundraising. However, he was a good schmoozer and would have to rely on his charm, as he often did.

The Spring Fling exhibit was to feature all local artists. Judith had the local theme approved by the board months ago. Coordinating the many artist participants was turning out to be a nightmare. Thank God there was still some time to prepare. Some of the artists were backing out, and whereas Judith would normally have back-ups, Thomas had not foreseen that and was running into the challenge now. He was used to giant professional exhibits being imported to museums. He was not used to dealing with the local artistic personalities and egos upfront. In fact, he had seldom met any artists in the California museums where he had worked. So, this was a pain. And now Lola Trahan had pulled out from her living garden exhibit. He had hired a gardener that Bitsy had found to take her place, but the Trahan woman was some kind of witch with plants. The garden was looking worse for wear already. On top of that, he constantly heard from the board how they were expecting great things from him. The pressure was great.

He had to make this job work so he could hang on here long enough to make his escape. It was not going to be easy.

But at that particular moment in time, he was not worried. He was joyous, breathless, and tingling with excitement about the new addition to his personal collection. He stood and continued to pack up the old exhibit, making sure to leave the forged piece along with a few others for when Bitsy returned. He would make sure to comment on the left-out pieces, so Bitsy would take note of them as she herself packed the forgery and saw to its "safe" return—just in case.

CHAPTER 27

The Gumbeaux Sistahs were resting in the new gallery after painting and decorating for a couple of hours. They had installed a plug-in cooktop in the food corner for serving hot dishes—like gumbo, of course. They also hauled a glassed-in pastry case that they'd found at the Habitat for Humanity store, so they could display baked goods. Helen was going to be baking and supplying most of the organic baked goods with the help of a young baker who specialized in cookies and cheesecake.

Sampling the baked goods was the next order of business that evening—that, and enjoying some red wine Dawn had supplied. They all agreed that the cookie samples were wonderful, and Helen's scones were perfect.

After a couple of glasses of wine, Dawn got a mischievous glint in her eye. She looked at her new partner and asked, "So, Judith, you've been working with Lola for a little while now here in the gallery. Has she told you how many men she's slept with yet?"

Judith almost choked, and Lola looked murderously at Dawn, who was laughing out loud.

"Well, no. I can't say that it's come up," laughed Judith. "Where did that come from? Is that some sort of rite of passage for Gumbeaux Sistahs—that Lola has to tell them all about her love life?"

"It sure as hell isn't," growled Lola. "Don't mind her. Dawn likes everyone to think that I'm an aging slut. It's all because of this one incident in the hardware store. That was the start of it all."

"Well, that, and the fact that she's slept with half the town," guffawed Dawn.

"Wait, what hardware incident? I've got to hear this." smiled Judith.

"You tell her. It's your story," said Dawn.

"I wish you'd let me keep it that way too," retorted Lola. "OK, OK. Here's what happened. It was just a big misunderstanding. I walked into Larry's Hardware—you know that cute, old-fashioned hardware store up the street from here? So, I walked in there because I was doing some work on my bathroom at home and needed some supplies. The store was full of men buying hardware-y stuff. The checkout is toward the back of that store, and when the clerk behind the counter saw me walk in, he yelled out, 'How can I help you, Miss?'

So I yelled back, 'I need some caulk!'"

At this, all of the sistahs burst into laughter. Judith joined them after a moment, as it dawned on her what those words must have sounded like in a room full of men. She almost fell over laughing when the light bulb went on.

"At least she's upfront about her needs," sputtered Dawn. "Man, that story never gets old!"

The scene kept playing in Judith's head, and she found herself laughing so hard that she was gasping for air.

"Well, needless to say, I got the damn caulk and then got out of there as fast as I could. You could have heard a pin drop in that store. I was so mortified!" said Lola, shaking her head with a burning red face. "I haven't been back there since, which is a real shame because, damn it, I love that old store."

"All I can say is—where is a gay man when you need one?" said Dawn, still laughing. "Wouldn't it have been hilarious if a gay man had been there and right after Lola said she needed some caulk, he would have said, 'Well, don't we all, honey?'"

That was it. The sistahs exploded with fresh gales of laughter.

"So, that's the hardware store story," laughed Lola. "And Dawn uses it every chance she gets to try and make me look like a hooker. I mean, OK, I've been a tiny bit of a floozy at times in my life. I'll admit that, but I've never been that bad. And there's something deeply disturbing about Dawn's interest in my love life, don't you think? I really have to wonder why it's so important to her. Do you think she could be jealous? Or maybe she's secretly in love with me?"

Bea broke in with her tinkling little laugh, "Oh, we're all in love with you, Sistah!"

Lola grinned at her, then suddenly frowned when Dawn said, "All I know is, just once I'd like to know how many men she's had for sure. She gets around, this girl does. And Judith, the guys still go gaga over her. I don't understand it. Maybe it's the landscaping dirt under her fingernails that turns them on."

"Obviously, it's this smoking-hot bod," grinned Lola.

"Oh well, maybe one day we'll find out," said Dawn with a sigh.

"And then what? You can die happy?"

Looking around, still smiling, Dawn said, "You know, this place looks great. And more importantly, it feels great. Helen, thanks for the sage smudging you did this afternoon. That always helps. I think that by smudging the gallery and adding our own energy by working together in here, we've created a nice vibe, and our guests' energy will only add to it. I for one look forward to many happy glasses of wine on future Friday nights—right here."

"The place does have a great feel about it," agreed Judith happily. "Have y'all noticed the additions Dawn and I made?" She walked over to a huge bulletin board next to the glass pastry case. "Here is the new Resource Center. We'll keep this bulletin board here for people to pin up business cards, job opportunities, and other announcements. We'll put the sign-up sheets for workshops here too. I'm also keeping this index card box right here. It's got categories tabbed inside and it can be a resource for people who need things like handy persons, rides to doctors' offices, travel buddies, etc. People can just add their business cards in a category, or fill out a blank index card to add to the box. So, let's say if someone wants to start music lessons, or needs a local attorney, or is looking for a ride to Florida, they can check here for a possible match in the index cards on file. Hopefully, it will turn into a good mini community resource."

"That's a fabulous idea, Judith," said Helen. "People can enjoy one of my scones or croissants with coffee and find a book club or lawyer while they're eating."

"And I see the Friendship Bench has arrived," smiled Bea.

"Oh, my goodness, I forgot to tell you, Bea," said Judith, slapping a hand to her forehead. "I don't know how you're getting the word out, but there was a lady sitting out there for a little while this morning already. I took her phone number, and told her someone would get in touch with her to let her know when the schedule started. I hope that's OK."

"That's wonderful," said Bea. "And guess what? I have two new volunteers to sit with people on the bench. They're a couple of women I know and trust—people that I wouldn't mind sitting on a bench with myself."

"That makes me so happy, Bea," said Judith. "I'm so proud to be a part of this insanely kind tradition that you and Helen started."

"Me too," said Dawn. "And I have some good news. I have some volunteers lined up for the opening night to help out as well."

"That's great. We're going to need it. This place is going to be so magical," said Judith happily. She suddenly twirled around in the middle of the room. "You women are magic!"

The sistahs smiled at each other. Then Dawn asked, "Judith, how are the paintings coming along? Will they be ready for hanging in the gallery soon? We've got to get something on these walls. Oh, and I had an idea. Do you think we could offer a mid-size painting for a raffle prize on opening night? We could market the heck out of that, and we could tell everyone that half the proceeds on the raffle go to support the women's shelter."

Bea and Helen spoke at once, "That's an awesome idea!"

Bea continued, "The women's shelter will love that. They need the funds badly."

"Yes, it's a wonderful idea, and I think I already have just the painting at home for it. Wow—I've got a genius partner!"

Dawn smiled smugly. "I just want to make sure that y'all heard that part—my partner said I was a genius. Did you hear that, Lola?"

"She's new," said Lola, laughing. "She'll learn."

Judith broke in, smiling, "And the new paintings are going well. I've got several pieces in different stages of completion, but they are all almost finished. And you'll love this. They are all different versions of us—the Gumbeaux Sistahs. I know I told you that I've been painting some version of these women all my life, remember? But now I know why I did that. I'm beginning to understand the true value of a supportive group of women. The paintings are taking on a life of their own. I think they may be the best work I've ever done. It's probably because I'm passionate about the subject matter. I can't wait for you to see them."

"Dibs!" shouted Dawn.

"What do you mean 'dibs?'" asked Lola, disgusted. "You can't call dibs. You haven't even seen them yet! And you have to leave something for the public to buy, you know."

"OK, you're right," said Dawn huffily. "But I want first pick is all." She turned to Judith apologetically. "I just love your work."

"You got it, partner," said Judith. "Without you, all this would not be happening. Without all y'all, actually. But we can't have any blank walls, so let's hang all the work in the gallery, and we'll just put a red dot next to the painting of your choice, and that way, people will know it's sold already. That will also give people the idea that the paintings are selling fast, and that they should snap one up before they're all gone."

"It's going to look great in here for the opening night," said Dawn. "And speaking of looking great, girlfriend, we've got to go shopping and look fabulous ourselves that night. What say you and I head over to the Columbia Street Mercantile tomorrow and spend a whole bunch of money? I saw something in the window that would look so cool on you, you know—artsy-fartsy, but elegant."

"How did you know?" asked Judith, fondly laughing with her new partner.

"See if they have something pretentious and blingy for Dawn," grinned Lola. Then she shook her head. "I'm just kidding. You always look put together and actually lovely, as much as I hate to admit it."

"Well, that goes without saying, Sistah. But look, while we're talking about things looking great, will the new garden be ready in time?"

"I'll have it done in time, all right. And wait till you see what I've got planned," said Lola dreamily. "I'll start installation in a couple of days. I've been getting all the pieces together, and once that's done, the work will go fast."

Judith said wistfully, "I wonder what the art museum will do with their garden."

"Well," said Lola, "I can't imagine how it's going to look by the event. Bitsy says it's already starting to look kind of sad, even though they've hired a gardener to work on it. But without my dad's secret formulas to nourish those plants, there's going to be trouble, and it's starting already. I hate to think of it, really.

"Speaking of Bitsy," continued Lola, suddenly wistful, "I sure hope she gets a chance to look around the museum for my lost ring. I've looked everywhere I can think, but it's just gone. It might be in the garden at the museum. Of course, it might be anywhere for that matter. I tend to take my jewelry off when I work, sometimes without even thinking about it. Then I'll find it later on a table, or a window ledge, or once, even in the refrigerator."

"If I see her, I'll remind her," said Judith. "And I'll ask her how the plans for their Spring Fling are coming along. The theme was to intake some of our better-known, local artists for the museum event, but that can be difficult to deal with for an event of this size. People don't always deliver what they promise, or they bring a different work than we discussed. Sometimes they bring too many pieces, and then get upset when you can't accept them all. Then there's the matter of where you hang the work. There are local rivalries, and some artists don't want their work hanging next to certain other artists' work. And some artists insist on hanging their work in only the prime viewing spots. There's a million problems, and I've always been the one to deal with them. Now it's all up to Thomas. Is it crazy of me? They did fire me, as you might remember, but I worry he won't treat the artists well enough."

"Just shows the size of your heart, dear," said Bea, nodding.

"And try to remember, partner," said Dawn, "It's not our problem anymore. Think of it this way. All those artists will be clamoring to get into our gallery after the opening night. We will get the crème de la crème of the artists. Plus, we can offer space to those up-and-coming in the art community, so all the artists have some exposure. If they are badly treated by the museum, then we'll be happy to make it up to them at our gallery."

"I didn't think of it that way," Judith said. "I don't wish bad treatment on any of them. But it's true—they would love it here. I'm going to treat them like queens and kings. I want every one of them to feel appreciated and supported here."

Dawn held out her glass to Judith for more wine. "Well, I'll feel appreciated and supported here if you would just pour me more wine."

Lola snorted, and then held out her empty glass too.

CHAPTER 28

The missing ring was bugging Bitsy. Three times Lola had asked her to look for it, but aside from a quick look around the museum, she kept forgetting to do a thorough search for her friend's missing jewelry.

"Lola could have lost it anywhere—on any one of her landscape jobs, or at home, or at her parent's house. Just anywhere," she thought. But it was still bugging her.

That afternoon, she had an idea. The security cameras in the museum streamed its video recordings to her office computer. She thought, *"Maybe I can watch videos of Lola when she was working on the Living Art garden. Maybe I'll get lucky and see something."* She thought it would be a little time consuming, but it might be worth a peek.

So that afternoon, while Thomas had a doctor's appointment, and she was alone in the museum, she hunkered down in her office and prepared to look through some of the videos. She figured it would take a few sittings to get through the ones she needed to see, so she might as well get started.

She smiled a little guiltily when she remembered the battle she had to wage to get the cameras in the first place. Lillian had beaten the idea down from the very beginning, saying that it was unnecessary. She insisted that they lived in a small city with little crime, and that it was a waste of money. But Bitsy, a firm believer in security and technology, had disagreed strongly. Judith had given her blessings already for the idea and let Bitsy herself approach the board for funding. But when Lillian shot down the idea right out of the chute, Bitsy approached another board member, Ed Bagrett. He proved to be sympathetic to the idea. Together, they managed to couch the expense in the budget for the Spring Fling that year. They added it to the security expenses category for the night, so it was not entirely misleading.

Since Bitsy did not go crazy and insist on the top of the line security package models, it had not been that costly, and the expense was easy to hide. As far as Bitsy could tell, Lillian spent more on superfluous printed flyers to advertise the event, which just got thrown away. So she did not feel too guilty about it. She was convinced that the museum would get its money's worth out of the cameras someday, if for no other reason than the peace of mind they offered. You never knew when those cameras would be needed. She went ahead and bought the kind of equipment that was hidden and disguised behind molding, fixtures, and electrical outlets.

The truth was, the cameras had not been mentioned once since that board meeting where most of them unknowingly approved the money for them. Bitsy doubted seriously if anyone even remembered that the cameras existed because she was the only one who installed, maintained, and used them. She doubted whether even Judith remembered them. And she knew for a fact that none of the others knew how to work them. But Bitsy had a variety of computer experience from back in her old California tech firm job, before moving to Louisiana. She had been hired by the Covington museum specifically because she was a "techy," and could match computer skills with the best of them. Not only was she handy with computers, AV equipment, and security systems, but also with social media, graphics, spreadsheets, and a whole bunch of other things. She was a useful person to have around.

Bitsy had installed the cameras, and then had kept quiet about them so Lillian would not find out. But Bitsy felt that one day they would all be grateful that they existed if there was ever some sort of incident at the museum. Today might be one of those days if she could help find Lola's ring. At least Lola would be grateful.

She settled into her swivel chair to watch. The air-conditioned office was chilly to everyone but Bitsy. She was one of those people who rarely felt the cold, and dressed as if to prove it. Her plump sixty-three-year-old self could usually be found in a sleeveless, colorful sundress and sandals year-round, except on the coldest days. They were nice sandals, but still sandals. She looked like the Southern California transplant that she was and definitely of the old flower-child ilk. She had natural curly, black hair, deep mahogany skin, and au natural makeup, meaning none to speak of. You always got the feeling she was wearing an invisible sign that said, "I'm Bitsy, take it or leave it." Fortunately, most people took her as is. Lillian had been known to look down her nose at Bitsy's work wardrobe, but Bitsy had the ability to not care one whit about that. Bitsy got along with everyone. It wasn't that she was wishy-washy or the type to agree with everything people said. Her likable quality came from her own soul. Bitsy just liked most people—and they knew it. That was one of several reasons why, even though Judith had lost her job, Bitsy was kept on to work with Thomas. That, and the fact that there was very little Bitsy Rogers could not do with a computer.

And while Bitsy liked most people, Thomas and Lillian were two of her exceptions.

Especially Thomas. It was not so much that she did not like him, but that there was something particularly snake-like about the man.

Of course, she did not like that he had replaced Judith, not that Judith and she were exceptionally close. Bitsy had been her usual friendly self, but Judith always kept her at a distance. They had a friendly but professional relationship. Judith was her supervisor and acted accordingly. They worked very well together though, and Judith had made sure that Bitsy was appreciated and received raises when she could. The relationship was strong enough that Bitsy felt terrible when Judith was fired, but not close enough for her to run to Judith's side or invite her out for drinks and consolation. She figured even if she had, Judith would politely turn her down as she had done on other occasions. As far as Bitsy could tell, Judith turned everyone's company down not just hers. Still, Bitsy missed working with Judith and hoped fervently that she would land on her feet after being let go. She would try and do what she could to help her, even if Judith did not welcome her with open arms.

But Thomas was something else again. She got the creepiest feeling from the guy, but she could not quite put her finger on the exact reason for it. Even thinking of him at that moment gave her an unusual chill up her sleeveless arms. She pulled on a sweater, which was almost unheard of for her, and started up the security camera footage on her computer, trying to solve the mystery of Lola's missing ring.

CHAPTER 29

Dawn had never called an emergency meeting of the sistahs before, but that is exactly what happened on Wednesday. She texted out an urgent sounding message: *"Be at St. John's tomorrow at 9!"*

It was hard for the women to contain their curiosity, so they rushed to the coffeehouse first thing in the morning. Dawn beat them there and was brimming with excitement. The sistahs could hardly wait for their orders to be served at the counter, so they could hurry to their table and hear what Dawn had to say.

Dawn wasted no time and blurted out, "Trinity has summoned us!"

Gasps went around the table, followed by excited laughter.

"Oh, you're kidding!" said Lola. "When? Where?"

"Who cares!" said Helen. "Let's go!"

Judith was mystified. "Who's Trinity?"

"Trinity is my baby sister," explained Dawn.

"Trinity is my idol," said Helen. "I don't know anyone who has more fun than that girl."

"Judith, you've never met such a character," said Lola. "If you think Dawn is bad, and by that, I mean crazy, wait till you meet her baby sister. She's a hoot!"

"So . . ." said Dawn, "In case you forgot, Friday is my birthday, and Trinity has invited us all to visit her in New Orleans. She wants to treat us all to lunch as my birthday present."

"She's lives in New Orleans?" asked Judith. "Great! I haven't been to the city in about a month."

"She lives right in the French Quarter, and she has owned the Royal Gala Art Gallery on Royal Street for probably twenty years now. Her condo, which is one of the most exquisite you've ever seen, is right above the gallery. It overlooks the St. Louis Cathedral gardens, and there's always a party out her front door. And Trinity is the queen of all she surveys," laughed Dawn.

"I think she knows everyone in town, and she's so much fun to visit. We haven't been there in about a year now, so it's time. She married into old oil money, right?" said Helen.

"Yes, Trinity is rich as Midas. Her husband owns River Oil and is such a nice man too—she got lucky. But listen, I spoke to her yesterday, and she wants us all there about ten A.M. Can everyone make it? Of course you can. None of us have anything to do that's more fun than this," said Dawn. Then her tone changed, and she asked sheepishly, "Lola, will you drive us . . . you know I have trouble with that. . ." Her voice trailed off.

"Do you still have that little problem, dear?" asked Bea.

"Well, yeah, I guess I do,"

"Are you kidding me?" yelled Lola. "Still?"

"What is it?" asked Judith. "What problem?"

Lola looked disgusted. "Dawn's a grown-ass woman, and she's afraid to drive over the Causeway bridge!"

"What? Really?" asked Judith.

Dawn hung her head.

"Seriously, the woman will get in a plane and fly to Paris over the freaking Atlantic Ocean, but she won't drive the bridge over the lake."

"It's twenty-four miles long. It's the longest bridge in the world over water, and it's straight out over Lake Pontchartrain," whined Dawn. "You can't even see the other side of the lake when you start out. It's not right, I tell you."

"People drive it every day. I cross it at least once a week. It's as safe as any other street!"

"C'mon, leave her alone," said Helen. "Dawn will get over it when she's ready."

"OK, OK, I'll drive," said Lola. "But you have to swim back, Dawn."

"Funny. But thanks for driving. Oh, and listen, I told Trinity about us being the Gumbeaux Sistahs now. She just went nuts over that, as you can imagine. And I also told her what's been going on with Judith and the museum, and she said she has an idea for us that she'll tell us about when we get there. No telling what she'll come up with."

—✶—

On Friday morning the sistahs piled in Dawn's big SUV, and Lola drove. Just as they were about to get on the Causeway, Dawn covered her eyes. "Oh Lord! Tell me when we're on the other side!"

"You're going to shut your eyes for twenty-four miles? Why don't you just look at your phone? You're glued to that thing twenty-four seven anyway," said Lola.

"You're always telling me to get off my phone. Now you're telling me to get on it? You can't have it both ways," cried Dawn, cringing in the back seat.

"You know, it's really too bad you're so crazy. You're missing a great drive. The lake is beautiful today," said Lola.

"I've always loved this bridge," said Bea. "I like to pretend I'm in a fishing boat, looking out over this quiet, gorgeous spot."

"I love it when the whole lake gets real calm and smooth—like a sheet of glass. It doesn't seem possible that a body of water this size can be so still," said Helen.

"And it's amazing when the pelicans glide alongside your car, just a few feet away. You get the feeling they're playing a game with you," said Judith.

"What are you actually afraid of, Dawn?" asked Judith, glancing back at her friend who was cowering down in her seat.

"Well, OK. I'll tell you," said Dawn, her voice muffled from the back seat. "The Causeway is obviously as straight as an arrow, right? Everyone knows that. But when I drive it, I keep thinking that the road curves towards the right. I just know that I'll get confused somehow, make a right turn, and plummet the twenty-five feet down, right into the water. I have terrible nightmares about it. Now I can't even look at it."

"We're going to have to help you with that, dear," said Bea. "You're missing out on too much. I know you don't want that."

As they made their way across the bridge, the skyline of New Orleans came into view on their left. They could make out the Superdome and several tall buildings emerging from a mist, like the Emerald City in the Wizard of Oz.

"You're missing out, Dawn. This view is always so beautiful," said Helen.

But true to her word, Dawn kept her eyes covered the whole trip across the bridge, and then some. The sistahs played a little joke on her by telling her, "We're almost there" and "Just a little bit more!" By the time they finally told her she could open her eyes, they were all the way down in the French Quarter. Dawn was mad and pouted for a few blocks, but could not keep it up once the spirit of the Quarter got under her skin. They found a parking spot for the day by the river, right next to the docked Steamboat Natchez, which was playing a catchy tune on its big pipe organ.

It was a beautiful, sunny day. The Quarter was lively with people, street musicians, good smells, antique buildings, and so much charm it made your heart ache.

They reached the Royal Gala Gallery and went inside then entered into a private elevator. Dawn used a code that transported them to the second floor, and the elevator opened right into Trinity's living room which was a plush, harlequin study in black and white.

"Darling girls!" shouted Trinity, swooping into the room. She hugged every one of them, and then laughed. "Big Sis, you're a sight for sore eyes. Happy Birthday!" She was younger than Dawn by about six years, but you could tell they were sisters from across town with their coloring and height. Trinity was even taller than Dawn, close to six feet, with curly, brown-streaked hair, and an exquisite, red, tailored pantsuit that probably cost a month's salary for Judith. Not only was she taller than Dawn, she was bigger too—bigger hair, bigger voice, bigger dress size, bigger jewelry, and bigger than life. She had a generous mouth that easily moved into a large, red-lipped smile. Her intelligent, large brown eyes held a mischievous glint. There was something about Trinity that made you think she might do something naughty when no one was looking.

"Come on in, girls. I'm all ready for you." She led them further into the living room to a seating area and picked up a gold tray filled with cocktail glasses. She handed them out, and the sistahs gladly took one, getting into the Trinity spirit.

"What's this, Trin?" asked Dawn, eying the concoction in her glass.

"You're gonna love it! It's a new drink I invented called a Sistah Sling—in honor of you Gumbeaux Sistahs."

"You're kidding!" said Judith, sipping her drink. "You made this for us? I love that!"

"You think of everything. This is so delicious," said Dawn.

"We aim to please. I'm so excited that you're calling yourselves the Gumbeaux Sistahs. That's inspired! I wish I had thought of it. Now come sit down and tell me everything," she said.

They sat in Trinity's lavish room, and the sistahs introduced Judith. At the same time, Dawn whipped out her phone to show her sister photos of Judith's art on her website.

"Oh! I have just got to have one of the paintings from your Pieces of a Life series—they're fascinating!"

"You two not only look like sisters, you must think alike too. Dawn bought a painting from that series—along with one of the Gumbeaux Sistahs paintings as well," said Judith.

Dawn looked at her sister sternly. "Hey, you know I have first dibs on all good art," said Trinity, smiling, then turned back to Judith. "It doesn't surprise me. Dawn and I are two peas in a pod. We shared everything when we were kids—clothes, toys, food. She took good care of me. A better big sister could not possibly be found anywhere."

Trinity then passed around another tray with tempting cookies on it, and the girls dug in. "Save some room for lunch, but try these. I gave them a special name. I know that Louisiana cooks use what they call the Holy Trinity in much of their cooking—onions, celery and bell pepper. But I have a sweet tooth and figured my Holy Trinity was chocolate, coconut, and nuts. These cookies have all three, so I call them my Holy Trinity cookies. Kind of goes with my name too," she laughed.

The sistahs groaned over the amazing cookies and Dawn immediately grabbed another one, "I love these things!"

Trinity turned to Judith. "So, I want to talk about what's been going on with you. I've been getting the scoop from Dawn on all that has happened. I could just spit nails at those museum people. They treated you horribly after all the years you worked for them."

Judith sighed. "Well, I hate to talk about this now. It's such a bummer. But it's been a tough time, alright. Thank God I've had these girls around me to talk me down off the ledge."

"Well, I've got an idea, and I'd like to give it a shot, if that's OK with you. In fact, where's my phone? Let me do it right now while you're here, and we've got it in our minds. Then it won't bug us while we enjoy our lunch. Now, who is that horrid woman in charge of the museum over there? What's her name?"

"Lillian Deslattes is head of the board. Are you going to call her?" asked Judith, surprised.

"Of course. It's the best way to meet this problem. Head on. What's her number?"

Judith shrugged, thinking she had absolutely nothing to lose. She rummaged through her purse for her phone and found it.

"OK, let's do this," laughed Trinity.

"What are you up to?" grinned Dawn.

"Oh, you're going to like this."

Trinity dialed the number and had just finished putting the call on speakerphone so all the sistahs could hear when a female voice answered. Trinity asked, "Is this Lillian Deslattes?"

"Yes it is. Who's calling, please?"

"It's Trinity Hebert. We haven't met, but I am the owner of the Royal Gala Art Gallery in New Orleans."

"Oh yes, Miss Hebert, I've been there several times—it's a beautiful gallery. How can I help you?"

"Thank you. I'm calling because my husband and I are admirers of your little museum. It sets such a good example for smaller cities in promoting culture and art—two things that are near and dear to our hearts. My husband is Harry Hebert, president of River Oil. Maybe you've heard of him? We've been to your museum several times."

"How nice of you to say," said Lillian, perking up because suddenly she could hear the distinct sound of a cash register cha-chinging.

"The reason I'm calling is this—we are interested in becoming sponsors of the museum, with the intention of promoting the city museum idea to other small cities in our state and across the south. We're interested in making a sizable donation to this worthy cause."

"Oh, that's wonderful. The museum will be thrilled, Ms. Hebert. May I call you Trinity?"

"Probably," said Trinity, and Dawn had to shove a throw pillow in her mouth to keep from bursting out laughing at that.

Trinity went on, "Here's the thing—we know several of your other sponsors, and they speak highly of your museum manager— Judith Lafferty. So she, of course, will be handling our business with the museum."

There was a long pause, and the sistahs held their breath.

"Oh dear. I'm afraid Ms. Lafferty is no longer with the museum."

"No? Oh, that's the worst news. My friends all tell me that they wouldn't trust anyone else to deal with the size of the donation that we have in mind. Ms. Lafferty is a known commodity. I'm told she's trustworthy and quite capable of following up on the wishes of the sponsors' intentions and wishes. I'm sure you understand."

"Well, yes of course, but we have people who can be relied on completely," Lillian rushed to say.

"Hmm . . . is there any way it can be arranged for Ms. Lafferty to return to the museum to help with our accounts? I feel certain the museum will see that it will be worth their while."

There was a pause. The sistahs could hear Lillian thinking on the other end of the phone. "I'm afraid that won't be possible."

It was Trinity's turn to pause. "Oh dear, that's such a shame," she drawled. "I would hate to have to retract our offer over a little thing like this."

Lillian struggled for words then desperately blurted out, "I heard that she died."

Judith, wide-eyed, choked on her cookie, and Lola patted her on the back till she got things under control again. The other sistahs looked at each other in disbelief.

Trinity couldn't help but laugh out loud. "What? Oh Lillian, how can that be? My friend spoke to her just yesterday, which prompted me to call you."

Another pause. Then Lillian's chilly voice came back at them and demanded, "Who is this, really? Are you a friend of Judith Lafferty's by any chance? Is this some kind of joke?"

"As I said, this is Trinity Hebert, and this is not a joke. You can google my husband and me. In fact, go ahead, I'll hold while you do."

"I'm not googling anything," said Lillian, all ice now. "Judith Lafferty does not work here now, and for all I care, she could be dead. She won't work here in the future either, so don't bother calling and wasting my time again."

"OK, I'll be sure not to. But after we get off this phone, Lillian, do look us up on Google. You'll see what a huge mistake you just made. Huge in terms of dollar signs. I just wish I could be there when you kick yourself up and down the street for it." With that, Trinity hung up.

On her end, Lillian put the phone down and immediately opened her laptop to Google's search window. After a moment, she shook her head. "Oh hell."

—m—

Trinity looked around at the sistahs and said, "Well, it was worth a try. That is one stubborn woman."

"First she fires you, Judith, now she's trying to kill you!" said Helen.

"She probably thinks Trinity is Judith's sister—somebody's sister anyway," laughed Dawn.

"Thanks for trying," said Judith. "I'll admit I admire your nerve."

"Oh, Trinity's all nerve," laughed Dawn.

"Sounds like someone else I know," said Lola, rolling her eyes at Dawn.

"Yes, but Trinity has Auntie Mame-level nerve! She makes me look like Agnes Gooch."

"No one could make you look like Agnes Gooch, dear. Not ever," confirmed Bea.

Trinity laughed, "You just think that, Dawn, because I live in the French Quarter, and I'm surrounded by party-loving, crazy people. You would be that way too if you lived here. In fact, I'd bet you'd be swinging from the street lamps."

"That's probably true," admitted Dawn, then laughed. "Maybe it's a good thing I'm afraid of the Causeway."

Her sister went off in gales of laughter, "Oh no, still? You need to drive it more to get over your fears."

"Can't see that happening anytime soon," said Dawn.

"Speaking of happening soon, it's almost time for lunch. I've got Bill standing in line for us at Galatoire's, so we need to get ready and go." Trinity explained that because Galatoire's did not take lunch reservations, it caused people to stand in line for hours to get into the revered old restaurant, especially on Fridays. The local regulars have learned to hire line-standers who will hold their place in line on the sidewalk out front, for a flat one hundred dollars per group.

"I keep telling Harry that if he ever leaves me, I'll get a job line-standing at Galatoire's. I might as well, since I'm always there anyway." Her face went serious for a moment, "Promise me, Dawn, that if that ever happens, you'll bring me champagne at my post to keep me fortified."

She stood up and said, "Ok, so listen. Friday at Galatoire's gets a little crazy. Everyone's glad for the coming weekend, and lots of folks show up. It's noisy and the energy level can lift the roof straight off the building. So we have to dress the part. Ladies, follow me please."

The sistahs looked at one another and then at Trinity's retreating back, and shrugged. "Here we go!" smiled Dawn.

Trinity led them down a hall and opened the door into another world.

"Look at this!" said Bea, in a whispered tone.

"I love it!" shouted Helen.

Inside the room were racks and shelves full of costumes, hats, boas, costume jewelry, makeup, and wigs. Along one wall was a full-length mirror. "Everyone I know in New Orleans has some version of this room," explained Trinity. "It might just be a trunk, or a closet, or just a big box in the attic. But there are times when you simply need a costume in New Orleans, because we do things big here. I just took it to a new, bigger, fun level because—well, what the heck—I'm rich, and I could," she laughed. "I love my costume room! Now, what we need today are hats. Big beautiful hats for a ladies luncheon."

Trinity matched each of their outfits with a feathered, outlandish hat. Judith was a bit hesitant at first, thinking she might feel silly in it, but seeing all the women come to life in their getups, she felt freed-up and ready to meet the public.

"Y'all look completely divine," said Trinity. "Off we go!" They grabbed their purses, and Trinity picked up a paper bag she had waiting on a table by the elevator door. They rode downstairs and walked out into the sunshine on Royal Street. Galatoire's was only a few blocks away, so it was an easy walk. But first, Trinity took them on a tiny detour to Jackson Square which was crowded with city visitors, musicians, and artists who lined the outside fence. Trinity stopped at the first artist, reached into her bag, and handed the artist a small, cellophane bag of her Holy Trinity cookies. After a brief, friendly conversation, she moved onto the next artist, and the next, always extending bags of cookies and heartfelt greetings. The sistahs followed in her wake, admiring the beautiful art work.

Dawn explained about the cookies. "Once upon a time, Trinity was one of these struggling artists. She studied art at LSU and tried to make a go of it. After many years of being a Jackson Square artist, she was able to open the Royal Gala Gallery, and it's been going strong since. She has an uncanny flair for the business, but she's never forgotten her fellow artists on the Square. So she likes to bring them snacks and customers when she gets a chance."

Getting into the spirit of supporting the local artists, Judith and Helen each ended up buying a small art piece. Then, it was on to Galatoire's.

They passed by a local street band in front of the restaurant as they met up with their line stander, Bill. He saw to it that they were the very next patrons allowed in the building. They were seated, and Trinity immediately ordered two bottles of champagne for the table. She made sure everyone had a glassful, except Lola who was driving. Lola stuck to club soda and lime.

Judith was relieved to see that their lavish hats were not out of place at all. In fact, she might have felt underdressed in Trinity's group without it. The crowd was boisterous and simply out for a good time—celebrating each other and life in the Big Easy.

Trinity then proceeded to drag Dawn up and down the aisles to many tables, introducing her big sister to dozens of people. There were very few people she did not know. When they got to one table where three women were sitting, Trinity told her sister, "I was especially excited for you to meet these three ladies—would you like to know who they are?"

Dawn looked confused, prompting one of the women in a tiger-print feather boa to grin and shout out, "We're your Gumbeaux Sistahs!"

"What?" asked Dawn, smiling but perplexed.

"Yep, we're starting a Gumbeaux Sistahs group in New Orleans!" Trinity was grinning from ear to ear. "And these ladies are the first sistahs! Dawn, this is Jessica, Ginny, and Jaenne."

All three ladies stood up and gave Dawn a big hug. "Oh, this is such a great surprise! I can't believe it."

"Yes," said Jessica. "And our first meeting is this week. We're going to invite all our friends."

Trinity explained, "From what you tell me, Dawn, the Gumbeaux Sistahs are all about helping out other women —or sistahs. So that's what we're going to do. Every month, we'll pick a new project in which we can help someone out who needs it. We'll brainstorm on what we can do, and then organize how to do it. Then, the following month, we'll celebrate and choose a new project. Of course, we'll serve gumbo and Holy Trinity cookies, and Sistah Slings too. Don't you think it's a great idea?"

"Speaking of which," said Ginny, holding up her cocktail glass, "We had the bartender here whip us up a batch of Sistah Slings. Cheers, Sistahs!"

"What an amazing idea, Trinity! It may be the best idea I've ever heard. The Gumbeaux Sistah groups should keep in touch with each other—maybe even have a yearly get-together, don't you think?" She turned to the three women at the table. "Oh, and if you can, please come to the Gumbeaux Sistahs Gallery opening."

"We wouldn't miss that—Trinity already told us about it," said Jessica. "We can't wait to bring you good luck on opening night."

Dawn could not wait to tell her own sistahs the amazing news, and hurried back to their table to share. Once they heard it, Bea, Helen, Lola, and Judith rushed back over to meet their new sistahs. There was a lot of rushing back and forth, but in that crowded, happy place, no one even noticed.

"It's such a good idea to meet regularly and choose an official project," said Bea enthusiastically. "We've been doing that haphazardly, but we should start meeting regularly too—on a monthly basis is perfect."

"Especially now that we have an official place to meet. The gallery is perfect for it," said Judith.

The two groups promised to stay in touch and to catch up at the gallery opening night. When the sistahs got back to their table, they talked over all the possibilities that a Gumbeaux Sistahs group might hold. They were tremendously excited by the idea.

They finally got around to ordering their meal and when it came, they could not have been happier. All of the sistahs started with a small cup of gumbo, of course. Then they each went their separate ways on the entrees. Some of them opted for the Duck Cassoulet and others veering towards the Trout Almondine with Rockefeller Spinach. The food was simply delicious, and they smiled happily all the way through the bread pudding for dessert.

After the meal, Trinity excused herself and went out the front door into the street.

"Where's she going now?" whispered Judith to Dawn.

"Oh who knows, but I'm sure she'll be right back."

And indeed she was, with a huge grin on her face, followed by a street band they had passed earlier. Drummers tread on the heels of trumpet and tuba players, who trouped right into the crowded restaurant. There they loudly played their booming, brassy rendition of *Happy Birthday* to Dawn. It was total mayhem as all the diners cheered and sang. Trinity made Dawn get to her feet and take a bow, which she did with a flourish.

They sistahs were thrilled with the whole scene. Dawn actually cried with happiness.

Later, when they finally left the restaurant late in the afternoon and said their goodbyes, they promised Trinity they would make Dawn come see her sister soon.

"I'll see y'all on opening night too. It's my turn to cross over the Causeway, Sis," said Trinity, and she hugged Dawn one more time.

On their drive home, Judith said, "Your sister is the greatest, Dawn. What a day!"

Dawn answered with eyes shut, since they were back on the Causeway. "Yes, she is. And this was the best birthday ever. And, oh my God, can you believe it? We've got new sistahs!"

CHAPTER 30

L illian's laptop was open on the conference table so that she could look over the announcements of the upcoming Spring Fling while sipping from a mug of coffee. The museum had taken out a large ad for the event. The Spring Fling was also mentioned in the calendar of events sections of the local newspaper and the City of Covington website.

She was noting the ad placement on the page and taking a sip when something caught her eye, and the coffee went down the wrong pipe. The coughing fit that ensued lasted a good three minutes.

Gasping for breath, Lillian grabbed the laptop and went back to reading the announcements, hardly believing her eyes. She read:

> *Joining the lineup of participating businesses in the Spring Fling in downtown Covington this year will be The Gumbeaux Sistahs Gallery, a new art gallery and gift shop, located at 413 Columbia St. Owners Judith Lafferty and Dawn Berard offer music, libations, and a not-to-be-missed exhibit of Judith Lafferty's bold, colorful paintings. Other award-winning local artists and artwork will be featured as well, including the grand reveal of the Gumbeaux Sistahs Living Exhibit by Lola Trahan, creator of the famed Living Art Garden formerly in the Covington Art Museum.*

"*It's them!*" she thought, white-hot anger rising so that she actually had to stand up to process it. "*They're the ones who are opening the new gallery down the street! I should have known they were up to something—they never quit! And look what they told the paper—that the Living Art Garden was* formerly *in the Covington Art Museum. Formerly! It's still here! That's so underhanded."*

She sat back down with her hand across her forehead, warding off an oncoming headache and trying to calm down. After a couple of minutes, she grudgingly had to admit to herself that the stunt sounded like something she might have done. She wondered what other stunts she might have pulled in a situation like this—and a light went on.

She suddenly smiled slyly and thought, *"Guess they forgot who they were dealing with."*

She reached for the phone, looked up a number that was already saved in her contacts and dialed. A voice answered, "Barry's Traffic Control, how may I help you?

CHAPTER 31

All day, Dawn and Judith worked like dogs to get everything ready for their grand opening that night. The event would start at five P.M., and they were just about ready.

Signs appeared in the early morning on lamp posts and traffic signs up and down Columbia St. warning drivers not to park on the street after one P.M., or they would be blocked in by barricades.

At about one-thirty P.M. a big truck with a sign that said *Barry's* on the side appeared, and men hopped out. They began setting up free-standing, metal barricades, surrounding three whole blocks for that night's event. Unfortunately the Gumbeaux Sistahs Gallery was on the corner of the fourth block. The sistahs were effectively locked out of the event.

When Dawn and Judith saw what was happening, they ran out to the barricade truck shouting, "Wait, wait!" A man sitting in the truck, stepped out and they told him hurriedly, "We're supposed to have barricades on our street too—we're in the fourth block of Columbia."

He reached back into the truck and pulled out a clipboard, read something printed there, then pointed to it so they could see. "No, I'm sorry, ma'am. Got the work order right here. Three blocks of barricades were ordered. Actually, it looks like there was a change in the order just this morning. The organizers said that they had originally ordered four blocks but then said that three blocks-worth were all they needed. I'm sorry, but I can't change it up at this point. I don't even have the barricades here to change it if I wanted to."

His phone rang and he turned back to his truck to answer it. The sistahs were left with their mouths open, panic rising fast.

"Without the barricades extending in front of the gallery, people won't know that we're included in the event. They won't bother to walk down to the opening!" said Judith, horrified.

"C'mon," said Dawn, turning back to the gallery. "We've gotta do something."

They headed back across the street, and Dawn went straight for the refrigerator. "What in the world are we going to do?" asked Judith.

"I'm going to drink," said Dawn, removing a bottle of wine from the fridge and reaching for a glass.

"Well, make it two," said Judith anxiously. She thought, *Oh my God! We're going to fall flat on our faces before we even open.*

Another thought occurred to her. "You know, this has all the earmarks of something Lillian would do. Do you suppose this is some sort of sabotage?"

"Now that you mention it—of course it is," said Dawn, shaking her head with anger. "Boy, you just can't underestimate that woman, can you?"

"I didn't think she'd stoop this low. She's trying to drag us down into her dark little world of hers. What can we do?"

Dawn took a deep drink of wine. "It's looking pretty dark, all right. We need to think—and fast. The barricades end only about thirty feet from our front door. There's got to be something we can do."

Judith asked, "Do you think we should call the Gumbeaux Sistahs together for an emergency meeting? Maybe between the five of us, we could shine a light on the problem."

Dawn stopped with the glass halfway to her mouth. She stared at Judith.

"What? Did you think of something?"

"No, you did, partner!" grinned Dawn and gave Judith a big hug. She then reached for her phone and dialed. "Dan, I need your help! Can you drop everything and do something for me—like right now? Yes? Oh my God, thank you. You know that's why I love you, right?" she laughed. She explained what she needed to Dan, then hung up and dialed Lola, "Lola, dig out your Christmas decorations. It's an emergency!"

CHAPTER 32

Opening Night

By three o'clock, having worked like madwomen, Judith and Dawn had the food service equipment set up across the street from the gallery and inside the barricades. Then they quickly assembled all the rental tables, chairs, and a few pretty umbrellas they had rented for the event in front of the food station. Lola arrived, ran an extension cord from the gallery, and arranged twinkly Christmas lights all over the barricades surrounding the tables. She left a sidewalk-wide space between two barricades and covered that area especially well with lights. On the other side of the street, in front of the gallery, she placed the lights everywhere she could, so it looked like a continuation of the food area. That way, people would get the idea that they needed to cross the street to get to the gallery.

Helen and Bea arrived at four P.M., carrying pots and trays and helped set up the food station. Meanwhile, Judith set up a drinks table inside the gallery itself so that people would have to cross the street and go into the building if they wanted champagne, ice-cold sweet tea, or a Sistah Sling.

Dan showed up at around four-thirty in his truck with his contribution. "I got them, Dawn!" he yelled to his wife. "They had a red one and a white one, and I didn't know which one you wanted, so I got both." He unloaded two machines and set them up with extension cords on the sidewalk in front of the gallery, a little ways from the entrance. When he flipped the switches, both searchlights, red and white, blazed straight up into the sky. It was a little early for people to show up, but in about an hour when it got dark, no one at the event could possibly miss that there was something exciting happening at the end of the block.

At five o'clock that evening, the gumbo was hot, the champagne and pitchers of Sistah Sling cocktails were chilled, and the Sistahs stood ready at their stations. Judith opened the Gumbeaux Sistahs Gallery doors to the public for the first time. Bea was behind the cash register, Helen was in charge of serving up gumbo and cookies, and Dawn handed out drinks. Helen had made the cookies, and all the Sistahs donated gumbo with their usual competition and banter. They had pots of the delicious concoction, no two alike, and all of them extraordinary.

The first four people through the front door were none other than Trinity and her three friends from Galatoire's, the new members of the New Orleans Gumbeaux Sistahs group. They had driven across the lake from New Orleans, and they trouped inside, decked out with big hats and feather boas.

"Oh my God, Trinity! You're a sight for sore eyes, thank you for coming," said Dawn happily.

"We wouldn't miss it," said Trinity, and her friends smiled in agreement. They were handed the first of many Sistah Slings served that night.

"Oh, you made my cocktail! I'm honored. And thirsty!" she said, laughing.

"Y'all look divine!" said Judith, delighted. "The four of you are going to bring this party to a whole new level. If you wouldn't mind, could y'all please circulate and make everyone feel that they are in the 'place to be' tonight?"

"That's why we're here," said Jessica, then grinned. "We'll make this place divine. We're good at it!"

Judith and Dawn started circulating among guests while music played over the speakers they had set up inside the gallery, as well as outside on the sidewalk. The crowd seemed happy and excited. Judith could have sworn that there were almost as many people coming through the gallery as they usually had at the event in the museum. She saw many familiar faces and greeted them happily while showing the various art pieces on the walls. Dawn and she sold a ton of raffle tickets for the painting that she had set up on an easel in the middle of the main room. Judith named work "Opening Night," and people seemed drawn to it. Half of the proceeds from the raffle would benefit the Safe Home for women and children. The organization always needed funds and had even sent a couple of trusted volunteers to the event to help with raffle sales.

Lola had pulled out all the stops in setting up her living art installation. She called it the *Gumbeaux Sistahs Living Exhibit.* In addition to her magic plants, which were trained with wire to resemble human forms, she had added lighting so that it was nothing short of dramatic and extraordinary. To top it off, she had even added a small fountain to the exhibit, so that the sound of calming waters would be welcome at times when the gallery was a little quieter. Lola had several offers to purchase the exhibit, and she finally had to put up a handmade sign that said *For Display Only.* She gave away enough business cards to ensure new business for quite some time.

But that night was anything but quiet. The night air crackled with excitement. Dawn had produced a microphone at one point in the evening. She and Judith stepped forward together in front of the crowd, welcoming everyone and thanking them for coming. Then Dawn said, "I'm Dawn Berard, co-owner of The Gumbeaux Sistahs Gallery and I'm also co-owner of Berard Accounting. And this is my new partner and co-owner of our gallery, and also our main artist, Judith Lafferty. And just so you know, we are not the only Gumbeaux Sistahs for which this gallery is named. There are others sistahs here too—Bea Walker, Helen Hoffmann, and Lola Trahan, all of whom had a hand in this gallery's very existence. Our New Orleans Gumbeaux Sistahs contingent is here tonight also. Raise your hands, Trinity, Jessica, and Jaenne! We also want you to know that Lola Trahan is also the creative genius behind the amazing *Gumbeaux Sistahs Living Exhibit* inside, and I think you will agree with us that she is so talented—she might just be a plant witch!"

She shot a grin at Lola, who winked back. People clapped with humor and appreciation, and Lola flushed with pleasure.

Dawn continued, "I'm going to turn this mic over to my partner and Gumbeaux Sistah, Judith Lafferty. Her artwork just blows my mind, so much so that I had to go into business with her." She laughed and people cheered. It was Judith's turn to blush, as she took the microphone.

"Good evening, everyone, and welcome. Many of you know me from the Covington Art Museum. I was a fixture there for many years, but it was time for a new chapter in my life. I've always been an artist, and my heart yearned to find more time to create and live that life. The paintings you see tonight are all from my Gumbeaux Sistahs series. I've been painting these women all my life. I was drawn to these images, and I wasn't even sure why that was. But now it's all come full circle, and I understand. When I met these other Gumbeaux Sistahs—Dawn, Bea, Helen, and Lola, they showed me true friendship and community. They brought it all home for me. Women supporting each other in friendship and compassion—it's a powerful thing. It can make a life, and it's made mine. I thank you, dear sistahs. This gallery and this wonderful night would not be possible without you. And I thank you, dear people, for coming out here to be with us tonight. I hope to see much more of each of you, and I hope that you will consider yourselves to be our Gumbeaux Sistahs—and brothers, as well!"

Dawn took the mic again. "One more thing. I just wanted to say something about the Gumbeaux Sistahs Gallery. Yes, we are a gallery, but we are also a community. We will offer a place to feel comfortable, visit, take workshops, meet friends, and have a cup of coffee and one of Helen's scones or cookies. There will be live music at times and, trust me on this, we will serve the best gumbo on the planet. We will also serve as a resource for people who want to meet like-minded folks for coffee, conversation, lunch, travel, art, art workshops—you name it. Music lessons will be offered here. And there will be a community bulletin board to let you know what's going on. Plus, we will gather information on recommended services and products. If you need a music teacher, or gardener, or lawyer, or a ride somewhere, we hope to become a resource for you. We offer Judith's amazing art, of course, but we will also have a wall for the artwork of some of our other local artists. And gift items, as well. So hopefully, we will offer something for everyone. Come on down anytime, especially on Friday evenings, and have a glass of wine with us. Hang out and listen to musicians play and be reminded of how good life is in Covington. We thank y'all so much for coming and . . . speaking of musicians, we have a little surprise."

On cue, the All Ukulele Band stepped forward, including Judith, and they played and sang *I'm Yours* by Jason Mraz. The crowd ate it up. It turned into a big sing-along as the group played several old favorites. At one point, Lola joined in on her saxophone, and Bea joined in on a portable keyboard they had borrowed.

On another cue from Dawn, a trumpet player and drummer, both of whom had been hired for the evening, appeared next to Lola on her sax. They started walking around the crowd, followed by the ukulele band. Meanwhile, Dawn and Trinity handed out white Second Line parasols and handkerchiefs, along with kazoos, to people who would join in the parade behind the musicians. They played several favorite New Orleans hit tunes, and everyone danced with their parasols and waved their white kerchiefs in the air. The kazoos buzzed along with the music. The Gumbeaux Sistahs from New Orleans twirled their feather boas and danced merrily with the crowd.

Then Dawn grabbed a picket sign she'd prepared, which said "FOLLOW US!" She jumped in front of Lola and led the whole crowd up the street one block to the Covington Art Museum. Judith and Helen stayed behind with the volunteers to take care of business.

The Second Line stopped in front of the building and played their music, whooping, hollering, and dancing all at the same time, catching the attention of many of the museum guests. As Louisianans are always wont to be, the visitors in the museum were ready for a good time. A Second Line is a hard thing to resist joining, and not many did resist. Dawn gave them each a free handkerchief and a kazoo, and they dove right into the fun.

At one point, both Lillian and Thomas appeared in the museum doorway, "What the heck is going on out here?" asked Thomas, as people filed past him and joined the line outside.

"Do something, for God's sake!" hissed Lillian.

Thomas threw his hands up, exasperated, and asked, "Like what?"

Dawn kept waiving the picket sign gaily, and the line attracted many new members. It started moving again, and the crowd paraded right back down to the gallery. Dawn grabbed the microphone again, and welcomed all the newcomers to the Gumbeaux Sistahs Gallery. She invited them all to enjoy the free gumbo, wine, cookies, music, and art.

In one fell swoop, they had all but emptied the museum, doubling their own attendance, and leaving Thomas and Lillian and several board members with their mouths hanging open.

The musicians kept playing, but Judith had to stay busy tending to customers. Her artwork was selling, and it was all she could do to keep up. She could not remember a better night. Her work was appreciated, people were having fun, and best of all, she had friends with whom she could share the experience. She and Dawn kept high-fiving each other throughout the night. It came as a surprise to her, but Judith found that she actually enjoyed selling her own work. Each piece had its own story. Sometimes she told the story to customers, and sometimes the customers wanted the painting to reflect a story in their own lives, so she kept her original story to herself. Every time she placed a "Sold" red dot next to a painting, she would catch Dawn's eye. Then Dawn would shoot her a thumbs up sign back to Judith.

At one point, Dawn noticed a man talking to Lola by the living art garden. He had been there quite a while, so Dawn whispered to Judith with a smirk, "Who is that guy hanging around Lola? Don't tell me another victim is falling prey to her charms."

"I don't know," answered Judith. "But good for her. He's cute!"

Judith walked away to talk to people in the crowd. She noticed how working the room at her own event differed from working a room in the past. At the museum, she was on automatic and professional with people, filling wine glasses, handing out artist brochures, and talking up events to come with potential fund providers. Here she was genuinely enjoying herself, chatting, and feeling welcome in people's presence. She welcomed their company too. What a difference a little exposure to the Gumbeaux Sistahs had made to her. She felt gratitude well up inside for her new friends.

People stayed later than Judith ever remembered them staying at the museum's events. They were simply having fun, plus many of them wanted to see who won the raffle that would be announced late in the evening. They eventually ran out of gumbo, but they had plenty of cookies and wine, and kept them circulating.

At one point, Bitsy showed up at the gallery. She had snuck out of the museum and hurried down the block to the gallery. She told Judith and Dawn, "I can't believe this! It's like a tomb down the street. And I believe that Thomas and Lillian might just kill each other before it's all over with. They just keep bickering."

"Looks like Lillian's golden boy is showing a little tarnish at last," said Dawn. "Of course—it's Lillian he's dealing with. She doesn't get along with anyone—it was just a matter of time."

"But you girls are kicking ass!" Bitsy exclaimed. "Look at all this. It's amazing!"

"We sold a bucket-load of raffle tickets too," said Dawn.

Helen added, "And we got so many signups for the first art workshop we're offering that we will probably have to split it into two groups!"

"Seriously, I'm in heaven," said Judith, who couldn't stop smiling.

Lola said excitedly, "And Bitsy, we've had reporters from newspapers, radio, TV, magazines, and even an impromptu podcast interview. They're going to be talking about us all over."

"It's really happening," said Bitsy. "I'm so happy for y'all. And so proud of you. I have to run back now, but we'll talk later. Oh, and Lola, I don't suppose you've had any luck with finding your ring yet?"

"No, not yet. I'm not giving up, though. It's important to me."

"I'll keep looking, too," said Bitsy, and ran off back to the museum.

The raffle painting was won by a well-dressed woman in head-to-toe white linen and a large, artsy necklace. Her name was Alice Couvillon, a former schoolteacher and current president of the local chapter of the Retired Women of Covington networking group. Before she left for the night, Judith and Dawn loaded Alice up with flyers and postcards about the gallery that she could take back to her group for distribution. Judith told her to invite them all to come out and be Gumbeaux Sistahs with her. She also offered the gallery as a venue where small break-out groups from the organization could meet. They would be more than welcome.

When the evening finally wore down, the five Sistahs were the last to leave. They locked the doors on a completely successful night and walked down the dark side street to their cars together.

"I wish we had some leftover gumbo, but Lola ate it all," Dawn said, laughing. "That's because it was my mom's recipe, and she knows in her heart it's the best."

Lola snorted, but was too tired to argue. She was, as were all the Sistahs, smiling in the dark.

CHAPTER 33

On the Monday after the Spring Fling, tensions ran sky-high at the museum board meeting. Ed Bagrett could be heard in the front gallery finding his voice at last. "You see, Lillian, I told you we shouldn't change things when they are working. We had a winning formula with Judith until you bungled it. She would have brought in the fundraising at the event, like she always did. You seemed to think your young man was going to be a miracle worker. You brought this guy in thinking his young blood would inject new life here, and now everything is falling to pieces. Obviously, age doesn't matter. 'What works' is what matters. And Judith worked. You let her go for nothing. The board should hold you and Thomas both responsible for this financial disaster."

"Don't point that finger at me, Ed Bagrett," snapped Lillian, rising to her feet. "Things change, that's all. We all thought bringing in new blood would shake things up. None of you disagreed with me when we voted Judith out."

She was right. Except for Ed, none of the board members had possessed the backbone to stand up to Lillian about anything—until, at last, today.

Betty Lauland, one of the younger members, spoke up, "The Fling was a disaster."

Marcy chimed in coolly, "I have to say, Lillian, you're right. Things do change. Board members can change too." She narrowed her eyes in defiance.

"Wow," said Lillian, taken aback. "So it's come to this. How quickly people can turn on you when you're trying to do something that needs to be done." She shook her head in anger and fear, sensing the lions circling. She knew she could lose her position if they decided to vote her out now that they suddenly were speaking up. She thought about Thomas, and for the millionth time that week, she wondered why she had bothered with him in the first place. True, he was handsome, charming, and a wonderful lover, but he was basically worthless around the museum. But if push came to shove, she would be damned before she took the blame for Thomas' fundraising failure. She had to do something. Then a light came into her eyes. "Look, I let Thomas take the lead in the event. Sure, I wanted us to shake things up, but I only wanted for us to do better. But perhaps we made a mistake. So here's what I propose. I know it's a bit irregular, but don't you think the board should hear about what happened at the event from the horse's mouth? Instead of getting a second-hand report from me? This is too important for us to make mistakes. We need to get this right before we say things we might regret later," she looked daggers at Marcy. "I think we should ask Thomas to step in and account for his performance himself."

After some deliberation by the members, the board agreed and hostilities were put on hold momentarily.

But Thomas was one step ahead. He could hear the goings-on in the meeting plain as day by standing in the hall outside the board room. He knew disaster was knocking on the door. He heard the tone of the meeting and the direction things were taking. Lillian could be heard all the way to Milwaukee trying to throw him under the bus. If he had any doubts about their relationship being over, he had none now. Something had to be done. He was not ready to leave this gig yet. All weekend, he had worried about what would happen because of the unsuccessful fundraising at the event, fretting that his worst nightmare was coming to pass. He had paced up and down in his apartment, eyeing his stolen collection, and now he was pacing up and down in the museum hall. He felt cornered and a little desperate. He needed a plan. He could just leave town, but he needed just a little more time at the job so he could use it to get a reference and step up to a bigger city museum job. As Thomas well knew, this gig was a windfall, and there was no telling if he would get another chance like this one.

In the back of his mind, an idea quickly formed. It was an idea he hated for several reasons, but when he heard Lillian gunning for him in the meeting, he panicked and decided to put it into immediate action. He ran to his office and reached into his bottom desk drawer.

When Ed stepped out of the board meeting he ran into Thomas, who was hurrying down the hall toward him. Ed asked him to join the meeting.

Thomas entered the board room and found many pairs of eyes staring at him—all but Lillian's.

She looked away from him when she said, "Thomas, it isn't protocol to ask you to be in this meeting, but it's time for you to speak up for yourself. As you know, the fundraising numbers were insufficient for the Spring Fling, and the museum depended upon them. Rather than our bank account being flush this time of year as usual, we are going to be in the hole. It was your responsibility to provide the funds . . ." Lillian turned and looked into his eyes, bringing her point home, ". . . and I can't tell you how disappointed we all are with you."

For Thomas it was like looking straight into a block of ice.

"She really is magnificent," thought Thomas, regretting their parting for one brief moment. He could not help but admire her resolution and feistiness. But then his self-preservation and lack of morals kicked into high gear. He took on an apologetic tone, "I'm truly sorry to hear that, Lillian. I would like to say that I take full responsibility for this, but I think we all know that this was a shared responsibility. I was promised support in this first effort at fundraising, and the only one helping me with anything was Bitsy, who has little experience at it. You all had a share in this disaster, didn't you?" He looked around, meeting the eyes of every member. "I suggest we work together to solve this problem so it doesn't occur again." This little speech amounted to a last-ditch effort to save his neck. It might have worked on a couple of the kinder board members,

but with Lillian, no such luck. He had expected her to react that way, but he had hoped otherwise.

"It was clearly on your head, Thomas," said Lillian.

"Now, Lillian, maybe there's something . . ." Marcy started to say.

"Oh, put a sock in it, Marcy. He's a big boy and the buck stops with him," snapped Lillian. "We have no other option than to let you go, Thomas."

Thomas watched momentarily, as the other members struggled with the idea. He could see on their faces that Lillian was about to win this one, as usual, and he could not let that happen. There was only one card left for him to play. It was a desperate one, but the only one he had. "Actually, I was on my way into this meeting even before you invited me," he said boldly.

That stopped Lillian, and curiosity made them all wait to see what he had to say.

Thomas went on, "I have a very serious matter to discuss, a much more important one than a little shortfall in the budget. I'm sure we can make up for that loss some sort of way, given a chance and help from you all. No, this matter involves the police."

The board perked up and stared at Thomas, curious and cautious. "The police? What's this about?" asked Ed.

"I just received an anonymous phone call regarding our last art exhibit—you remember the Chagall, Picasso, Cezanne one? It seems a valuable piece is missing from the returned collection."

"What? How can that be?" asked Marcy, horrified.

"That's what I want to know. Bitsy and I packed the exhibit ourselves. The caller wouldn't identify herself, and I don't understand why. If the call was from the New York museum that sent us the paintings, they would never call anonymously, right? It's very mysterious. The small missing piece is called *Romeo and Juliet,* and it depicts a dreaming couple floating over Paris."

"I remember that one," said Marcy. "It's missing?"

"We need to call New York right away and verify things," said Thomas. "But first, I suggest a museum-wide search for the piece right now—together. We shouldn't wait. It's more important than anything on your agenda. The museum's reputation is at stake."

"What? Good Lord! Who could have called us? This is so very strange, but I agree. If there's any truth to this, it only makes sense to see if we can find it right away," said Ed.

The board members, including Lillian, agreed to go from room to room together to make an organized search. They started in the shipping room since the artwork was last seen in there by Thomas and Bitsy, but couldn't find any sign of it. They stopped at Bitsy's office and pulled her into the effort. She was as confounded as they were. "I packed that piece myself," she said. "So I know it went out with the rest of the collection."

Next, they moved into the private offices. When they got to Thomas' office, he helped them search it himself. They looked on bookshelves and in the drawers of his desk, but no lithographs turned up.

Then they moved into Lillian's office. With her cooperation, Ed searched the desk. He stopped short after pulling open her lower desk drawer. There, under a single sheet of copy paper, was the missing lithograph. Ed pulled it out by its edges, and everyone gasped. "Oh my God, Lillian! Is this it? What is it doing in here?"

They all stared at her, and her face went sheet white. She turned sharply to look at Thomas. "What the hell is that doing there?" she said.

"Well, that's the million-dollar question, isn't it?" said Thomas smugly.

"But, but . . . I didn't put that there!" She looked around, "Ed . . . Marcy . . . you know me. I had nothing to do with this."

"This is all pretty suspicious, Lillian," said Thomas.

"Shut up, you bastard," said Lillian, her eyes blazing.

"I think we should call the police and get it all straightened out," said Ed. "Bitsy can you make that call, and also call the New York museum and find out what's going on over at their end?"

"Of course," said Bitsy, and took off.

"Ed, I don't know how to explain this," said Lillian, fear crawling into her voice.

The board members stared speechlessly at Lillian. Most of them secretly felt that if Lillian did steal the artwork, she would certainly pay the price and not get any leniency from them. Some of them actually hoped that she was guilty.

The police were called, and while they were there, Bitsy was able to confirm with the New York museum that there was indeed an irregularity with the returned artwork. They had a lithograph of that description, but it appeared to be slightly tampered with. They would get an expert on it right away. No more than twenty minutes later, a very furious New York museum director called to say that they demanded the original back, that they had a cheap fake in the frame, and that they planned to press charges if it was not returned immediately.

The police arrested Lillian on the spot for the theft, and she was led off to the patrol car, her high heels clicking across the museum floor angrily in her Manolo Blahniks as she left. They took the Chagall litho as evidence. Bitsy called Lillian's husband, and he said he would drop everything and meet Lillian at the police station.

As she was led out, Lillian struggled and cursed loud and long. She demanded to talk to a Sgt. Spencer. He was evidently someone she knew in the department. Several business owners and customers on the block, having seen the police car and heard Lillian's shouts, came out to see what the commotion was. Lillian loudly threatened to sue the police and every one of her staring, shocked neighbors as well, for good measure. Thomas watched her being led away with nothing but admiration in his cold, grey eyes.

CHAPTER 34

After the police left, the museum quieted down a bit, mostly because everyone was in shock. Thomas took a break and left for a while. He told Bitsy that he needed to get some air and maybe a bite to eat, and would be back soon.

Meanwhile, Ed, who watched Thomas walk out the front door thoughtfully, asked Bitsy to dig up some employment files for the board, saying that he had some things to check. After she delivered the requested files to Ed, Bitsy managed to sneak out for fifteen minutes and ran immediately down to the Gumbeaux Sistahs Gallery. She burst in the front door to find Dawn and Judith behind the counter.

"Oh my God!" screamed Bitsy, startling the other women while panting, "Lillian's in jail!"

"I wish," laughed Dawn. "Very funny, Bitsy. Nice try. Can we get them to throw away the key?"

"It's no joke. I ran down here as soon as I could. You won't believe it. She stole some artwork, and the police arrested her!" shouted Bitsy, trying to catch her breath. "I feel like this is some sort of terrible movie."

Dawn's mouth dropped open, "What in the world . . ."

Judith's face was pale with shock, "Bitsy, tell us what happened. I know Lillian is awful, but I would not have said she was a thief, for heaven's sake."

Bitsy told them quickly what had happened at the museum. "It's unbelievable, isn't it?" she said in a rush. "Look, I gotta get right back, but I'll keep y'all posted."

The minute she left, Dawn got on the phone and called Bea, who told Helen, who called Lola.

"Keep us up to date, dear," said Bea seriously. "I have to say, this is just weird. Lillian—a thief?"

"I know, Bea. Something's off somewhere. Let's talk later," said Dawn. She sat down with Judith, and they looked at each other, stunned.

—◊—

When Thomas left, instead of going for lunch, he went straight home to pack up his étagère. He did not know what to expect from all the morning's events, but he decided to be ready in case things took a turn for the worse. He packed up a box of his "re-homed" collection and placed it in the trunk of his car along with a packed suitcase of clothes and personal belongings, just in case.

He thanked the gods of chance that he had not moved the litho from his desk drawer at work to his étagère' collection yet. Something had told him to hold off for a little while, even though he was itching to place it in with his collection.

Because of his unfailing confidence in himself, he still felt he could make the situation work for himself. He just had to be smart and on top of the situation, and he felt he was. He thought, *"This might actually turn out to be a good thing. With Lillian out of the way, I may be able to bend this small-town museum board's will to my way of doing things. If Judith could do it, then maybe I can too. And it would just be until it's time for me to go."* He knew that it would not be easy, but he had turned Lillian's head and finagled himself a job. Maybe it would be possible to do it again. Or perhaps there was another middle-aged, female museum curator waiting for him somewhere else. Maybe this time she would be in a mid-sized city, moving him closer to a position in New York or Chicago. Vanity and overconfidence were not always Thomas' friends.

—◊—

Ed Bagrett sat quietly in the boardroom with the door closed. He was deeply upset by Lillian's arrest. He thought, *"Lillian is hard to take sometimes, but a thief?"* It was a horrible turn of events for both Lillian and the museum. He was studying an employment file that Bitsy had brought him and scratching his head. He was not sure what he was looking for, but he thought he might know it when he saw it. There were some puzzling issues with the file. Mostly because it was oddly sparse in details about the candidate. He decided that he would need to make some phone calls to clear things up.

When Bitsy got back to the museum, she was still shaken by the entire morning and not sure what to do with herself. She stayed busy with routine work until late afternoon when Ed poked his head into her office.

"Are you all right, Bitsy?" he asked. "What a crazy morning."

"I'm fine, I guess. How about you?"

"Hanging in there," he said, shaking his head. "I know Lillian can be difficult, but I never would have seen this coming." He told her that he was leaving and would be making more museum business phone calls at home, and they would talk tomorrow. He also told her that the board was reconvening for an emergency meeting at ten A.M. and he would see her then.

After he left, Bitsy did not really feel like going home. She was still too wound up, so she ordered a pizza delivery. While she was waiting, she went back to viewing the security camera videos, looking for a hint of what happened to Lola's ring. It was like watching a very boring, monotonous TV series full of people walking on and off screen. She was glad for the interruption when the pizza was delivered. She brought the box back to her office and continued watching videos. She had a piece of pizza halfway to her mouth, when the video suddenly stopped being boring.

CHAPTER 35

The next morning, Ed Bagrett opened the emergency board meeting with the words, "Thomas McCann's employment record isn't worth the paper it's printed on." He threw Thomas' file onto the conference table in anger.

"What's that supposed to mean, Ed?" asked Marcy, who was still upset about yesterday's events and was not in the mood for more excitement.

Ed opened Thomas' file again, "I spent a lot of time with this file yesterday and . . ." His speech was suddenly interrupted by the door bursting open. A small crowd of people rushed into the room.

Thomas led the way, and seemed to be trying to keep the rest of the crowd from entering behind him by saying, "I'm sorry, but there is a meeting in progress in this room." It was to no avail.

Pushing past him was Bitsy, carrying a laptop, and behind her were two police officers. Then came Lillian and her husband, Jack, and finally, Lola brought up the rear. Bitsy had called her a half hour before and told her to get down to the museum right away. She, like all the other Gumbeaux Sistahs, had heard about the theft and did not waste any time getting there to see what in the world could be happening now.

"Thomas . . . Bitsy," said Marcy, "What in the world is all this?"

"Lillian, did you get bailed out already?" asked Ed.

Lillian was the first to speak, "No, not bailed out, thank you very much. I was released. Period. I told you I wasn't responsible for what happened." Lillian was so indignant at having spent the night in jail and having to show up at this meeting wearing the same clothes as yesterday, that she literally sputtered when she talked.

"Well, tell us what happened—and why are you all here?" asked Ed, puzzled.

Lillian said coolly, "Let me introduce someone to you. This is Sgt. Brian Spencer of the Covington Police Department, and he's also my cousin. We're here to set the record straight and to get to the bottom of things."

Sgt. Spencer spoke up. "Here's the deal, folks. We have a good reason to believe in Miss Lillian's innocence. And now, as a favor to my cousin, we have a video that Miss Bitsy delivered to the police department early this morning. We would like for you all to watch this video because it clears my cousin's name beyond a doubt. It was very important to Lillian that you, her co-workers, see it for yourselves. Now, some of us have seen the video already this morning, but not in its entirety. Since then, Miss Bitsy says she has found more footage to add as evidence. I'm sure we're all anxious to see it and to clear up Lillian's good reputation, and get a few important issues straightened out around here."

"Of course," said Ed, as Bitsy fired up the computer, and they gathered around it.

As the computer woke up, Bitsy stammered nervously, "As Sgt. Spencer said, I found more footage in the last hour to add, so I'm actually the only one who has seen all of these videos so far. As you will see, Lillian had nothing to do with the theft. But I suggest you find seats. I've spliced together relevant pieces of the video, and there are certain parts of it that have come to light that are—well, unexpected. I've got to warn you that it's a bit upsetting." She looked around at several people in particular. "I think this may come as a shock, so just be ready."

Thomas started moving slowly toward the door, saying, "I'll be right back. Let me use the men's room first."

"That can wait, Mr. McCann," said Sgt. Spencer, standing in his way. "We all need to be here for this viewing, and it won't take too long."

Lillian chimed in with a sly smile, "Yes, let's all watch, shall we?" She looked pointedly at Thomas, and took a seat next to her husband who held her hand for support.

Unable to reasonably defy the policeman's request to take his seat, Thomas did just that with a resigned sigh. He kept on high alert, though.

The video started, and Bitsy explained, "As I said, this is a spliced version of events that took place over the last year. They are from the security cameras we set up in the museum some time back.

"What security cameras?" asked Thomas, wide-eyed. "This little museum has cameras?"

"Every office and room in this museum has a camera," Bitsy explained, and then hastily added with emphasis, "as approved by the budget from two years ago. The cameras, as agreed upon, were installed and maintained by me."

Lillian interrupted, "The truth of the matter is, I wasn't aware of these cameras myself until this morning, so some explaining definitely has to be done when this is all over. However, I have to say that they paid for themselves today. No matter what they cost, I, for one, am very grateful for them. Thank you for your diligence, Bitsy."

"Uh, well, hold off on that for a moment and let's all watch the video," said Bitsy, rolling her eyes with worry.

The video clip showed dates and times as people came and went in various offices and rooms of the museum. The first clip showed the Chagall exhibit when it was first hung on the museum walls. Several clips later showed Thomas admiring one particular Chagall litho, the stolen and recovered one, the *Romeo and Juliet*.

"I don't see why this is important," interrupted Thomas, trying to stand.

"Stay seated if you will, Mr. McCann," said the Sergeant firmly. "I wouldn't want you to miss anything."

The next clip showed Thomas touching the litho with his bare hands.

"What?" Ed spluttered. "What were you thinking, Thomas? You know better than that."

"Hold on, Ed, it gets better," said Bitsy, her eyes glued to the screen.

The next clip showed Lola at work on her living art exhibit garden. "This part is for you, Lola," said Bitsy. In the clip, Lola was reaching for her garden gloves. She was obviously focused on her work. Then, suddenly, she took off a ring and absent mindedly placed it on a pedestal nearby that held a large marble sculpture.

"My ring! You found it, Bitsy!" exclaimed Lola happily. "Do you have it?"

"Well, no," she answered mysteriously. "But I'll explain in a minute."

The next clip showed Lillian's office, wherein she and Thomas were talking and laughing. Lillian sat behind her desk and Thomas stood in front of it when he suddenly walked around the desk, leaned over and kissed her. It was not a little peck on the cheek, either. Lillian threw her arms around his neck and pulled him down close, kissing him passionately.

You could have heard a pin drop in the boardroom except for Lillian's loud gasp. Her husband turned a few shades whiter, dropped his wife's hand and yelled, "What the hell, Lillian?" Thomas put his hand to his forehead to keep his head from exploding.

Lillian was momentarily speechless, then she said tearfully, "Jack, I can explain!"

Several board members sat with their mouths open, and Ed finally burst out with, "Dear Lord! What's been going on around here?" Then everyone started yelling and accusing at once. It was not easy, but Sgt. Spencer quieted them all saying, "Look people, believe me there's a lot more things to deal with here. More than I bargained for, actually. That last part was a bit of a surprise, Lillian. So, let's quiet down and just get through the video first."

The next clip showed several people, including Thomas, walking by Lola as she worked on her plant exhibit. On one of his walk-bys, Thomas reached out a hand and quickly picked up Lola's ring, placing it in his coat pocket. It was then that Thomas let out his first groan from his seat next to the Sargent.

"Why, you little snake!" said Lola.

"A little snake that needs his ass kicked, I'd say," said Jack.

"That ring is a family heirloom. Just give it back right now!"

"We'll have to settle things like that later, Miss Lola," said the Sergeant. "Let's keep going, Miss Bitsy."

The next clip clearly showed the stockroom. Thomas stood by himself amid some packing crates holding a litho from the old exhibit. Suddenly he pulled out a short knife and used it to remove the original Chagall piece from its beautiful wooden frame. His movements were purposeful and efficient.

"What the hell!" said Ed, getting to his feet.

Thomas then replaced the litho with what was obviously a fake. When he was done, he sat down at the staff room table with a huge satisfied smile on his face, while admiring the Chagall and his own handiwork. The next clip showed Thomas in his office, placing the stolen litho in the bottom drawer of his desk. The clips then skipped forward to later that same day, showing Bitsy packing up the framed fake to be returned to the New York Museum.

A second round of groans could be heard from Thomas' direction. The board stared at him in shocked silence.

Lillian actually had tears running down her cheeks, and said softly, with fury, "You've forced us all down a fool's path, Thomas. You're an evil man and this is all your fault." Her husband just sat like an ice carving, ignoring his wife, but shooting Thomas a look that could kill. Lillian turned to him and whispered, "Jack, it's all his fault."

"Hold on, there's more," said Bitsy.

"I'm not sure I can take any more!" said Marcy.

The video kept going. The next clip was from just the day before and showed Thomas removing the Chagall from his office desk, and in the next scene, showed him placing the piece in Lillian's desk drawer.

"You set me up!" hissed Lillian furiously to Thomas.

At this point Ed said, "Well, actually this doesn't come as much of a complete surprise as it might have before yesterday. I was going to tell the board this morning, before all this started, that Thomas McCann's employment record is completely phony. There's not much in it, and what is there is all lies. I got suspicious yesterday, seeing as how I've never seen his file before. Plus, we've never had any trouble before in this museum till he came. Ever since he arrived, things have gone downhill. When I looked at his file yesterday, I found that there were no notes made in his file. There was nothing in there about the results of checking his references. So, I made several phone calls to these so-called references yesterday, and nothing was the truth on his resume. There is no telling who this guy is. I thought you checked his references, Lillian. Why did you hire him?"

"Don't give me that, Ed. You all agreed to hire him as well as I did!"

Sgt. Spencer stood. "Thomas McCann, I'm arresting you for theft. And I have a court order, issued this morning, for a search warrant of your property, including your office here at the museum. We'll start with your office right now."

The police escorted Thomas to the office where they immediately searched the desk where the Chagall originally had been hiding. In the bottom drawer, the first thing they turned up was Lola's ring.

"You found it!" Lola yelped.

"We'll have to take it in as evidence, Miss Lola, but don't worry, we'll get it back to you soon enough."

"I'm so relieved," she said. "I'm so freakin' mad I could spit nails, but I am relieved." She turned to Thomas, "You little snake! If I were you, I would sleep with one eye open."

Sgt. Spencer said, "Don't bother, Miss Lola, I doubt he'll be available for a very long time.

The police escorted Thomas to their patrol car. Unlike Lillian, who went kicking and screaming, Thomas walked like a zombie, dead white in the face.

Later that morning, a further search of Thomas' car turned up a very interesting boxful of treasures. The objects, along with Thomas' mysterious history, would bear some close investigation. Lillian was able to help the police by remembering that Thomas had mentioned working for a museum in southern California, perhaps in San Diego. Thomas was a liar, but he seemed to talk a lot about that city. That narrowed their investigation down tremendously.

Lillian and her husband left right after the police with Jack walking out angrily ahead of his tearful wife.

After they left, Marcy said, "I think working on this board may just kill me yet."

"Hang in there, Miss Marcy," said Bitsy, "I think the worst is over. I hope to God it is anyway."

Ed countered, "I certainly hope so too. We need to seriously think about this museum's future and its policies. But honestly, I think right now we all need a break. I was going to suggest a cup of coffee, but I could use something a hell of a lot stronger. It's barely noon, but I'm heading to the Southern Hotel for a Scotch. Anyone want to join me?"

Every single board member did. Bitsy and Lola joined them.

But first, Bitsy ran down the block, and burst into the Gumbeaux Sistahs Gallery. "Thomas has been arrested!" she cried.

"What the hell?" said Dawn, throwing her hands up in the air. "What kind of an organization are they running down there?"

Bitsy caught them up with everything that had happened that morning.

Dawn shook her head, "Bitsy, maybe you shouldn't go back down there. They'll probably be throwing you in the slammer next."

CHAPTER 36

On Friday morning, Lola was in the back of the Gumbeaux Sistahs gallery mixing up one of her secret Trahan plant formulas for the new living art exhibit. Judith, Dawn, Bea, and Helen were in the front, sitting at the tables by the pastry display. They were sampling some of Helen's new cranberry scones and drinking coffee.

On top of Dawn's head sat one of the large, feathered hats that Trinity and the New Orleans Gumbeaux Sistahs wore to the gallery on opening night. All four hats, plus matching boas, had been donated to the gallery by Trinity and left behind that night. Trinity told her sister later, "That's for all present and future Gumbeaux Sistahs that may walk through your door."

Earlier that morning, Dawn and Trinity had spent an hour on the phone, and now Dawn was telling the sistahs all about their conversation. "So, Trinity and her friends have had their first Gumbeaux Sistahs meeting, and it sounds like it went really well. At the meeting, they all voted on what they were going to do during the following month to help out someone they knew. They chose to help out their friend, Caroline, who had just built a shed in her backyard. Caroline just had hip surgery and she needed help moving all of her arts and crafts supplies into the new "she-shed." They christened the shed with champagne, of course, and then spent an entire afternoon assembling shelves, and getting it all stocked and ready. Afterwards, they celebrated with Sistah Slings and made a party of it." Dawn laughed, "Sounds like Trinity, doesn't it?"

The sistahs agreed wholeheartedly.

Dawn took a sip of coffee, and patted her large hat. "I could get used to this," she said. "It kind of suits me don't you think?"

Suddenly Lillian burst in the front door, interrupting them. She glanced at Dawn's hat, shrugged, ignored it, and got right to her point, "Look, I need to get some questions answered around here."

"Well, if it isn't the jailbird," said Dawn, laughing. "I'll bet the board can't wait for you to fly away."

"It may be hard for you to grasp, Dawn Berard, but I'm an innocent woman," said Lillian, hands on hips.

"Not *that* innocent, as I understand it," smirked Dawn, nodding at her meaningfully.

"Just be quiet," said Lillian. "You don't know what you're talking about. The board knows that I had nothing to do with the theft. And to their credit, they heard me out about Thomas and saw that they were just as much at fault as I was for hiring him. True, I didn't check his credentials, but then, neither did they. Needless to say, some policy changes have been implemented, and hopefully Thomas will be convicted and put away for a long time."

"Missed opportunity for the board, I'd say," quipped Dawn.

Lillian went on hotly, "And as to the personal side of that situation, I've come clean—both to the board, and to my understanding husband, Jack. And I've come down here to clear the air with you too, Judith. I hope you will do the same with me."

"Me?" asked Judith, confused.

"Yes you. Of course—you. Y'all know that there was an . . . indiscretion, if you will, between Thomas and me."

"Yeah," said Dawn, scratching her head. "A strange pair of ducks if I've ever seen one. I never would have guessed that."

"Now, give her a chance to say her piece, dear," said Bea gently to Dawn.

"Thank you," said Lillian. "As I said—it was an indiscretion. I've owned up to it and explained to the board that Jack and I were having some problems back then. The only reason it happened was because I was grieving the loss of affection from my spouse. There's no museum policy about relationships between employees, so there's no repercussions to suffer from that. And let's face it, I did get arrested because of all this. God knows how horrible an experience that was. I was afraid to use the bathroom—and those bunks! I thought I would die, OK? I've paid my dues for all this mess. But there's one thing that needs clearing up. Something that I can't bear until it's done."

She shook her head at the distasteful task ahead of her. "OK, so as I said, I was facing a loss of affection from my husband at the time. I knew in my heart of hearts that Jack was having a fling of his own back then. A wife just knows. And it sent me flying into a younger man's arms. Jack and I have talked things out, and we are going to work through this thing. We've been married too long not to try to salvage out marriage. But I have unfinished business that must be dealt with so the healing can begin. It's about *who* my husband was having an affair with. As a gentleman, Jack is not naming any names, but I know that it is someone in our immediate company. The truth is, I've known all along who it was."

She turned to Judith and looked her square in the eyes, "That someone was you, wasn't it?"

"What . . . *me?*" Judith managed to squeak out.

At that moment, Lola, who had been listening to the drama from the back room, joined the group.

Lillian went on, "Yes, you. Don't tell me I imagined it all. Jack admitted to me that he slept with someone. I knew it was you from the start."

"Me?" Judith said again, stunned. Recovering slightly and growing angrier by the second, she said, "Are you serious? It wasn't me!"

Lola sighed. "No, it wasn't. I'm afraid that would be me."

Dawn, who was taking a sip at that moment, choked and sprayed coffee out of her mouth, coughing.

"Dear Lord, Dawn—are you all right?" asked Bea, patting her on the back. Helen ran to get napkins.

Lillian ignored them. "You?" she asked Lola incredulously. She took a step forward, her eyes blazing.

"Yeah, it was me," said Lola, looking at the floor, deeply embarrassed.

Dawn, still sputtering, but delighted, said, "See I told you she was a slut! I didn't actually know that it was true, but now I do. Man, this is great."

Lola's face was as red as a scarlet letter. "Look, I'm sorry, Lillian. I only slept with him the one time, and I know it was wrong. I don't know what got into me. I was going through some pretty bad times, and Jack happened to be there for that one moment when I was looking for some comfort. But it wasn't comforting at all. In fact, it was a rock bottom moment for me—no offense to Jack. I know it's no excuse. But it didn't mean anything. Heck, it's barely even Jack's fault. I talked him into it. I'm really sorry, Lillian."

Lillian's mouth fell open, "Oh my God! All this time I thought it was Judith."

Realization flooded over Judith, "Wait. Is . . . is that why you fired me?" she demanded, suddenly so angry she was stuttering.

"Oh no, of course not," Lillian said quickly. "But I do have to be honest—I was relieved when it happened because you and Jack would be separated from each other. But Jack's affair and your firing were not connected. No way. Not at all." She shook her head, eyes nervously darting from face to face.

She went on, backtracking as fast as she could "But I can tell that's what you thought for a second, so maybe I owe you an apology for making you think that. Yes, I probably just owe you an apology."

"Ya think?" said Dawn. "You almost ruined her life is all."

"Yes, I do think. I'm sorry that you got fired, Judith. You were actually decent at your job, but you just didn't meet the quotas, is all."

"I think hell just froze over," said Dawn. "That was actually kind of, sort of—an apology."

"What? I am capable of apologizing!" said Lillian.

"Since when?" asked Dawn.

Lola interrupted, speaking slowly as she thought out loud, "So, even though Lillian says she didn't get you fired because of her husband, we all know she did. She actually used ageism as part of her plan to get rid of you. She convincing the board members to fire you because you didn't meet the new quotas while pushing the idea that a younger person could meet them, which he certainly couldn't." Lola shook her head. "It's amazing, isn't it? Some of the board members are young, but some of them are older than Judith. If Lillian got a majority to vote for kicking Judith out for that, then it's a sorry statement about how the museum board, and our culture in general, views aging. I hope this makes them think twice about their hiring and firing process in the future."

Dawn added, "The museum certainly paid for that mistake, too. I understand that the fund-raising coffers are pretty empty after the big Spring Fling fiasco."

"Yes, a fiasco that you all created," said Lillian hotly. Then she softened slightly, "But you're right. I feel terrible about the museum. It was the one that took the worst blow in all this mess. My husband and I have decided that we will try to make up for some of the shortfall with a donation of our own, since we had a very small part in this disaster."

"A very small part—yeah right," said Dawn, rolling her eyes.

Bea nudged Dawn, and then said approvingly to Lillian. "Your donation is the right thing to do, dear."

Dawn suddenly looked thoughtful, and said after a moment, "Yeah, it is. Hmm. You know, my husband and I have always supported the museum and didn't donate this year for obvious reasons. But the truth is, we still value the museum's contribution to the community, and I've been feeling a little guilty about it. So . . . you can put us down for our usual donation. It should help clean up this mess. I'll get a check to you this afternoon."

Lillian blinked in amazmnet. "Why, thank you, Dawn. That's very generous of you."

Then Judith said, with some hesitation, "Lillian, it's hard for me to admit this, but now that I finally know what was going on, I can kind of see now how it all happened. Of course, it was wrong. And while, yes, it was stupid, hurtful, and just awful to go through,

I understand now how it all went down. And let's face it, I got the better end of the deal in the long run, thanks to my sistahs here. But there's no reason that the museum and the gallery need to compete. We can help each other out with events. There's enough patronage to go around, and having more than one venue on the street may just bring out more people to events. It would make the events bigger and better. I think it happened at the Spring Fling, actually. There were a lot of people there, and I think that will only grow in time. And our new gallery won't always steal all the attention."

"But we'll try," laughed Dawn.

"Well, that's what I hoped for when I first heard about a gallery opening up the street. Of course, I didn't know that it was you all back then, but still. By the way, turning that Second Line parade into a guerrilla tactic was genius. Evil genius. It stole all our attendees away. I hope you understand that I will have to make you pay dearly for that."

"And now she's back," laughed Dawn.

"I've got to run," said Lillian. "And just so you know, the board is going to offer Bitsy the position of manager."

"You mean the 'Director's' position, don't you? That sounds much more influential. And you're getting the perfect person for the job. That woman can do anything." said Judith.

As she started to walk out the door, Lillian turned back and said, "And Lola, keep your hands off my husband—or I will kick your ass." Then she was gone.

"Message received," said Lola to the closing door.

Dawn said, "Wow, Lola, you never fail to entertain, do you?"

Lola looked down, still embarrassed, "Yeah, I'm sorry, y'all. It was really stupid."

Bea patted her on her arm. "Yes it was, dear, but we're all stupid now and then."

Dawn said, grinning, "Here's what I want to know. Do you think she really could kick your ass? I'd give good money to see that."

"I know I deserve it," said Lola contritely. Then she winked at Dawn, "But I'd like to see her try."

"C'mon, Lola. You've had a rough morning. Let's go over to the bar in the Southern Hotel, my treat. We'll teach them how to make a Sistah Sling. I have a feeling they're going to be making a lot of those for us in the future."

CHAPTER 37

Two hours later, Bitsy burst through the front door of the Gumbeaux Sistahs Gallery. The sistahs were back from lunch and discussing the morning's events.

"Doesn't anyone just walk through the door like a normal person anymore?" laughed Dawn. "Sheesh—what a day."

"I have something to tell you," gasped Bitsy.

"And we have something to tell you too," said Judith. Dawn, Helen, and she took turns telling Bitsy the morning's events with Lillian. Dawn made sure they didn't leave out the part Lola played in all of it by fooling around with Lillian's husband.

"What? Lola? Really?" asked Bitsy, then she laughed. "Man, you are a slut!"

"What have I been saying all along?" crowed Dawn.

"Now, dears, leave Lola alone. You know that Lola is as far from being a slut as I am," reprimanded Bea.

"Oh my God, Bea—you're a slut too?" said Dawn, cracking up.

Lola interrupted, "Thanks, Bea. And don't worry. I learned to ignore Dawn a long time ago. But seriously, I've been saying some serious mea-culpas over that little fling. I'm probably going to hell over it."

"Oh no. I guarantee you're going to heaven, girl. Nobody down there would have the patience to put up with you," grinned Dawn.

Bea gave her a look.

"OK, I'll back off," said Dawn. "Not about her being a slut, but about her one-off with Lillian's husband. I think she learned her lesson the hard way."

"Thanks, I think," grinned Lola. "Now, Bitsy, I'm definitely going to change the subject here—tell us your news."

Bitsy blurted out, "When Lillian left here, she came straight back to the museum and offered me the Director's job."

"Director, huh?" smiled Judith, cutting her eyes to Dawn.

"Yes. She tried to lowball me, but I held out till she matched Thomas' salary, which I happen to know because I do the payroll. His title was only Assistant Manager, but all this time he was making at least as much as a Director's salary, thanks to Lillian. That was ageist, sexist, and disgusting, but it ended up working out pretty well for me." Bitsy did a little dance then, whooping it up.

"Good for you, Bitsy," said Judith happily.

"We're so proud of you, girl," said Helen, giving her a big hug.

Then Bitsy sat down next to Judith and said privately, "It's time I told you a secret I've been keeping, Judith."

"A secret? What is it?" asked Judith, curious.

"In case you haven't figured it out yet—I'm actually one of the official Gumbeaux Sistahs too," said Bitsy shyly.

"Wait—what?"

Bitsy hurried on, "It's true. I'm sorry I didn't tell you. I thought because we worked together, you might somehow be more receptive to the sistahs if they were strangers to you and not connected to the job. You do tend to keep people at a distance, if you don't mind me saying so. I just knew you'd love them if you could give them a chance."

"Ohhh, well, now that I think about it—that makes sense. It was you who told them to be at St John's Coffeehouse the day I got fired, right?" asked Judith.

"Yes, I did, since I had a strong hunch that they were going to let you go that morning. Lillian had been making noises about it all week. And with the board meeting coming up, I just knew it was going to happen. So, I asked the sistahs to be at St. John's, just in case. Can you forgive me for all the secrecy?"

"Well, Bitsy," Judith said, shaking her head sadly. "I just don't know."

Bitsy looked horrified, "Oh no! I was hoping you'd think it was all for the good."

"Bitsy, it was, I'm just kidding you. It *was* all for the good. Sorry, I've probably been hanging around Dawn too much." She grinned.

"I heard that," said Dawn from the other side of the room.

"Listen Bitsy, it was probably the nicest thing anyone has ever done for me."

"I knew it was hard to make friends with you—God knows I've been trying for years," grinned Bitsy. "Sorry, but I'm just being honest here. So, I decided to be your friend, even if you weren't sure you wanted to be mine. I hope that's changed now."

"Everything's changed, Bitsy. I owe you big time. But tell me, how did you come across this group of crazy women in the first place?"

"It was about four years ago, when I first came to town. Remember how I moved here from California to be with my sister who was sick? And Judith, she was so sick. Breast cancer, as you know. I didn't talk about it much and kept it professional at work, but it was hard. I had to work and take care of her, and it was nearly impossible. I watched my kind, beautiful sister fade to nothing in front of my eyes. I thought it would kill me too. And I had no one to talk to about it because I was new in town, and didn't know anybody."

"I'm so sorry, Bitsy. My God! I so wish I had been a better friend to you. How did you ever get through it?"

"It was the Friendship Bench. I heard about the bench from my sister's doctor. Don't ask me how she knew about it, but word gets around about that bench. You'd be surprised. So, I sat with both Bea and Helen a few times, and it gave me someone to talk to. They were also such a help with the end-of-life decisions I had to make. I didn't know anything about that sort of thing. Because of them, I made it through when the time came. I knew what to expect. They came to visit my sister too. They got to know her before she died. I can't tell you how much that meant to me. Seriously, I needed them badly."

Judith reached out to hug her. "Bitsy, I'll never be a bad friend to you again as long as I live."

"You know, I've watched you become more and more isolated as the years went by. And now, I've been watching you do this incredible reversal. Being a part of the sistahs changes people. It's made my life better, and I think it's done the same for you. I wish that everyone on the planet had Gumbeaux Sistahs. If people reached out to each other more, there'd be a lot more happy people running around. And I'm not just talking about people our age. It's true for everybody."

"I know. The sistahs are not my biological family, but they are sure my logical one."

"So true. *Family* is exactly the right word for them," smiled Bitsy.

I wish that everyone on the planet had Gumbeaux Sistahs.

—Bitsy

CHAPTER 38

Three months later, Judith stood at a wooden easel in her home studio holding a paint brush that was dripping with Cadmium Blue. She worked on a large canvas displaying five colorful women playing musical instruments. *The Gumbeaux Sistahs.* As she worked, she wore an old paint-spattered apron and shoes, along with a huge grin.

For the first time in her life, she felt completely attached to what she did for a living. She was an artist. Her work identified her for herself, and presumably for others. Judith was shored-up on all sides of her world by her paints and her new-found friends. She had a heightened sense of purpose owing entirely to the fact that she was fortunate enough to have something to be purposeful about.

She thought about how it might have turned out if she had not met her sistahs. Instead of painting to her heart's content at that moment, she might be stacking groceries somewhere, or making phone calls as a telemarketer. These were perfectly fine occupations, but they would have never satisfied Judith's soul.

"Instead," she thought, *"I get to come and go as I please and do work that makes my heart sing."* Without her work, her art, and her friends, she would have been at the mercy of what had happened to her at the museum.

Since the opening night of the gallery, painting commissions had come in, one after another. She would be hard-pressed to keep up with the orders and keep the gallery walls filled at the same time.

Fortune, like the sun on a rainy spring day, had poked its head out of the dark clouds and smiled at her. Judith was everlastingly grateful.

CHAPTER 39

Dawn, Lola, and Trinity were in Dawn's big SUV, driving towards the Causeway bridge at ten A.M. right after morning rush hour and before the lunchtime one.

"OK," said Lola in the passenger seat. She reached over Dawn, who was at the wheel, to pay the toll. "Now don't worry. We're going to talk you through this."

Dawn looked at her and said in a deadly serious tone, "I'll give you one million dollars, right now, if you two don't make me do this."

"Well, don't think I'm doing this for you," said Lola haughtily. "I'm doing this because I love your sister, and she needs you to overcome this little obsession of yours."

"C'mon, Dawn. I've never known you to be afraid of anything in your whole life. I can't stand to think of you as too chicken to do this," said Trinity.

"Hey! No fair playing the 'chicken' card," said Dawn crossly. "I know it doesn't make sense to you two, but I just can't help myself. When I'm on this bridge, it looks to me like the road turns to the right. Of course, I know in my head that it's a perfectly straight bridge, and if I turn right I'll end up in the lake. But that's how it looks. It's got to be an optical illusion or something."

"An illusion that no one else can see," said Lola drolly. "This is all in your head, Dawn Berard."

"Just think," said Trinity reasonably, "If you conquer this, you'll be able to come over and visit with me more often. I would love that. I miss you, Sis."

Lola added, "And I promise that I'll come over the bridge with you for the first five times you cross it. You'll be completely cured of your insanity by then. Shoot, you'll probably be over it today once you see that it's not hard. You can do this, girl."

"And I promise that every time you drive over to see me, I'll let you choose a new hat or boa from my costume room. You'd like that, wouldn't you?"

"I sure would, but what if that optical illusion pops up again, and I start thinking that I need to turn right?"

"Wait, I know what will help," said Trinity. "Remember that kids' movie we watched some years ago—about a girl fish who was trying to inspire another fish to just keep moving forward in his life. She told him to 'Just keep swimming. Just keep swimming.' Remember that?"

"Yes I remember, and . . ?"

"Well, Lola and I will sing to you all the way across the bridge, 'Just keep driving straight. Just keep driving straight.'" And they both jumped right in and did exactly that—singing together and laughing. Even so, they were cautiously aware that they were either going to make Dawn successful at driving across the bridge, or she just might drown them all.

After a mile of their singing, Dawn rubbed her aching head and pleaded. "Look—I'm driving straight already! And I'll keep doing that if you two will just, please, shut up already."

"Can you throw in that million dollars you mentioned, just to seal the deal?" laughed Lola.

CHAPTER 40

Dawn, Judith, and Bitsy sat in the cafe section of the gallery. Dawn, tapping her pen against her clipboard and looking over her list of interview questions, said, "So, Miss Bitsy, let me ask you this. What do you know about our little company—the Gumbeaux Sistahs Gallery?"

"I know it's owned by a couple of crazy women," said Bitsy, nodding with a smile.

"Hmm, and how did you hear about this job opening?" asked Judith, trying to keep a straight face.

"As a matter of fact, those same two crazy women told me about it. They insisted that it came with an unlimited amount of days off and double my current salary."

Dawn snorted and rolled her eyes. "Yeah, not likely. But tell me, why do you want this job?"

"I don't!" said Bitsy, laughing. "Stop it already. I can't leave the museum. They need me. And you can't afford me."

"OK, OK," said Judith. "But it would be so great to work together again. Are you sure we can't convince you?"

A voice came from the doorway, "She's quite sure. Of course she's down here so often, you'd think she already worked here."

The sistahs looked up to see Lillian standing in the doorway with her arms folded.

"But let's get this straight—she doesn't work here and hopefully never will. You heard her. We need her a lot more than you do," said Lillian frostily.

"They know that, Lillian, they're just teasing," said Bitsy. "They need some help here in the gallery, and they're practicing their interviewing skills on me."

"So, business must be good," said Lillian, raising her eyebrows as a question.

"Oh, it is," said Dawn happily.

Bea walked in just then, right behind Lillian.

"Hey Bea," yelled Dawn, "Tell Lillian here that we're not stealing her number one employee, but that she needs to give Bitsy a raise."

"Oh, I'm all for that, dear," said Bea, her eyes twinkling as she set down her purse and poured herself a cup of coffee.

"I'm heading back to the museum, Bitsy," said Lillian. "I was looking for you because I need to talk to you about the incoming exhibit. There's a small problem and you're needed back at *your job*." Lillian said the last words loudly, while looking back at the sistahs.

"Sure, no problem," Bitsy said, then turned to wink at her friends. "Let's walk back together. Maybe we can talk about that raise."

The two walked out just as Lola and a man were walking inside. Lillian took one look at the hunk besides Lola, and raised her eyebrows appreciatively at Lola as they passed but did not say anything.

Dawn, however, watched the two walk in and said in a teasing voice, "Well, well, well, who have we here?"

Lola smiled, but she looked at Dawn warningly. "Whatever you're thinking of saying—just don't. We're heading down to St. John's for coffee, and I thought it might be nice to introduce y'all. So, Dawn, Helen, Judith, Bea . . . this is Bud. Bud Broussard."

Realization dawned on their faces as the name rang a bell. Helen said it for all of them, "Bud Broussard? As in—you were once married to each other, Bud Broussard?"

"The very same," laughed Bud. "And it's so nice to meet the famous Gumbeaux Sistahs. I was here at the opening night, which was fantastic. Everyone was so busy that I didn't get a chance to say hello then. But y'all did a great job."

Bea reached out her hand for his. "Bud, dear, you are very welcome here." She shot a warning glance toward Dawn.

Dawn ignored it. "OK, I have to ask. You two look pretty cozy—is there something going on here?"

"You must be Dawn," laughed Bud.

"Bud and I are simply walking down the street to get coffee. You can read as much or as little into that as you'd like," Lola said with a sly grin. "And we really have to go, so I'll catch up with y'all a little later."

"You bet your ass you will, Lola Trahan!" called Dawn after them as they walked out the door. Then to the others, "Well, how about that? Do you think she's coming back around full circle to her ex? Ooh, this is going to be interesting!" She stood up suddenly, grabbed her purse, and headed out the door, shouting back, "Actually, she's not getting away with this—I'm going to follow them and find out."

Right then, Judith glanced out of the front window and said excitedly, "Oh look, Bea, there's a woman sitting on the Friendship Bench already. You're not even open for business yet today, are you?"

"That's OK, dear. It's nearly time, and I'm ready for her now that I've got my coffee." She opened the front door and looked back at Judith. "You know, I've met with this woman before, and I think this one might make a great Gumbeaux Sistah!" She smiled, winked with her twinkly blue eyes, and was off.

"Go get her, Bea," whispered Judith. She started to close the door, but stopped to watch her little Velvet Hammer friend in her old straw hat make her way to the bench to spend more of her life offering love and assistance to someone else who needed it.

Judith thought, *"That's a pretty amazing way to spend this short life we have to live."*

Then, just before the door clicked shut, she heard that loving voice say, "Hello, dear".

ACKNOWLEDGEMENTS

Thanks to those who helped bring the Sistahs to life. The girls had been waiting in the ether for some time and would be there still if not for the unbelievably helpful editing efforts of friends and professionals. And yes, it needed much help—just in commas alone! As all of these people know at this point, I have the nasty habit of dropping a bunch of commas on the side of a page and then letting them crawl around finding completely inappropriate spots in which to inhabit.

So first, thanks to Rob Bignell, my editor, and an author in his own right, who got me pointed in the right direction over and over again. Deep thanks go to my sister, Ginny Hoffman, and her buddy, Vicki Johnson, both of whom are experts at comma extermination/relocation. Thanks to my good buddy, Dian Lusher, who spent hours poring over the manuscript with a special look-out for verb abuse. Not verbal. Verb. Thanks to my eagle-eye daughter, Elizabeth Frey, who never misses a thing and can make a joke funnier than anybody I know. A special thanks goes to my Veritas group—Dian, Pemmie, Ellen, Betty, Triness, and Maurer—for listening, reading, and Florida girls' weekends (yay, Chad!) Also thanks to my Breakfast Tribe—Connie, Sandra, Cathy, Sue, Ellen, and Mary—for inspiration, much-needed encouragement, and enthusiasm. Thank you to Lucy, my pug, for being great company during this process. And a very special thanks goes to my four children, Tony, Jessica, Erika, and Lizzy, who always tell me I'm funny—when I ask them to.

And finally, thanks to you, dear reader, for coming along on this journey with the Sistahs and me. Geaux Sistahs!

ABOUT THE AUTHOR

Born in New Orleans, Jax Frey came into this world, whooping and hollering, with a sense of celebration of Louisiana culture, food, family, and fun. Translating that celebration into her writing and onto canvas is her true calling. Her colorful art depicts everything Louisiana, from her dancing Gumbeaux Sistahs paintings, to her popular line of original Mini paintings. Because over 25,000 of the mini paintings have been created and sold into art collections worldwide, Jax holds a World's Record Academy record for *The Most Original Acrylic Paintings on Canvas by One Artist*. Jax is also the co-founder of the Women of Infinite Possibilities, an empowering women's organization started in Covington, LA, where Jax lives today with her loveable, tornado-of-a-pug named Lucy.

More Gumbeaux Sistah Info

For more information or—
to Purchase Gumbeaux Sistahs gift items or—
to sign up for The Gumbeaux Sistahs Blog, please visit—
www.gumbeauxsistahs.com
FB and Instagram – Gumbeaux Sistahs

———

For Jax's artwork: www.artbyjax.com
FB: Jax Art & Gifts, Instagram: Jax Frey

JUDITH'S MOM'S CHICKEN/SAUSAGE/ SEAFOOD GUMBO RECIPE

Serves about 8 main dishes

1 chicken, cut up
Garlic powder
Cayenne pepper
1 cup finely chopped onions
1 cup finely chopped bell peppers
1-3/4 cup finely chopped celery
1-1/4 cups all-purpose flour
½ tsp salt
½ tsp garlic powder
½ tsp cayenne
Vegetable oil for deep frying
About 7 cups chicken stock
1 lb. sausage, cut up (Andouille or smoked sausage)
½ lb. cooked peeled shrimp or crab if desired.
1 tsp minced garlic
Hot cooked white rice

Remove excess fat from the chicken pieces. Rub a generous amount of salt, garlic powder, and cayenne pepper on both sides of each piece, making sure each is evenly covered. Let stand at room temperature for 30 minutes. Meanwhile, in a medium sized bowl combine the onions, bell peppers, and celery, set aside. Combine the flour, ½ tsp salt, ½ tsp garlic powder, and ½ tsp cayenne in a plastic bag. Add the chicken pieces and shake until chicken is well coated. Reserve ½ cup of the flour.

In a large heavy skillet heat 1-1/2 inches of oil until very hot. Fry the chicken until crust is brown on both sides and meat is cooked, about 5-8 min. per side. Drain on paper towels (and try not to eat it all before you can add it to the gumbo!). Carefully pour the hot oil into a glass measuring cup, leaving as many of the browned particles in the pan as possible. Scrape the pan bottom with a metal whisk to loosen any stuck particles, then return ½ cup of the hot oil to the pan.

Place pan over high heat. Using whisk, gradually stir in the reserved ½ cup flour. Cook, whisking constantly, until roux is dark red-brown, about 3-1/2 to 4 minutes, being careful not to let it scorch or splash on your skin. Remove from heat and immediately add the reserved vegetable mixture, stirring constantly until the roux stops getting darker. Return pan to low heat and cook until vegetables are soft, about 5 minutes, stirring constantly and scraping the pan bottom well.

In the meantime, place the chicken stock in a 5-1/2 quart saucepan or large Dutch oven. Bring to a boil. Add roux mixture by the spoonful to the boiling stock, stirring until dissolved between each addition. Return to a boil, stirring and scraping pan bottom often. Reduce heat to a simmer and stir in the sausage and minced garlic. Simmer uncovered for about 45 minutes, stirring often toward the end of cooking time.

While the gumbo is simmering, bone the cooked chicken and cut the meat into ½ inch pieces. When the gumbo is cooked, stir in the chicken (and shrimp or crab if desired) and salt and pepper. To serve as a main course, mound 1/3 c. cooked rice in the center of a soup bowl and ladle about 1-1/4 cups gumbo around the rice.

HELEN'S MAGIC SOUP RECIPE

1 Tbsp olive oil
5 cloves of garlic minced
1 med. onion diced
3 lg. organic carrots thinly sliced
3 organic celery stalks chopped
1 tsp ground turmeric
1 tsp sea salt
¼ tsp pepper
½ chopped fresh organic basal
2 tsp chopped fresh organic parsley
6 c bone broth or organic chicken broth
1 whole clean organic chicken, cut up
1 c organic frozen peas
1 c chopped organic spinach
1 c chopped organic kale
1 c yellow miso paste

Add olive oil to a stock pot over medium-high heat. Allow to heat for a few minutes then add the garlic, onion, carrots and celery. Cook, stirring occasionally for 2-3 minutes or until onion becomes slightly soft. Add the turmeric, salt and pepper and sauté to combine. Once combined, add the broth. Stir briefly to mix then add the uncooked chicken to the pot. Adjust and stir to make sure the chicken is completely covered by liquid.

Turn heat up to high and allow the soup to come to a boil. Once boiling, reduce heat to medium-low and simmer uncovered for 25-30 minutes or until chicken is fully cooked reaching an internal temperature of 165 degrees F.

Once the chicken is cooked, remove it with a slotted spoon and transfer to a cutting board. Debone it and then, using two forks, shred the chicken (or you can just chop it). Add miso paste to soup and stir to combine. Add peas, chopped chicken, kale, parsley, basal and spinach and stir.

Store in airtight container in refrigerator for up to one week.

HOLY TRINITY COOKIES

1-1/8 cups flour
½ tsp baking soda
½ tsp salt
½ c butter softened
1/3 c sugar
1/3 c brown sugar
1 tsp vanilla extract
1 egg
1-1/2 c semi-sweet chocolate chips
1 c sweetened coconut flakes
¾ c chopped pecans

— Preheat oven to 375 degrees.
— Use a whisk in a bowl to combine flour, baking soda & salt. Set aside.
— Use mixer to cream butter and sugars. Add vanilla & egg and mix till incorporated. Slowly blend the dry mix into the creamed mix. Stir in chocolate chips, coconut and pecans.
— Drop by 1-1/2 Tbsps onto parchment covered cookie sheets. Bake 9-12 minutes. Cool for 10 minutes before moving to cooling racks.
— Serve these to people you love!

SISTAH SLING COCKTAIL

An original and official Gumbeaux Sistahs cocktail
Created by Erika Frey

1-½ oz Gin or Rum
½ oz Sweet Vermouth
½ oz Cherry Liqueur
1 oz Lemon Juice (fresh)
½ oz Pineapple Juice
1 oz Simple Syrup
Dash of Angostura Bitters
3-4 oz Soda Water
Garnish: Lemon Twist with a Cherry

Add all ingredients (except soda water) together in a shaker with crushed ice. Shake vigorously. Pour into a tall glass and top with the soda water and garnish. Makes 1 cocktail - Cheers Sistahs!

To make a batch of Sistah Slings, add all ingredients into a punch bowl (including soda water) and also add 4 oz of water per cocktail. Just measure ahead of time how many cocktails you can fit in the punchbowl and keep measuring out the ingredients. (You might want to make a note of the amounts for the next time you make a batch) Then add ice and serve!

READERS GUIDE
THE GUMBEAUX SISTAHS
BY JAX FREY

Discussion Questions:

1. Which of the Gumbeaux Sistahs do you relate to the most? What characteristics or actions of this Sistah can you picture yourself portraying or acting out? What do you admire and not admire about her?

2. How does ageism and sexism draw the characters together? What else do they have in common?

3. Have you ever had an ageism experience in your life? Could you imagine yourself making a new friend through a shared ageism experience? What would that look like?

4. The Sistahs come from diverse backgrounds. How do their differences help bond them together and foster their friendship?

5. How would the Sistahs ultimate outcomes be altered if they had never become friends?

6. The relationship between women and men is a prevalent theme in the book. Discuss the effects of each of those relationships on the Sistahs.

7. Food, particularly gumbo, is often described in the book. What role does it play in different settings, such as the informal meetings at their houses, the opening night at the gallery, the times when Judith, Lola, and Dawn were first invited to meet

with the Sistahs, and the meal served to Dawn by her husband when they reconciled?

8.   If you were to write a sequel to this book, how would it go? What do you think the future holds for these characters?

How to start your own Gumbeaux Sistahs Group

In the books, the Gumbeaux Sistahs are all about helping a sistah out. They brainstorm and come up with ideas to help solve each other's problems and the problems of women that show up at the Friendship Bench.

A Gumbeaux Sistahs group is all about helping out too. The Sistahs choose a project/problem to work on every month at their regular meetings. They brainstorm, use their resources, and create a plan to help solve the problem—and have a ridiculously great time doing it!

Interested and want more information? Please visit:
https://www.gumbeauxsistahs.com/gumbeaux-sistah-groups

Free Gift

Sign up for Gumbeaux Sistahs news to
receive a FREE, emailed, pdf version of:

18 Gumbeaux Sistahs Steps to
Living Happily Ever After

18 steps that can change your life—try them!
Visit: <u>www.gumbeauxsistahs.com</u> to sign up.

Coming Soon

Gumbeaux Love
A Novel

Judith Lafferty meets the biggest challenge of her life —falling in love after sixty!

Southern Artist, Judith Lafferty, confesses offhandedly to the Gumbeaux Sistahs that she is occasionally lonely and would like to meet a nice boyfriend. She should know better. The sistahs tackle her problem with their usual extreme, evil-genius schemes and plots, and in doing so, unwittingly uncover the many flavors of love in the lives of this over-fifty crowd.

Sign up for Gumbeaux Sistahs newsletter to be notified of release date:www.gumbeauxsistahs.com